P9-AOI-636

THE MIDNIGHT ORCHESTRA

A MYSTWICK SCHOOL NOVEL

THE MIDNIGHT ORCHESTRA

A MYSTWICK SCHOOL NOVEL

BY JESSICA KHOURY

ILLUSTRATED BY FEDERICA FRENNA

CLARION BOOKS

An Imprint of HarperCollins*Publishers*

Clarion Books is an imprint of HarperCollins Publishers.

The Midnight Orchestra
 For information address HarperCollins Children's Books, a division of HarperCollins Publishers, 195 Broadway, New York, NY 10007.
www.harpercollinschildrens.com

ISBN 978-0-35-861291-9

The text was set in Garamond MT Std.
Typography by David Hastings
22 23 24 25 26 PC/LSCC 10 9 8 7 6 5 4 3 2 1

First Edition

For Bryony,
my magical girl

CHAPTER ONE

The Element of Reprise

AMELIA JONES, ARE YOU prepared to lose *everything?*"

I stare hard at Jai Kapoor, and he glares back, his violin tucked under his chin. His dark bronze face is set in a determined frown, while a breeze makes his black hair flop over his eyes. With a scowl, he pushes it away, all without breaking eye contact.

We're standing on the front steps of Harmony Hall, the grand building at the heart of the Mystwick School of Musicraft. The high mountain peaks in the distance shine with fresh snow, and despite the sunny sky, the air is cold enough to turn my breath into pale, frosty mist. Dozens of other seventh-graders sprawl on the grass and sidewalk, watching the pair of us poised like two fencers about to clash swords.

"Try not to cry when I destroy you, Kapoor."

He gives a harsh laugh, his British accent ringing out across the grounds as he replies, "Such big talk from such a puny girl! I'll let the violin do *my* talking."

"That whiny, off-tune thing? There's not much difference."

The other kids laugh.

Jai scoffs. "It's time to settle this . . . Darby!"

Darby Bradshaw, leaning on one of the carved mustangs holding up the roof, now straightens and raises a whistle to her lips. As usual, her clothing is ironed and pleated to perfection, from her khaki skirt to her Mystwick sweater to her polished shoes. A headband pushes her shiny black hair away from her pale face. "Keep it clean, you two. No bloodshed if you can help it."

I purse my lips over my flute, my heart drumming in my ears.

Darby blows her whistle, and we dive into the spell, our eyes locked. I sway with my flute, and Jai scrapes his bow over his strings. The duet is a tripping, frantic onslaught of notes, an aggressive Celtic reel that soon sends tentacles of yellow magic coiling through the air. Like all magic, it gives off a faint scent, in this case, lemon zest.

Though we play together, our spells are two separate forces that lock horns, pressure building between us. His magic snakes through mine and tries to knock away my flute. I back up and lean harder into the melody, fingers tapping keys, breath pouring through the barrel of my instrument. Jai grins, ducking as a rippling streamer of my magic cracks like a whip.

"Easy!" warns Darby. "Disarm, don't disable!"

I grin apologetically and send another punch of magic at Jai's violin. He dodges and gives me a dirty look.

He retaliates with a burst of staccato notes that wash me in sparks, and I have to dance backwards to keep them from clogging my instrument.

Back and forth we spar, music and magic crackling between us while the kids below cheer and clap in tempo. A few Maestros and older students wander over to watch.

I yelp when a lash of magic stings my cheek, and Darby blows her whistle at Jai, marking his first foul.

"Sorry," he mouths.

When Jai challenged me to a Sparring duet, I thought he meant it to be somewhere more private, like one of the practice rooms. But I should have known better. There's nothing private about Jai. The bigger the audience, the happier he is.

Besides, he has an ulterior motive.

"I have to prove to the Sparring Club that I can do this," he'd said. "They almost never let seventh-graders join. But if I show them how *awesome* I am at it, they'll have to let me in, right?"

It doesn't take long for Jai's magic to overpower mine, golden light encasing my hands like gloves, freezing them in place, preventing me from pressing the keys.

Jai completes the spell with a triumphant flourish, then bows dramatically to the applauding audience. But his face falls a little as he looks around. I don't think any of the Sparring Club members showed up for his exhibition.

"Make sure you tell everyone what you saw here today!" he tells the audience. "Jai Kapoor! Already a Sparring champion at age twelve!"

"Literally the only person you've Sparred with is me," I point out as the crowd begins to break up.

"And *literally* I have never been defeated," he adds, giving me a grin that clearly says *shut-up-right-now-you're-ruining-everything.*

"Fine! I surrender. You're the champion. Though I don't get why you're going out for Sparring. I thought you were finally going to sign up for the rock elective?"

"Yeah . . ." He toes a clump of grass. "About that. My dad sort of found out about it, and, well, let's just say he can be very persuasive."

"Oh, Jai."

"Don't *oh, Jai* me. You don't know the guy." He shudders.

Jai's an incredible violinist, but I know his heart is in a different kind of music. I'd thought he finally worked up the nerve to tell his dad, but I guess not.

Clearly not wanting to talk about it more, Jai exchanges a fist bump with me before rushing off to his strings ensemble class.

I shiver as a sudden cold wind rolls over the campus, making the Echo Wood that surrounds the school creak and rustle.

The last few leaves of autumn break loose and tumble through the sky. Kids pull on their heavy coats as they head to their next classes or to the library, hauling instrument cases of every size and shape. Someone's thoughtfully left a knitted winter hat atop the statue of Beethoven; the old Composer looks as miserable as ever despite its happy shades of pink and yellow.

Darby nudges me. "Did you get a note this morning from Phoebe?"

"Yeah. Something about a meeting tonight in the Shell. Do you know anything about it?"

She shrugs. "It's probably about whoever's been leaving hair in the shower drains again. Sometimes I think she takes this dorm captain job a little too seriously. They could appoint her Maestro of room checks."

"Speaking of new Maestros . . ." Unable to hold back a grin, I continue, "My Composing teacher is supposed to get here tomorrow."

She raises her eyebrows. "Nervous?"

"You could say that." It's only been a few weeks since I learned I *could* Compose, or create new spells, a rare ability among musicians. And it's been just a few days since one of my Compositions—a spell that *kinda* accidentally loosed a horde of ghosts—nearly tore the school apart.

Since I'm the only person at the Mystwick School of Musicraft with this strange ability, there wasn't anyone to tell me what it all meant and what I should do next. Which is why the Maestros are bringing in a real, live Composer to be my teacher.

"Well, see you at this mysterious meeting of Phoebe's," Darby says. "I'll save you a seat."

She blends into the crowd of students heading to the cafeteria for lunch. I smile to myself, watching her go.

It's been less than a week since Darby stopped hating my guts, and it's been nice to actually have a friend for a roommate. Now I spend every meal sitting between her and Jai. She even started telling me about her life outside school—about her parents, her summers spent with her grandparents in Japan, and how she's hoping to join the famous Tokyo Philharmonic after graduating from Mystwick.

Darby's a bit like a hedgehog. Prickly at first, but the more you get to know her, the softer she turns out to be.

I have a bit of time, so I stop by my mailbox in Harmony Hall. There's the usual care package from Gran, this one informing me that soon she'll be heading out on her first-ever cruise, she's sure it'll be a terrible experience, and here's twenty dollars for allowance and a purple scarf and hat she knitted for me.

But there's something else today as well—a black envelope with no return address on it. Inside is a matching black note card, the paper velvet soft and the letters metallic silver calligraphy.

Amelia Jones,

You are invited to witness the Midnight Orchestra.
A doorway will be provided on the next full moon.

Cordially,
Mr. M.

Weird. I look around, but everyone's gone now, and there's no telling who wrote the note or what on earth it means. What's a Midnight Orchestra? Who's Mr. M? What *doorway?* I have no idea when the next full moon is.

It's probably just some stupid prank, but I refold it and put it in my pocket. Maybe Jai or Darby will know something about it.

I head back outside and breathe in the chilly cedar-scented air, my breath a frosty cloud. The campus is quiet, the grounds still and serene. The snowy mountains reflect on Orpheus Lake, which is as smooth as a mirror today, especially around the edges where the water is slick with ice. The Echo trees surrounding the school have shed the last of their golden leaves, and piles of them dot the grass where the grounds-keepers have been raking. Slender white trunks stretch high in all directions, but even bare, their branches knit together to form a magical protective barrier around the school.

There's almost no sign now of the events of last week, when I accidentally unleashed a horde of malevolent ghosts on the school—as well as the spirit of my own mother. Staring at the dock on the lake, where I'd last seen her, I can almost envision her hovering there, translucent blue. I can hear her last words to me and feel the tug of a question I never got to ask her . . .

Out of nowhere, I hear a strain of piano music, faint and distant. First I glance over my shoulder into Harmony Hall, where the shining grand piano sits in a beam of sunlight. But no one's at the keys.

Then the air at the bottom of the steps starts to . . . *wrinkle*. It looks like a hot road in summer, when the rising heat makes everything go wavy and warped. The scent of cinnamon fills my nose, so I know there's only one possible explanation:

Teleportation spell.

Sure enough, purple smoke starts swirling on the drive. Then, with a swelling crescendo of piano music, the smoke parts, and a long, sleek limousine appears, engine idling, windows tinted black.

I look around. No one else is in sight to greet the limo.

As the music fades, I hesitantly move down one step. I'm pretty sure Mystwick doesn't have any teleporting limos.

Who could it be? Obviously someone important. Someone *fancy*.

Like . . . my mysterious Composing Maestro? Maybe they're arriving a day early.

Stomach filling with butterflies, I walk down the steps and approach the car just as the driver—a man in a black suit with spotless white gloves—exits. He ignores me and goes to the rear car door, opening it crisply and then standing back. I can just glimpse the telltale black-and-white keys of a piano, built into the vehicle itself. A pair of pale, delicate hands runs over them, completing the teleporting spell with a long, sustained note.

I pause, uncertain. They never told me *who* my new Maestro is, so I have no idea what to expect.

The hands pull away from the piano keys, and then a leg pops out, clad in a shiny red boot.

Another follows.

Then a girl slithers out of the car. She's wearing a fuzzy pink coat and sparkly sunglasses. Shiny brown hair tumbles in waves down her back, and the earrings she's wearing look like actual diamonds. She wobbles a bit, the heels on her shoes giving her trouble on the gravel drive.

I blink. I'm pretty sure the new Maestro isn't supposed to be a girl my own age.

"Ugh!" She looks around and wrinkles her nose. "I knew

this place would be a dump. I told Daddy this would be a disaster! But *nooooo.* 'It'll build character,' he said. Whatever. *Straighten you out* is what he meant." She squints at me over her sunglasses. "*Hello?* You, girl! Are you just going to stand there staring, or are you going to take my bags?"

The man in the suit opens the trunk and hands me two heavy suitcases. I take them, because I'm so bewildered I don't know what else to do, and I struggle not to fall over from their weight.

"Are you the only person they sent to greet me?" the girl asks in an offended tone.

"Uh . . ."

"Typical." She yanks off her glasses.

And I *gasp.*

Because I do know this girl.

I've seen her before, not in person, but on the internet. In magazines. On television.

In a little silver picture frame above Darby's bed.

I stammer. "You're . . . you're . . ."

"Oh, great, a fan." She sighs. "Hello. Yes, I'm Amelia Jones."

CHAPTER TWO

A New Arrangement

THE MYSTWICK CAFETERIA BUZZES like a beehive in a hurricane.

Kids stand on chairs and tables, craning to see over each other's heads. They completely drown out the voices of the Maestros telling them to get down. Flashes of light spark as my classmate Jingfei shoves her camera wherever she can to get a good shot, taking her new job as reporter for the school newspaper *very* seriously. Claudia, a clarinetist from my Aeros class, sobs dramatically on the floor, her friends trying to calm her down.

And I sit frozen on a plastic yellow chair, my hands clasped on my lap, staring at Amelia Jones.

The *other* Amelia Jones.

Alive and in the flesh.

Is this really happening? I feel like I'm stuck in some sort of dream. Not just because the other Amelia happens to be rich, famous, and a musical prodigy—but because she's supposed to be *dead.*

But there she stands in the center of the room, a space cleared around her, as if fame surrounds her like a barrier spell. I hadn't known what else to do with her but bring her to the cafeteria, where all the Maestros would be eating lunch. Only seconds after we walked in, Claudia had recognized Amelia Jones and started screaming.

Chaos followed.

Through all the commotion, one person drifts through the crowd, as if in a trance, to take Amelia's hands in her own. A reverent space clears around the two girls.

"It's really you," Darby whispers.

The other Amelia squeezes my roommate's hands. "It's me, Darbs."

"It's just . . ." Darby swallows. "I'm having a hard time believing it. You wouldn't be the first ghost I've seen this month, Mia."

Darbs and Mia. They have their own names for each other. But then, of course they do. They were—*are*—best friends. Because Mia is definitely no ghost.

I should know.

"I don't understand," Darby says. "*How* are you here?"

That's the question everyone around us is trying to answer.

But finally Mr. Pinwhistle takes out his trumpet and plays a silencing spell. A fog of yellow magic spreads through the room, muffling all sound but that of his trumpet. With a loud, final note, he lowers the instrument and glares at everyone.

"Enough!" he growls. "All of you, sit down and finish your food. You two"—he points at Darby and Mia—"come with us."

He and Miss Noorani gather the girls and escort them out of the cafeteria. I start to follow, then stop myself. This doesn't really have anything to do with me.

And yet . . . it kind of has *everything* to do with me.

After all, when I first arrived at Mystwick, it was only because I'd received the other Amelia's acceptance letter by mistake. They said she'd died, and so her letter got rerouted to me by magical accident. The Maestros had given me a second chance anyway, letting me prove that I had what it took to be a real Mystwick student.

And I had done just that—though not exactly without some trouble along the way. In fact, I've only been an official, permanent Mystwick student for one week now. Everything has only just started to feel normal.

Until today.

I sit beside Jai and stare at the peas and mashed potatoes on my tray.

"Well," he says, staring wide-eyed at me. "Wow."

"Wow," I agree.

"I mean . . . *wow.*" He gives me an odd look. "You okay?"

"Of course she's not," snipes a voice. It's Claudia, who leans in between us. "The *real* Amelia Jones has arrived, so what does that mean for our little impostor?"

I roll my eyes. "Give it up, already. I earned my place here same as you."

"It's not like they're going to kick Amelia out," Jai says. "And if they try it, we riot." His face splits into a sunny grin. "Hey! A rhyme!"

As Claudia sniffs and goes back to her seat, Jai does a dance, chanting, "If they try it, we riot. If they try it, we riot. If they—*ow!*"

I jab his rib. "I'm not gonna get kicked out, moron."

"Then why do you look like you swallowed something slimy?"

"It's a lot to process! I mean, as far as we all knew, the other Amelia died in a boat accident months ago. But suddenly she just shows up, alive and well and ordering people to carry her luggage?"

"Wait a sec," Jai says, lifting a finger. "If she's been alive this whole time, why did her Mystwick acceptance letter go to *you* all those months ago? I thought it only found you because she was supposed to be dead."

Spidery unease crawls over my skin. If she wasn't dead, why *did* I get Mia's letter?

"There must be some other explanation. Maybe we'll never know what it is."

Picking up my fork, I mix my peas into my potatoes and shovel them into my mouth, but I have to force myself to swallow, because my stomach is doing gymnastics.

What will Mia do when she learns I took her place at Mystwick?

What does this mean for me and Darby, who just started becoming my friend?

"What do you think they're talking about?" I wonder aloud, staring at the door Darby and Mia went through.

"Oh, you know," chirps Jai. "The usual things you say to a person you thought was dead but was actually marooned on a desert island on the other side of the world for four months."

He switches voices, pretending to be Darby and Mia but sounding more like a shrill British granny, his hand flung over his forehead. "'Oh, darling, it's you, it's really you!' 'Yes, darling, it's me! I'm alive! It's a miracle!' 'I had a funeral for you and everything!' 'Oh, I hope it was nice!' 'It was the *nicest!*'"

Sighing, I stand up and swing on my backpack. "Right. Well, miracle or no miracle, I've got math class."

"Hey," says Jai. "Just remember, you're one of us now, no matter what. Nothing's gonna change."

As I trek out of the cafeteria, I spot Darby and Mia in the shade of an oak tree, hugging each other while a knot of Maestros gather a few steps away. Mia's eyes flicker up and meet mine, and there's something very strange in her gaze. Something . . . intense and knowing, as if she could read my thoughts.

Then, slowly, she smiles at me.

I can't tell if it's my imagination or not, but it doesn't exactly feel like a *nice* smile.

And I can't shake the feeling that Jai's wrong . . . and that everything is about to change.

After a hectic afternoon of classes, I run back to my room to drop off my textbooks, but when I get there, I find my bed already occupied—by Mia Jones.

Darby sits on her own bed, hugging a pillow. Her face is blotchy from crying. They both stare at me when I bust through the door.

"Amelia!" Darby smiles.

"Hey," I say, glancing nervously at Mia. "I was just gonna change real quick. Didn't mean to interrupt."

"No, this is good," says Darby. "I know you already met, but—"

"But that was *before* I knew who she was," cuts in Mia.

She stands, smiling sweetly, and picks up one of my red

curls and runs it between her fingers, as if she's considering buying it.

"Amelia Jones," she says. "Funny coincidence, isn't it? Same name, same age, same school."

"So funny," I say faintly.

"Wanna know a secret?" She leans close and whispers in a flat tone, "I don't really believe in coincidence."

"Oh?"

She steps back and laughs, but her eyes are serious. She has the most piercing gaze I've ever seen. I feel like my brain is being x-rayed. "You're welcome, by the way," she says.

Behind her, Darby winces. "Mia . . ."

"Welcome for what?" I ask.

"Um, all of this?" Mia steps back and spreads her hands wide. "Darby told me everything. How you got my letter by accident. How you wouldn't even *be* here if it weren't for me."

"Oh. I . . . uh . . ." My cheeks have to be redder than tomatoes. "I'm glad you're safe. It must have been terrifying, being shipwrecked all those months."

She flicks her hair. "No big deal, really. I decided to treat it like an extended vacation. With, like, a *lot* of coconuts."

"And your family? Are they okay?"

Her eyes lower, her laughter gone. "My father, yes. But . . . they haven't found my mom yet."

"Oh, no. I'm so sorry."

"It's fine. I know she's alive. It's just a matter of time before they find her."

"I'm sure you're right." I glance at Darby, who looks at her friend sadly, and I can tell she doesn't share Mia's confidence.

But Mia doesn't look the least bit worried about her mom's fate, which I find a little strange. If my Gran were lost at sea, I'd be a wreck.

"Anyway," Mia says, "Darby's told me *everything* about you. How you're a Composer, how you saved the school . . ." She tilts her head, her eyes narrowing even though her smile doesn't fade. "How much *fun* she's had hanging out with you."

"Really?" I blink. "She said all that?"

"I was almost worried that she'd gone and *replaced* me." Mia chuckles, giving Darby a shove that's a little too hard to be playful. Darby laughs back, but her eyes flicker to me.

"Of course not," Darby says. "Nobody could replace you, Mia."

"You sure?" Mia teases. "The whole school seems pretty obsessed with Amelia Jones the great Composer. You're practically a wondergirl. Is it true that you Composed a *black* spell?"

"Well . . . kind of. Yeah."

"Oh, don't look so scared!" Mia says, grinning. "C'mon now, Wondergirl, I can tell we'll all be best friends. Special as you are, I'm sure to keep a *very* close eye on you."

"I'm really not that special."

"Oh, I think you are. I think you have no idea how special you are. A girl who can raise ghosts? You must be *very* interesting to a lot of powerful people."

"Um . . ." I glance at Darby, then at the door, wishing for an excuse to leave as quickly as possible.

"Oh, loosen up, Wondergirl!" Mia clutches my hand and Darby's with such earnestness that I can't help but smile back. Maybe she is just teasing, and I shouldn't take it so personally. I remind myself of all she's gone through in the last few months and decide that she's allowed to be a little bit weird. Who wouldn't be, after being marooned on an island?

"In fact, speaking of best friends . . ." Mia gives Darby a meaningful look.

Darby clears her throat. "Oh, yeah. Um. Amelia . . . you know how Mia and I always planned on, well, being roommates at Mystwick?"

My stomach sinking, I nod.

"Well . . ." Darby scrapes a stain on the carpet with the toe of her shoe. "It's just . . ."

"You want her to move in with us," I finish for her. "D'you think there's room for another bed?"

"In *here?*" Mia gives our room a distasteful look. "My closet back home is bigger than this. Of course there's not room. Which is why Darby thought maybe you could . . . you know."

I look from her to Darby. "You . . . want me to move out."

Darby winces. "I—I hoped maybe they'd have a three-person room in the dorms, but there isn't one. So . . ."

I've never seen Darby like this, stammering, nervous, her voice barely a whisper. Even when she hated my guts, she'd at least been straightforward about it. I don't know *this* version of Darby at all. It's as if the moment Mia arrived, she pulled out a whole brand-new personality.

"If you don't want to—" Darby starts, but I jump in.

"No, it's fine. Of course you two should be roomies. It's only right."

"Really?" Mia says. "Oh, Wondergirl, you're the best!"

"No problem. I mean, as long as it's not against the rules to switch rooms."

"Rules?" Mia says the word the way a fish might say *Shoes?* As if the concept has never really applied to her.

"I'm sure it'll be fine." I yank open the closet to pull out my suitcase. "Maybe one of the other girls has an empty bed I can have."

But it turns out that everyone else already has a roommate. So with help from Miss March, the dean of students, and Phoebe, the senior dorm captain, I move all my things into an empty room on the far end of the hallway. It's dusty, and there are cobwebs in the closet, but I pretend to love it, because Darby's standing anxiously in the doorway.

"She's real," Darby murmurs, looking a bit dazed.

Dropping my suitcase, I walk over to her. "I thought you were going to pass out the moment you saw her. How do you feel? I mean, it's not every day someone comes back from the dead."

"You'd know better than anyone," she points out. "I don't know *what* to feel. I mean . . . happy, of course. Shocked. Confused. It's like a dream."

With a smile, I impulsively reach out and hug her. "I'm glad you got your best friend back, Darby."

"Thanks," she whispers, hugging me too. "And . . . Mia's not that bad. You have to give her time, that's all. She always comes off as a little *much,* at first."

"I'm sure she's great." I pull back, still forcing the smile. "Sounds like she went through a lot."

She nods, biting her lip. "Are you really okay with all this? The room, I mean?"

"Absolutely!" I nod vigorously. "You two should room together. It's only right."

"I'm kind of jealous," says Mia, poking her head in and making us both jump. "A room all to yourself! It's like VIP treatment."

"Totally," I say, patting the bed. "I love it."

"Great! See, Darby? She loves it. Now let's go. I want to see *everything* this school has to offer. Please tell me there's a sauna? I positively cannot *live* without a—oh! I left my bag in the room. Darbs . . ."

"I'll get it for you!" Darby runs off like an eager Labrador.

Mia turns back to me, her eyes narrowing to slits.

The temperature in the room seems to drop.

"So. You and Darby, huh?" she says. "Don't you think you've stolen enough from me?"

"What? I—"

She snaps her fingers, cutting me short. "Want a word of advice from someone with far more talent and experience than you? Don't get comfortable here at Mystwick."

"What's that supposed to mean?"

"It means life has a way of changing so fast it'll make you spin. Trust me—I know." She looks me up and down, her lip curling. "*Amelia.* You're supposed to be a Composer? Please. Even your *name* isn't original. Stay away from Darby."

She turns with a flick of her hair, her face transforming back to a carefree smile as Darby returns with her bag.

"See you around, Wondergirl!" she chirps, and with a wave, she links arms with my former roommate and they exit out the door.

Ho-ly Bach.

Mia Jones is the most terrifying person I've ever met.

And I've met *dead people.*

My stomach turns like its being operated by a tiny, over-caffeinated hamster. It's so quiet I can even hear the faint, distant drone of the upper-class orchestra practicing in the Shell, as we call the school concert hall.

Mia Jones's words linger in the air.

Don't get comfortable here at Mystwick.

What I can't decide is, did she mean her words as advice . . . or a threat?

CHAPTER THREE

A Score to Settle

AT DINNER THAT NIGHT, all anyone can talk about is Mia Jones.

She and Darby aren't even there. I guess Darby is helping her settle in. Or maybe, on account of being famous, Mia gets a fancy private dinner somewhere else. I poke at my meat loaf, not very hungry, and listen to Claudia brag about how she *knew* Mia wasn't *really* dead, that she'd felt it in her heart all this time.

Rolling my eyes, I deliver my tray to the dish room and then head out for Phoebe's meeting.

"Amelia, wait!"

Jai runs up to me. His knitted hat is pushed up on his head so that his large ears stick out, which seems to defeat the whole point of the hat.

"Can I come with?" he asks.

"To the girls' dorm meeting?"

He shakes his head. "What? No. The meeting in the Shell. There are a bunch of guys going too, so I don't think it has anything to do with nail polish and hair braiding, or whatever it is you girls do all night."

"That's definitely what we do. Okay, whatever. I'm sure it'll be boring, though."

"I heard Kjersten's going to be there," he admits. "The whole Sparring Club too."

So that explains his eagerness. Kjersten's captain of the Sparring Club, and she's the one Jai has to impress if he's going to be let in.

We walk briskly, hands deep in our pockets, taking the shortcut behind the gym. Somewhere in the Echo Wood an owl hoots, but otherwise the night is frozen and silent.

"So. Darby and Mia are roommates now, eh?" says Jai.

"Yeah."

"You okay with that?"

"I mean . . . they were supposed to be together to begin with. It's not like they stopped being best friends."

"Still. Tossing you out of your room? Bit rude. Why didn't you just say no?"

"Because Mia's right," I point out. "I did take her spot at Mystwick, and her room, *and* her roommate. It was only fair."

"But none of that was *your* fault."

"Well . . . it kind of is. I mean, it's true I did those things.

What do you want me to do, tell her *no,* that I won't change rooms? I don't want to start a fight."

"Well, it's unfair. She might as well be blaming you for her getting shipwrecked in the first place. You can't go around taking blame for things that aren't your fault."

"I don't want to talk about it."

"Hmm." He acts like he's going to say more, but he doesn't.

The front doors of the Shell are locked. I knock, then shove my cold hands into my pockets. That's when my fingers brush against a folded paper, and I suddenly recall the note I got in the mail this morning. *You are invited to witness the Midnight Orchestra . . .*

I start to tell Jai about it, but at that moment someone appears in the dark lobby and opens the door for us.

"Phoebe? What's going—"

"Shhh!" The Australian senior presses a finger to her lips, her face shadowed by a black hoodie. She gives Jai a severe look. "You weren't supposed to bring guests, Jones."

Jai beams at her. "Top o' the evening, Phoebe!"

"Hmph. Come in, then, but don't cause any trouble."

"Trouble? *Me?*" Jai presses a hand to his heart, dramatically aghast.

"What's this about?" I ask.

"Just follow me," Phoebe says.

She leads us through the dark lobby to a tall glass display

case on the back wall. It holds the many trophies and awards won by Mystwick students over the decades, with accompanying photos of various orchestras, ensembles, and soloists.

We're not the only ones here. About thirty other kids have already gathered, seated on the floor. Most, like Jai and me, are wearing expressions of confusion. They're nearly all from higher grades. The only other seventh-graders are Amari and Jamal, the violin twins, Victoria, the guitarist, and . . .

"Darby!"

She looks up. "Hey, Amelia!"

"Of *course* Wondergirl is here," says a voice.

I step aside as Mia plops down beside Darby. She's got her fluffy pink coat on over her Mystwick uniform.

"Oh. Hi, Mia." I step back, unsure whether she'll show her sweet or sour side.

"You can sit with us," Darby says.

"No, it's fine. I'm with Jai, anyway."

"Ooooh, the cutie with the ears?" says Mia. She flutters her fingers at Jai and smiles, and he looks ready to pass out.

I push him away to a clear spot while he swoons. "Did you see that? Amelia Jones knows who I am! I mean, the *other* one, the famous one, not—er—you know what I mean."

"She called you a cutie." I gag.

"Of course she did. I mean, have you *seen* me? I'm adorable."

"Silence!" hisses Phoebe. She stands in front of us, her

hands clasped behind her back. "Sit down. Nobody speak. Nobody move."

She exits down a dark hallway, leaving us all bewildered on the floor. Mia yawns and lies back, shutting her eyes, as if she can't be bothered with it all.

Then I jump as a sudden, strange sound echoes through the lobby, like the tingling, warping notes you'd hear in a horror movie. The music groans and shudders with high-pitched shrieks and bonging sharp notes that make me flinch.

Chills run over my skin. I grab hold of Jai's arm. The sound gets louder and louder.

From down the dark hallway, the eerie glow of blue elemental magic begins to shine. Watery wisps of light float like snakes through the air, illuminating the faces of the five seniors marching toward us. Phoebe's one of them, and like her, they're all wearing dark hoodies. The magic flowing around them casts dancing shadows on their faces.

One of them is holding a strange instrument I've never seen before. It's like a metal bowl with a bunch of stainless steel spikes around the rim, which the student strums with a violin bow, creating the shivery notes that crawl up my spine.

"Waterphone," Jai whispers, grinning. "Sweet. I always wanted to try one of those."

The elemental spell causes water to flow from the drinking fountains at the back of the lobby. Thick, twisting streams swirl through the air and collect in gently glowing globes all around us, hovering at about head height.

The students march a full circle around us before stopping, and the magic from the waterphone burns steadily. The last notes fade away, but the glow of magic lingers in the orbs of floating water. They cast a shimmery pattern on the ceiling, walls, and floor, making it feel like we're sitting in a huge aquarium.

The boy who steps forward next is the student body president, Trevor Thompson. A bunch of the girls around me sigh a little. Trevor's got a handsome brown face, curly black hair, and a movie-star smile, all of which he shows off by dramatically flinging his hood back. Since arriving at Mystwick, I've noticed several of my classmates dreamily doodling his name next to theirs more than once.

"Welcome, my brothers and sisters in magic," he intones, making his voice deep and resonant. "You have all been handselected by us, your senior student body, for a most sacred and crucial mission. Well, *most* of you, anyway." He glances at Jai. "We are *very* proud, of course, to welcome Amelia Jones."

My stomach flips until I realize I'm not the Amelia he means.

"Just *Mia* is fine," she says, blowing a kiss, and a couple of students clap.

"Right . . . so." Trevor spreads his hands. "As I was saying, your mission, should you choose to accept—"

"Oh, stop blabbing and just say it," says Rosa Guerrera, who stands beside Trevor. She's wearing a black hoodie embroidered with grinning skulls.

I've had run-ins with Rosa and the other members of Rebel Clef, the school rock band. I know just how terrifying she can be. She seems as affected by Trevor's charm as a black hole is by a flashlight.

"Fine," he says. "Friends, you're here to right a great injustice. To restore the honor of our proud Mystwick!"

"Woohoo!" Jai cheers, pumping his fist. "I'm in!"

"*Quiet,* Kapoor!" Phoebe snaps.

"Direct your attention behind me," says Trevor. He turns and lifts a hand over the glass display case. "Behold, the greatest shame of our school."

The spot he indicates is . . . empty, except for a little note card.

"For the first *century* of its existence," Trevor says, "Mystwick was the proud owner of the holy grail of academic Musicraft, a *very* precious item."

He pauses to look pointedly at Phoebe.

"Oh! Sorry," she says, holding up a school-issued tablet and turning it on, showing a picture of . . .

"Ew!" someone shouts.

"Gross!" yell other students. "Look away!"

"A selfie of Phoebe's chin zit," says Rosa. "Nice."

Phoebe squeals. "No! That's not—I thought I deleted that!" Frantically, she swipes to the next photo. *"There."*

Everyone leans forward to get a better look.

"The Crystal Lyre!" proclaims Trevor, like he's announcing royalty.

The lyre—a kind of U-shaped harp—is indeed made of crystal, and it shimmers atop a pedestal. Its prismatic surface casts dancing rainbows on the walls around it. It's beautiful, and it looks fragile enough to break if you actually tried to play it. At about two feet tall, it does appear to be exactly the right size to fill the empty spot in the trophy case.

"It's the shiny thing you get if your school wins the Orphean Trials," says Rosa in a bored voice. "Whoopdedoo."

Students start nodding and whispering like they suddenly understand what's going on, but I couldn't be more lost.

Jai raises his hand. "Wait. The *Orphan* Trials? Um, is it mandatory to be an orphan, because I—"

"Or-fee-uhn," pronounces Trevor, looking irritated. "As in the Greek god of music, Orpheus? As in Orpheus *Lake?"* He points through the glass doors to the dark waters across campus. "Decades ago, the Crystal Lyre was stolen from us when the Souza Musicraft Academy notoriously sabotaged the

Mystwick orchestra's instruments just before they performed at the Trials, and the scum *got away with it.* Souza won the Lyre that day by playing dirty, and they've won it every year since."

He opens the glass case and takes out the note card sitting where the Crystal Lyre once stood.

"This is the message left to us by our predecessors," he says. "These are the words of the Mystwick students of generations past. A holy mandate, which we are honor bound to—"

"It says, 'Avenge us,'" Rosa interrupts.

Trevor cuts her an annoyed look. "Right. And so, for the first time in nearly twenty years, Mystwick will enter the Orphean Trials, avenge our wronged predecessors, and take back what's ours!"

Everyone starts cheering, except for Mia, who yawns, and me, who's still confused. None of this explains why we're meeting like this, or why there's such a small group of us, or why on earth *I* was hand-selected for this little meeting.

Everyone starts chanting *"Mystwick Musicats! Mystwick Musicats!"* There's a flag in the corner with the school crest on it—a harp surrounded by ivy—as well as the mascot, the musicat. A kid grabs it and waves it around, nearly taking out several eyeballs in the process. The pointed tip pokes one of the water-globe-lamp things, and it bursts, drenching the kid. He shrieks and drops the flag.

"All right, all right!" Trevor waves everyone quiet again.

"Here's the deal. The Trials take place in just six weeks. There are five of them in all, and points are awarded for each. It's simple. Get the most points, win the lyre, and tell the Souza Sonogoats to shove it."

Phoebe swipes to a video of a sonogoat—a weird animal whose screams are known to produce a sonic wave so powerful it can knock a person over. But someone's edited the video so that the goat chokes on its own scream and swells up like a balloon before floating into space.

Trevor explains further. "Let's break down the plan. Once you all agree to join us, we'll go to the Maestros for approval to enter the Trials. They're more likely to say yes if the whole team is already on board. Then, once we're in, Rosa here and the other Rebel Clef players will take the first trial, Battle of the Bands."

Rosa grins like a shark.

"Next is the Gauntlet, which will be handled by the twins."

Amari and Jamal exchange baffled looks. "We'll handle *what now?*"

"It's basically an obstacle course made up of spinning logs, cliffs, traps, things like that. You have to guide each other through sections of it, with one of you blindfolded and the other playing spells to get them to the finish line safely."

"You sure we're up for that?" asks Amari. "We're just seventh-graders."

"It's a strategy. You're smaller than all the other contestants, who'll be seniors and juniors, making it easier for you to navigate the obstacles." Trevor winks at her, and I swear Amari swoons a little. "Besides, you bring that whole twin power thing—you know, where you read each other's minds and stuff."

"That's a stereotype," says Jamal.

"But we'll let it slide," says Amari, still with heart-eyes.

"Next up is the Musical Arts Installation, which the ice sculpting club will handle under Phoebe's lead," Trevor says.

"We have an *ice sculpting* club?" I whisper to Jai.

Trevor raises a hand. "And then there's the Sparring Tournament, obviously led by the Sparring Club captain, Kjersten."

The senior holding the waterphone waves. Kjersten is short, blond, and, as Jai has wistfully told me many times, a Sparring champion back in her native Norway.

Jai's hand closes on my arm like a guitar capo.

"Did you hear that, Amelia Grace Jones?" he whispers. "I will be on that Spar team, you can bet your flute on it."

"Finally," says Trevor, "there's the main event. The trial, in which we *all* participate, a full orchestra. The one that counts toward *fifty percent* of our total score. The one they broadcast on live TV so everyone in the world can watch. In fact, you can lose all the other trials and still claim the lyre if you win this last one."

He looks around, trying to stare intently at each one of us. In the awed silence, the glowing water orbs continue revolving in midair, making our shadows dance.

"I'm speaking, of course," Trevor says slowly, "of the *Composium*. Which brings me to the reason we're all here, the reason why, after twenty years of being ineligible to even *enter* the Trials, we can finally take our rightful place as the best of the best." He raises both of his hands like a priest giving a blessing. "Our own Amelia *Jones!*"

This time, there's no doubt which Amelia he means.

Because everyone turns to stare at *me*.

"Wh-what?" I whisper.

"You're the first Composer we've had at Mystwick in years," Trevor says. "Which is why we haven't been able to compete in all that time. The Composium's rules are simple: we can perform any spell, but it has to be written by a student Composer at our school. *You,* Amelia Jones, will write this spell. You will lead us to victory. I mean, come on, we all saw what you did last week. You literally took on an army of *ghosts!* This should be a cakewalk for you, right?"

Every eye in the room drills into me.

"Well," says Trevor. "What do you say, Jones? Will you help us steal back the Crystal Lyre?"

My throat is so dry I can't even swallow. It suddenly feels like a hundred degrees in here.

They're all waiting for my answer. Holding their breath. Looking at me like there's a flood coming and I'm the only raft around.

"Oh, c'mon, Wondergirl!" Mia calls out. "Isn't *stealing things* your specialty?"

Darby shushes her.

I blink hard, then shake my head. "I don't know . . ."

"Please, Amelia," says Trevor. "You're the only one who can set things right."

He holds out a hand, indicating the empty space on the shelf.

But my eye travels to the faded photo sitting next to it—and my blood freezes in my veins.

In a daze, I stand up, barely even aware of everyone watching, and walk to the back wall. I open the glass door and take out the picture, which is lacquered onto a wooden block.

"That's the last Mystwick team to compete at the Orphean Trials," says Trevor. "They're the ones whose final performance got sabotaged by the Souza kids."

The picture is old and faded, showing five students with old-fashioned hairstyles and Mystwick sweaters. Their names are written below them.

Forgetting Trevor, forgetting everyone else in the room, I stare at the pretty girl with huge bangs and a smile like sunshine.

Mom.

Hanging over her shoulder is the very same flute case I'm holding now. She looks happy and confident, beaming into the camera.

SUSAN JONES, it reads below her picture. COMPOSER.

Then, with growing dread, I look at the boy next to her, the one with his arm around her shoulders, his fingers knitted with hers. He's wearing a jean jacket over his Mystwick uniform, his thick, dark hair combed back from his pale face. He's smirking at the camera. Below him, his name is written in fading ink.

ERIC NEAL.

But I know him by a different name.

Dad.

Gran told me that my parents met at Mystwick. But ever since I arrived, I only ever imagined this place as belonging to Mom. I'd pictured her walking across the grounds countless times. I'd thought of her sitting in the library and canoeing on the lake and hiking in the Echo Wood.

But it occurs to me now that not once have I ever imagined *him* here.

No no no no NO.

My chest gets tight, as if my ribs are squeezing together. When I try to breathe, a knot of panic clogs my throat.

"Amelia?" Trevor asks. "You . . . okay?"

Don't think about him, I tell myself. *He's nothing to you anyway. Forget him. Think about* her.

I close my eyes and picture my mom leading the Mystwick student orchestra through a spell of her own making, laughing and cutting up just like any other kid. I picture her shock and anger when she realized that their instruments had been sabotaged and her spell had been all for nothing. I picture her until, slowly, *he* fades from my mind.

Opening my eyes, I turn and face the others. "I'm in."

Cheers erupt, and Trevor and Phoebe take my hands and lift them high. I grin, even as my belly fills with queasy butterflies.

As soon as they let go of me, I shove the picture back into the case and close the door so hard the glass rattles.

CHAPTER FOUR

Oh Me, Oh Maestro

THE LAST BELL RINGS just as I leave the dorm the next day. Everyone floods to the common areas, probably to gossip about the Trials. Word has spread fast, and now the whole school is buzzing about the competition. Trevor Thompson beams his toothpaste-commercial smile and gives interviews to the student newspaper, the *Mystwick Bugler*. Phoebe's art club designs T-shirts emblazoned with our mascot, a snarling musicat that looks like Wynk, Mrs. Le Roux's pet. In between classes, kids I've never spoken to in my life wish me luck.

I push my way through them to reach Harmony Hall, where, according to my note from the headmaestro, my Composing class is to be held in room 713. I look up at the big building and frown; there are only six floors.

So where's 713?

After searching the building from top to bottom with no luck, an amused senior finally points me in the right direction —which leads up a long, creaky stairway.

"It's in the attic?" I squeak.

"Good luck, guppy." He laughs before leaving me alone.

I ascend slowly, positive that I've been pranked, but sure enough, at the top of the steps is a door with Room 713 written on it in faded Sharpie—like it's some third-grader's secret clubhouse and not a real classroom at all.

I knock, fully prepared to turn and flee down the stairs depending on what answers the door.

But nothing does.

Slowly, I twist the knob, and the door opens to a dark, dusty attic, the ceiling arching cavernously above. All around, dark, vague shapes loom, and the air smells of old paper and dust. A spidery shiver crawls down the back of my neck.

"Hello . . ." I whisper. No one answers, but I'm pretty sure that somewhere in the back of the attic, something *scurries.*

I assemble my flute and play an illumination spell; if there are any working lightbulbs in the attic, the magic should make them turn on.

Soon lights being flickering on through the room—not lightbulbs, but candles. Sputtering flames dance uncertainly, as if they've been extinguished for so long they've forgotten how to burn. In the soft orange light I see that the attic is even bigger than I'd thought. It must stretch the whole length of Harmony Hall, with no windows or other doors. Bare rafters hold up a pitched roof so high it feels like a cathedral, filmy with cobwebs. Everything is covered in a layer of dust. There are a few old desks set in front of a chalkboard, words still scrawled on it.

COMPOSING 101.

My heart skips. This *is* a classroom, but one that's not been used for a long time.

A few papers are tacked to a bulletin board on one wall: half-finished spells; a magical classification chart; instructions for what to do if you accidentally start a fire, unleash a flood, call down lightning, or create other magical disasters. It's all so old, the papers are turning yellow.

I wander to a tall shelf packed with binders, notebooks, and folders.

"Student Compositions, 1950–1952," I whisper, reading the spine of a leather folio. They're all labeled the same way, covering more than a hundred years all together, probably back to the day Mystwick was founded.

My pulse jumps.

Does that mean . . .

I run my finger over the spines until I reach the years my mom would have been a student here. I find the folio at the very bottom of the shelf, the last in a long line.

The notebook is brown, with the word COMPOSITION stamped on the front in faded gold letters. The spine is worn from age and use.

Sliding it out, I hold my breath as I let the pages fall open in my hands. A cluster of white candles on a nearby table provide just enough light to see . . .

That half the pages have been ripped out.

On the inside of the notebook's cover, I find her name: SUSAN JONES, along with a doodle of music notes with little happy faces in them. The remaining pages have blank staff lines, waiting for notes to be penciled in. But the pages that were torn out had to have been used; the barest lines are visible where my mom pressed down hard with her pencil tip—tiny, ghostly notes left behind.

But the actual spells she Composed are gone, leaving only jagged edges.

Where? Did she take them with her?

Or did someone steal them?

"Oh, let me have a peek," says a syrupy voice behind me. "I do love a good snoop."

My soul jumps out of my body and lands somewhere around Neptune.

Slamming the book shut, I whirl around to see a woman perched on the desk behind me, grinning like a Cheshire cat.

"Who—who are you?" I stammer. "Where did you *come* from?"

She's tall and dark-skinned, with a pile of graying dreadlocks towering precariously atop her head, and layers upon layers of flowing clothes in several clashing prints—zebra, floral, tie-dye, polka dots—all over a T-shirt that reads PEACE. LOVE. MUSICRAFT. Heavy beaded necklaces and bracelets clack when she moves. She looks like she ran full tilt through a clothing rack and came out wearing whatever stuck. On her collar glitters a golden Maestro pin.

"Hmm," she says, closing her eyes and tilting her head, as if listening to a spell I can't hear. "Who am I, who am I? Today . . . yes . . . today I am a crane, regal and swooping, alighting upon this earth with wings full of the sun."

I blink, take a step back. "Um."

"And who are *you?*" she asks, opening her eyes to peer at me with intense curiosity.

"I'm . . . Amelia?"

"You seem unsure of that. Good! An excellent start. *Question everything.* Let go of the past. Fling yourself into a pool of infinite possibilities."

"You're my new Maestro?"

She raises her arms, stretching them gracefully away from her body. "Maestro, student, these words are so *limiting.* There is much for me to learn, isn't there? And much for you to teach."

"Uh . . ."

"Now, my dear." She presses her hands together. "Tell me

what you *are.* Not your name. No labels. Pssh! We're moving beyond all that. Go on, girl. Tell me what you *feel* you are."

"I'm confused."

"Honest. Yes! I like that. What else? What emotions can you harness like wild horses in the wind? For what is music but emotion, and what is emotion if not power?"

"Power?" I feel anything but powerful right now. My head is still spinning, trying to figure out how she crept up on me.

The woman bursts up in an explosion of colorful fabrics and rushes to the chalkboard, flipping it over. The reverse side is blank.

"My name," she says, scrawling with the chalk, "is Mathilde Motte. And you are here to forget everything you have learned. The first and only rule of Composing is that here, *rules don't apply.*"

I raise a finger, a hundred questions crowding my brain, but she rushes on, still scribbling with her chalk.

"Composing is *feeling,* and feeling is power. So let's dig deep! Let's unearth the ugliest and best parts of you and set them free. We are here to crack you open, Amelia Jones, and let power ooze out."

"Crack me open?"

"Like a coconut!" She laughs so loudly, spiders scurry for cover.

Miss
Motte

Holy Bach.

My Composing Maestro is terrifying.

"Aha!" cries Miss Motte, stepping back from the chalkboard to reveal that she's drawn a rather terrible picture of . . . well, *me,* I guess. There's curly hair sprouting from my head in all directions, one arm is way longer than the other, and my legs end in jumbled scribbles rather than feet. But there's no mistaking the flute in my hand or the freckles she dots onto my face with an exaggerated flourish.

"Amelia Jones," she murmurs, tapping her chin with chalk as she studies her artwork, leaving little white smudges on her dark skin. After a moment, she shoots me a sideways look and whispers, "You should know, I've never actually *taught* anyone before."

"Oh," I say weakly.

She extends the chalk toward me. "Go on. Write what you are. Show me who Amelia Jones is."

I take the chalk uncertainly and step toward the board, then turn back to her. "The thing is, Miss Motte, there are these Trials coming up. Maybe you heard about it? See, I kinda need to Compose a super awesome spell and—"

"Yes!" She dashes her hand through the air. "Eager, I see! Good! Write it down."

"What?"

"*Eager!* An excellent word. Write it down!"

"Okay . . ." I scribble the word on the board.

"Yes, yes! Give me *more*. What are you, Amelia Jones?"

I think a moment, then write FLUTIST and GIRL. "Like that?"

Miss Motte clicks her tongue. "No, no, not *labels*. Write down what you *feel*."

Exasperated, I write CONFUSED.

"Superb!" says Miss Motte. "Go on!"

Okay, then. I add EXCITED and NERVOUS and HOPEFUL, and she practically swoons.

"Yes, Amelia! Yes! In Composing, emotions are everything. They are your power. Your inspiration. Your *magic*. There is no spell on this earth that was not Composed out of love or envy or *rage*. But then, you should know this already." She smiles. "You've Composed before."

"Yeah, I guess."

"So tell me. What did you feel when you Composed the spell to summon your mother's ghost?"

"You know about that? Um . . . well, I guess it was sadness," I say softly.

Her smile fades, her eyes brimming with empathy. "Grief can be powerful indeed."

"So . . . that's it? The whole secret to Composing is just to . . . feel something?"

She spreads her hands wide. "Exactly! An *A-plus* for you, Amelia Jones! Congratulations on passing your first Composing class. Ha! This teaching thing is easier than I'd thought. And to think my sister was worried I would be too scatterbrained for the job! Ha!" She picks up the wooden pointer leaning against the chalkboard and thumps the floor with it. "Hear that, Euphonia? I *can* teach."

"*Mrs. Le Roux* is your sister?" I asked. It's hard to imagine the serene, dignified headmaestro of Mystwick having any family. She seems so . . . timeless, like one of the statues of the famous Composers erected all over the campus.

"My *baby* sister," says Miss Motte with a wink. "By five years. A fact she likes to forget. Now, I suppose that's it for us today, so—"

"Wait, that's it? That can't be it. I have so many questions. Are there books I should be reading? Composers I should study? And what about the Trials? Everyone's counting on me to have a spell ready."

"Hmm, you're probably right." She strokes her lip. "Ah! Of course!"

She begins pulling open drawers in the desk, sorting through sticks of broken chalk, old Conductor's batons, a broken metronome, chunks of resin, until finally she lets out a shout and produces a slim notebook bound in black leather. After flipping through it, she nods and pushes it into my hands.

The pages inside are all blank staff lines waiting to be filled with music.

"Every Composer should have a blank page ready at all times," says Miss Motte. "A stray thought could wander through your head at any moment, and you must be ready to pin it to the page."

Smiling, I clutch the notebook to my chest. My own Composition book—just like my mom had. It makes me feel a little bit more like a *real* Composer.

"Your homework," says Miss Motte, "is to listen, to breathe, to dream. No thought is too insignificant to be written down. Remember: true inspiration comes not from *here*"—she taps my forehead—"but from here." Her finger moves to my heart.

I nod vigorously. "I'll get started on some melodies right away!"

She gives me a bemused look. "Melodies? Oh, no, no, child. I don't want you to write down *music*."

"Huh?"

"*Emotions,* Amelia." She pats my cheek. "Record your emotions, your feelings, big and small. The music—pah—the music is just notes and sound. But the emotions? Those are *everything*. Those are what the music must flow from. Those are your power."

"Right," I murmur. "So . . . you don't actually want me to Compose."

She blows out a breath, then gives a little weary laugh. "I suppose there might be more to teaching than I thought. Well, never mind. It's only day one, and we have plenty of time. Go on now, flutter away, my butterfly. Record your feelings. Listen to your heart."

I nod as if I understand. I really, really don't.

But then, this is Mystwick, after all.

What else is new?

CHAPTER FIVE

In Portal Danger

"HMM, HMM, HMMM . . . **No.** That's not it." I stare at the gym floor, where someone's sneaker has left a black scuff mark, and hum to myself some more. *"Hmm. Hmm, hmm, hmm . . . hmm?"*

Ugh! That's not right either.

"What are you muttering about?" Jai asks.

Flinching, I look up at him. I'd almost forgotten where I was — or that I was supposed to be stretching my hamstrings. I cross one leg over the other and reach for my toes. "Just trying to think of a melody."

I know everyone is waiting for me to produce some amazing spell for the Trials. I know because this morning at breakfast, no less than nine kids stopped by my table to ask how the *amazing spell* was coming along, and I had absolutely nothing to give them but a queasy smile.

"Still nothing? What about your new Maestro? Isn't she helping?"

I wince. Miss Motte's teaching has been, so far, the opposite of helping. I'm more confused about how Composing works than I was *before* I had a Composing class. In the week since she arrived, I've recorded every mood I've had, learned fourteen yoga poses, folded six origami horses, painted eight rocks to represent the eight basic emotions, drank six cups of ginkgo tea, learned how to tie-dye . . . and Composed exactly *zero* notes.

"My brain feels constipated." I groan. "I'm going to walk up on that stage at the Trials and have absolutely *nothing* to play."

Maybe the judges will accept my new collection of tie-dyed bandanas instead.

Coach Phil blows his whistle and barks, "Jumping jacks! Go!"

With a sigh, I throw my arms half-heartedly into the air in a sudden flashback to my week at sports camp last summer. I can still hear the bleat of the camp counselor's whistle and his favorite slogan booming in my ears: *You haven't failed until you've given up!*

Well, I haven't given up.

But I still feel like I'm failing.

Jai and Darby bounce on either side of me. This may be a school for Musicraft, but regular PE is a rite of passage no student gets out of. Strong bodies make for strong music, the

Maestros like to say. So every Thursday afternoon, all the seventh-graders sweat it out in collective misery. The gym echoes with the squeak of sneakers and gasping breaths punctuated by occasional moans of despair.

"Take it easy," Jai says. "We've still got six whole weeks."

"Five, actually," says Darby. "And that includes the time we have to actually *practice* Amelia's spell."

Not all the sweat in my armpits is from the jumping jacks.

"No slacking, Jones!" shouts Coach Phil. He rolls his wheelchair in front of me and glares. He's got arms like show hogs, which he likes to display by always wearing tank tops. "How are you supposed to kick Souza's butts when you can't even get your *own* into gear?"

Ugh. Even the *gym teacher* is on my case.

He's about to yell some more, but then Miss Noorani, the Maestro of strings, walks into the gym for her afternoon Pilates, and his face goes red. "That is, uh, keep up the good work, kid."

He wheels quickly to the other side of the gym, says hello to Miss Noorani, then begins doing pull-ups, lifting himself, wheelchair and all.

The pull-up bars just happen to be located right in front of the Pilates mats, so Miss Noorani has an excellent view of Coach Phil's biceps.

"Good timing, Maestro," says Jai as he and half the other

kids stop jumping and just lift their arms up and down. With Coach Phil distracted, the rest of us can go easy. "I was starting to worry that she wouldn't show up today."

"Maybe I could Compose a spell to help Coach chill out," I mutter.

"Maybe you should try trusting Miss Motte's process," suggests Darby. "I'm sure this is all leading somewhere."

"Is it?" Jai gives her a skeptical look. "Don't get me wrong. I'd give my *teeth* for a class as easy as this one sounds. What was your homework yesterday, Amelia? Napping?"

"Meditation." I sigh. But yes, it had turned into a nap. "I need more time. Like, a year maybe. Or two."

"Or . . ." Jai spreads his hands wide. "Maybe we could do another brainstorm session."

Darby snorts. "The last one we did, your idea was that she Compose a spell to unclog toilets."

"Hey! I live in a guys' dorm. It's a *problem*."

"What Amelia needs is to stay disciplined, keep practicing, and trust the process."

"What Amelia needs is help—"

"What Amelia *needs*," I interrupt, "is some space. Maybe a long walk, to clear my head."

Thankfully, Coach Phil blows his whistle, ending class and giving me the chance to do just that. I change into warm clothes, pull on the purple and gray scarf and hat Gran knitted for me, and wave goodbye to Jai and Darby. With an hour of free time before dinner, I head for the one place at Mystwick I know I can be alone: the Echo Wood.

But when I slip out of the locker room, I bump smack into Mia Jones.

"Wondergirl! Where are you sneaking off to?"

"I wasn't sneaking. I'm going for a walk in the woods."

"All alone? Weird." She puts her hand on the wall, her arm blocking my path. "You know, I saw you talking to Darby."

"What? In gym? We have five classes together, Mia, I don't see how—"

"I told you to stay away from her. And trust me, you *don't* want me as an enemy."

Geez Louise, this girl has control issues. "I don't want to be enemies. Honest. But you know, Darby's allowed to have other friends besides you."

"Yes, just not *you*." She pushes off the wall and walks away, her hair swinging behind her. "See you around, Wondergirl. Watch your step out there. It can get pretty *icy*."

Seriously, what is her problem? All week long, she's been keeping Darby close to her like she's some kind of pet. Maybe it has to do with her shipwreck and her missing mom, and she has some kind of paranoia about losing people. But I'm starting to get the feeling it's more personal than that.

Just not you.

Clearly, she's still holding my acceptance to Mystwick against me. But why? It's not like my being here got her kicked out or anything. How long will she keep this grudge?

I rush outside into the cold and the trees, never gladder for the quiet and solitude of the forest.

When the wind blows hard enough, the Echo trees will sing out Canon in D, the protective spell that wards the school. But today, in the lightest of breezes, the trees only rustle, their swaying bare branches humming with soft tones — sweet flute, sharp violin, vibrating cello. Like an orchestra tuning up before a performance, the trees play dozens of notes that somehow create harmony despite their different keys.

If only people worked that way.

I don't go more than five steps into the woods before I hear a shiver of music deep in the trees. I stop for a minute, turning my ear to it. At first I think it's just the Echo trees' natural sound.

But the more I listen, the more I pick out the faintest melody . . . and it's not Canon in D.

Curious, I go deeper into the forest, my steps crunching on the frost-covered leaves. The sound gets louder and louder, and it's definitely some kind of spell. Who'd be out here practicing in the freezing cold?

Then I push through a thicket and see it.

A glass piano sits in a frozen glade. Its top open, it glows in the dim forest as if there's a spotlight shining from the sky. Tiny butterflies made of ice flutter all around, leaving trails of glittering dust. Meanwhile, the piano keys play of their own accord, and the air shimmers with swirls of purple magic.

Purple? A teleportation spell?

There's no sign of a musician.

The hairs on my arms rise. If this is another ghost thing, I swear . . .

I approach the piano cautiously. "Hello? Is anyone—"

But the moment I step into the glade, it's like I trigger some hidden switch. The piano vanishes in a flash of light—it was just an illusion all along. The keys, however, zoom into the air in a long black-and-white chain, and the music does not stop. The keys begin spinning in an oval above the ground, forming a kind of doorway. Through it, purple light ripples like the surface of a pool.

Purple magic . . . A piano-key doorway . . .

This is definitely some kind of portal situation.

Oh . . . no.

No way. That's a double-triple-*quadruple* NO from me.

I am not getting involved in any kind of ghostly weirdness. Not this time. I've learned my lesson. I choose *normal* from here on out. Just call me Amelia the Ordinary. Amelia the Boring. Amelia the Too Smart to Enter Strange Portals in the Woods.

But before I can turn around, words appear on the watery purple curtain in the doorway.

Amelia Jones,
You are invited to witness the Midnight Orchestra.

I gasp, then plunge a hand into my coat pocket. Sure enough, the black note card is still there, where I'd stuffed it the day Mia Jones arrived. Seeing her had completely driven it out of my mind. But now I hold it up and see that even the handwriting on the portal matches that on the card perfectly:

A doorway will be provided on the next full moon.

I guess I know what *that* means now. Though there's no moon; it's four in the afternoon.

Well, I don't know what a Midnight Orchestra is or why I'm invited to see it, but I have absolutely zero intention of finding out.

I turn and run, racing through the Echo trees, my exhales little white puffs, my shoes crunching on the leaves. If I had a tail, I'd tuck it right between my legs. My plan is simple: run all the way to school, right up the steps to the headmaestro's office, and report everything to her.

Let the grownups deal with this.

But whoever is out here playing tricks is not playing fair.

Suddenly the portal appears *right in front of me*—and, unable to stop in time, I hurtle right through it.

CHAPTER SIX

The Sand of Silence

I LAND ON MY STOMACH with a gasp, my skin shivering from the plunge through the portal. Whatever that shimmering doorway was made of, it hit me like a blast of ice.

Winded, I lie there for a second, waiting for my head to stop spinning and desperately hoping that I'm lying on the floor of the Echo Wood.

But . . . as I push onto my hands and knees, I see not crunchy leaves beneath me, but *sand.* The purest sand I've ever seen, so smooth and clean it's almost like liquid.

Climbing to my feet, I look around in dismay. Dunes curve and slope away, glowing white beneath a full moon that shines larger and brighter than I've ever seen it. Wait—it's *night?* That's not right. Gym class ended at four o'clock.

Across the black, billions of stars burn, so many it almost hurts to look at them. The dusty band of the Milky Way arches from horizon to horizon, a river of stars and galaxies and nebulae. The quiet of the desert is like nothing I've ever heard, a silence so deep and so absolute that my ears feel *empty* with it.

This is *not* the Echo Wood.

This is like nowhere I've ever seen.

"Miss Jones?"

I nearly jump out of my skin.

Spinning around, slipping on sand, I spot an old man standing a few steps away. He carries a massive set of bagpipes with one hand, while the other runs over his long white beard. Beneath that is a tuxedo jacket, and beneath *that* is a plaid kilt. His bare knees wobble slightly, and he's got white socks pulled up over his shins. He wears a tartan mask over his eyes.

What is he, some kind of Scottish desert Santa-slash-superhero?

"Miss Amelia Jones," he says again. "We are pleased to see that you accepted our invitation."

I stare at him a moment longer. He must think I'm an idiot.

Invitation? *Invitation?* That wasn't an invitation! It was a kidnapping!

I whirl around, hoping to leap back to the Echo Wood, but the portal is *gone.*

Of course it is.

Of course it is.

I'm stranded here. Wherever "here" is, with somebody's

kilted grandpa, probably a zillion miles from Mystwick, and nobody knows where I am—

"Miss Jones, please take a breath." The old man steps closer.

I move back warily. My flute is back in my dorm room—we're not supposed to bring instruments to gym class—so I have no way of defending myself.

"You are in no danger here," Bagpipes Santa says calmly, which makes me feel no better. "Word of your talent has impressed Mr. Midnight, and he requests you be his honored guest for the evening."

"Where am I?" I ask, my voice barely above a squeak.

"You are in the Saharan Desert," he says. When I don't reply, he adds, "In the north of Africa . . ."

"I know where the Sahara is!" That explains why it's nighttime. I must be seven or eight time zones ahead of Mystwick—right at Saharan midnight. "*Why* am I here? What do you want from me?"

"We wish only to serve and entertain you. Once the performance is over, the portals will be reopened and you will be free to return home."

Right. This must be his polite way of saying I'm *not* free to leave until I've seen whatever it is he brought me here to see.

I decide to play it nice, remembering some kidnapping survival tips Gran made me memorize after she watched too much late-night news: Speak calmly. Don't run. Obey instructions. Be observant. And try to make your kidnapper see you as a *person.*

"I'm Amelia," I say. Then I remember that he already knows my name. "I'm twelve years old. I . . . like to play the flute."

"Yes," he says with a bemused smile. "We know. I'm Mr. Stewart, manager of the Midnight Orchestra. Please follow me."

Obey instructions, Gran seems to whisper in my ear.

So I start walking, staying a few steps behind the old man. My shoes slip and slide in the sand, and I shiver. It's even colder here than it was back at Mystwick.

Explanations run wild through my head:

This is some kind of test sprung by the Maestros without warning.

I tripped in the Echo Wood, hit my head, and this is all a dream.

Or . . . they have the wrong Amelia Jones.

Hey, it's not as if that hasn't happened before.

Finally we come to a large split in the dune, where an ancient-looking pillared archway parts the wave of sand. Beyond it, pale stones pave the ground, making it easier to walk. This must be some kind of ancient ruin.

"Welcome to the Midnight Orchestra," says a woman

standing in the archway. She's very lovely, with long black hair and a black, lacy dress. She wears a mask too, black lace molded perfectly over her beautiful face. Next to her is a little stall with a red curtain over it.

"Please," she says, pulling aside the curtain, "choose."

"Uh . . ." I lean over to see an arrangement of masks—the fancy kind you'd wear to a masquerade party. There's glitter and feathers and rhinestones, even one mask that looks like it's made of crocodile skin.

What in the world?

This is getting weirder and weirder. But, eager to make them see how obedient I am, I pick one at random and put it on; it's an orange fox face with tall ears tipped in black.

"Excellent, Miss Jones," says the masked lady. "Right that way. Find a seat. The performance will begin very soon."

She gestures toward an amphitheater sunk into the sand. It makes me think of a history program Gran and I watched about ancient gladiators. There are people there. Dozens of them mill around, all wearing masks, whispering in little groups. Everyone is dressed in fancy clothes, tuxedos and glittering gowns, some waving fans or tapping jeweled canes. I don't see any other kids. It reminds me of a grownup's holiday party, but for people who look extremely rich. Many of them are carrying instrument cases.

Have I been kidnapped by some creepy desert cult?

Hoping to get more info from Mr. Stewart, I turn around, but he's gone.

"Is it your first time here, young lady?" asks a voice.

I start, looking from mask to mask until I see the one talking to me—a woman in an emerald green dress and a peacock mask.

"Y-yeah. Hi." *Make them see you as a person*, I remember. "My name is—"

"Shhh!" She flutters a peacock feather fan at me. "No names at the Midnight Orchestra, dear! That's part of the fun." Her laugh is like a tuba, brassy and deep.

"What do you mean?"

"Think of it as a very exclusive club, dear. Only the most interesting and powerful musicians are invited to join, an honor very few people ever receive." She cocks her head. "You are the first child I've seen here, though. How odd. You must be quite remarkable . . ."

I remember something Mia said: *"You must be very interesting to a lot of powerful people."*

Is that what this is about? My black spell? It never occurred to me that people outside of Mystwick might have heard about it . . . or that it would make me seem interesting or powerful. Whoever made this guest list is going to be pretty disappointed when they learn I'm just a normal kid who has no idea what she's doing half the time.

"So, when the performance is over, they send us home?" I ask.

"Of course, dear! Oh, bless your heart. You look like a mouse in a lion's den. Don't worry, you're perfectly safe here. Mr. Midnight treats his guests *very* well. You'll see. Now, sit, sit! It begins soon."

The other guests, if that's what they even are, have begun to take seats around the amphitheater. I do the same, hoping Mr. Stewart was telling the truth and that when this is all over, I'll be allowed to go home. The lady in green sits nearby and gives me a friendly flutter with her peacock fan, then points at the stage.

A hush falls over the crowd, as below us, a single violinist appears—a man in a long, dark coat with a plain black mask over his face. He waits motionlessly for absolute silence, and when it falls, he raises his violin and begins to play.

As the sweet notes rise, curling ribbons of blue light, the air over the stage begins to shift. There's some kind of invisible dome placed over it. But the violinist's solo deconstructs it before our eyes. The illusion melts away like sugar under heat, shimmering and sparkling. And as it dissipates into thin air, it reveals the musicians gathered beneath it.

They'd been there this whole time, hidden from view. As still as statues, dressed all in black, they wear matching porcelain masks painted like doll's faces.

Then the violinist's spell ends, and he raises his bow high.

"Esteemed guests, welcome."

His voice is deep and resonant, like a cello tuned to a dramatic pitch. Everyone in the audience leans forward, breath held, eyes fixed on him. It's almost as if he's cast a spell over all of us to utterly hold our attention.

"I am Mr. Midnight," he says, "and this is my orchestra."

CHAPTER SEVEN

The Midnight Orchestra

WHEN THE MIDNIGHT ORCHESTRA begins to play, every hair on my arms rises.

The breath leaves my body.

My soul leaves the ground.

There is no bombastic flare of trumpets, no loud, clashing first notes. Instead, they play deliberately, slowly, easing into their piece with a precision that holds everyone around me speechless.

The melody is like a forgotten dream, familiar and strange, sinking into my skin and wrapping around my bones, making me feel heavier and lighter at the same time, as if my spirit were lifting right out of me.

The man in black—Mr. Midnight—has vanished, and no conductor appears to take his place. There are only the musicians below us, seated in a spiral. They play with such discipline that they look almost like dolls, especially with those painted masks on. No sheet music is arranged in front of them, no music stands are assembled. None turn to look at the others, but focus only on their own instruments or, when they have a rest, stare straight ahead.

I try to imagine the Mystwick students performing with such perfected movements. Even the best of the seniors couldn't sit that still.

Soon, magic begins sparkling from the instruments as the spell's strength grows, pale yellow light blossoming and stretching like a brilliant, flourishing garden. Deep, rolling drumbeats send up bursts of magic like fireworks.

Sand begins to rise from the desert around us, streaming in glinting rivers to gather over the orchestra. Sparkling like glass, it swirls in a great, glittering cloud over our heads. Then, slowly, the magic sends out tendrils, flowing rivers of sand that slowly arc through the sky and pour downward.

Where they touch the ground, they gather into the shapes of horses.

One appears right in front of me—honey-gold, its hide almost but not quite solid; here and there I can still see the rough texture of the sand, as if the creature might return to the desert at any moment. It has a saddle and a rope halter with tassels, also made of flowing sand, and its mane and tail stream into the ground. It's hard to tell where the horse ends and the desert begins.

All around the amphitheater, guests start climbing onto

the horses, as though that's what the creatures were waiting for.

"Um . . ." I look around and see that most of the guests have already mounted, and their horses are starting to trot away. I've never ridden on a horse. I don't much want to, either.

At least that's what I tell myself.

The creature is just so *beautiful* . . .

Before I half know what I'm doing, I put my foot in the stirrup, only to grab in vain at the saddle and drop down.

It's just as well. For all I know, this is how the kidnappers really get me—by tricking me into riding this thing off to my doom.

The remaining guests are on their horses now, some sitting sidesaddle. The orchestra plays on, its golden magic dancing all around us, infusing the sand horses' manes and tails, their hooves glowing with it.

I'm the only person still on the ground. The musicians don't seem to notice. In fact, they don't seem to notice anything. They play on with robotic stillness, never looking up from their instruments to see the magic they're unfurling. If I didn't know that magic can only flow from living musicians, I might think they're animatronic.

"Give me your foot, girl," says a soft, deep voice.

I turn, my eyes widening. The man himself stands there—Mr. Midnight, the guy who runs this whole show. His dark blue eyes stare at me through the narrow holes in his mask. They're the only part of his face that I can see.

"Excuse me?" I say.

"Your foot." He kneels on one knee and laces his fingers together, his black leather gloves probably more expensive than anything I've ever owned. And he wants me to put my dirty shoe on them?

Obey instructions. Make them see you as a person.

I plant my foot on his hands and he lifts me up easily. Settling into the saddle, I blink at him.

"Thanks."

He stares at me a moment more, then says, "Amelia Jones, is it? The little girl who rent a tear in the veil between life and death. Most impressive."

"Um . . . you've heard of me?" So I was right—this *is* about my black spell.

"I make it a point to know all my guests," Mr. Midnight says. "Especially the ones with gifts like yours." He leans closer, his hand on the sand horse's neck. "What if I told you I could make you the greatest Composer of your generation?"

Uneasily, I tighten my hands on the saddle. "I already have a Composing Maestro, thanks."

With a scoff, he dashes a hand through the air. "I assure you, the things I could teach you, no Maestro would dare. They will treat you like a child. They will hold you back from your true potential. But I know you could be a *star.*" He reaches into an inner pocket and takes out a small glass vial, which he hands to me. "Let's call this our first lesson."

I hold it up to see a single dandelion seed inside. "What is it?"

"To most, it is nothing. To *you?* It is everything." He taps the vial. "It contains a single memory infused with emotive energy —a spell's greatest source of fuel. When you're ready, simply bite the seed and absorb the memory, and you can Compose a spell that would rattle the sky."

"Seriously?" I've never heard of such a thing. Then again, I know practically nothing about Composing to begin with.

Mr. Midnight tips his head. "All great Composers borrow memories for their magic, but I'll bet your Maestros would never tell you that."

"Okay, but . . . isn't that sort of cheating?"

Even through his mask, I can tell he's offended. "Cheating? Is it cheating when a painter uses a model for reference? Is it cheating when a sprinter wears the best running shoes? Here at the Midnight Orchestra, we deal in magic and favors and wonders beyond imagination, not *cheating.*"

"What's it cost?" If there's one thing I've learned from Gran's TV shopping channel habits, it's that most deals that sound too good to be true *are.*

"Never mind that. Let's call it a favor for a favor. An

investment in a young musician I find to be exceptionally promising." His eyes crease as he smiles under his mask. "I never ask for payment a guest cannot afford."

"I don't know . . . I think I'd better not." I start to hand it back, but he steps away and bows.

"Handle it with care, Miss Jones. There is great power in that small vial."

Mr. Midnight whistles, and my horse leaps into motion, cantering up the amphitheater steps to join the others. I kick myself; I just talked to the guy in charge of this whole thing! I should have asked him why I was here, and what he wanted from me, and when I could go home.

I'd been so overwhelmed, my brain seemed to just shut down.

And what's with all the *I could make you the greatest Composer* weirdness? I know a shady deal when I hear one.

And yet Mr. Midnight's voice echoes softly in my head. *I know you could be a star . . .*

Then, all at once, my horse's hooves leave the ground and I forget all about Mr. Midnight and his offer. I still have the dandelion seed in my hand, and I slip it into my pocket so I can hold on.

The horses take flight together, trotting on empty air. All around the amphitheater, borne on a cloud of music, the enchanted creatures begin rising in a spiraling path to the stars.

Sand falls away from their manes and tails; motes of gleaming magic dance around their hooves. Sparkling dust floats between us and all around.

It's like a carousel in the sky.

These kidnappers have style, I have to give them that.

Beautiful as it all may be, I cling to my sand horse and hope to Bach the whole creature doesn't suddenly disintegrate. Or that I topple off. Either seems unnervingly likely.

Higher and higher the horses fly, spiraling toward that huge canopy of stars. It really does feel like riding a carousel, the horse's motion smooth and serene, and gradually I relax. Well, a little bit, anyway. My death grip on the creature's mane loosens a tad.

Far below, the musicians of the Midnight Orchestra slide seamlessly into the next movement of their symphony, the tumbling measures propelled by the rolling drumbeats of the percussionists. Humming violins produce banners of magic that flutter upward, chased by the bright sparks of light sent flying from the French horns, oboes, and clarinets. When the trombones come in, a burst of magic shimmers upward, robust and swelling, like the bubbles in the champagne Gram always pours for herself on Christmas Day.

The air is thick with more magic than I knew could exist in the world at once. The night crackles with energy and light;

magic runs through the sky in golden veins, pulsing gently in tempo with the symphony.

It feels like no time at all passes, or perhaps the entire night. It's hard to tell, because I feel half entranced myself. Perhaps there is some white magic threaded through the orchestra's yellow, working its mental enchantments, because my mind feels foggy with wonder. The tension eases out of my brain, worries popping like the bubbles of magic around me.

And then, all at once, I realize we've landed in the same spot we took off from, so lightly I didn't even notice. The carousel ride is over.

Sliding down, I land on my feet, swaying a little, as if I've just got off a long boat ride and the ground is unsteady. With a shake of its mane, the horse collapses, a pile of sand once more. Sadness tugs at me to see it go.

All the other guests look just as dazed as I feel, wandering around in a dreamlike way. In the amphitheater, the musicians begin to close their spell.

As their notes fade out, the glassy dome that had first concealed the Midnight Orchestra forms again, swallowing them up and then sealing itself over their heads before turning completely opaque. Once more, it looks like an empty stage, and silence falls over the amphitheater and the desert beyond.

All around me, people burst into applause.

"Distinguished guests of the Midnight Orchestra!" It's Mr.

Stewart, standing near the doorway in the dune. "We hope you have enjoyed tonight's performance. Your home portals will be reopened momentarily. We hope to see you all again, under the next full moon."

Guests stream out of the amphitheater, a long line of masked faces. The lady in the emerald dress waves at me cheerily.

"This way, Miss Jones." Mr. Stewart ushers me through the archway.

"How do I know you'll send me back to Mystwick?" I ask him, mentally adding, *And not the middle of the ocean or the surface of Mars or some creepy basement in Kansas?*

"Because, Miss Jones, I'm about to open a Midnight Orchestra exclusive: a cerebrodirectional, interdimensional, geoextensional portal."

"A what?"

"When you step through, think of where you want to go—and you'll find that place on the other side."

Before I can say another word, he fires up his bagpipes and blasts a spell. I have to step back, hands over ears, as the sheer *volume* of the sound hits me like a blast of wind. Purple magic erupts from the pipes and swirls in front of me, opening a portal like the one I saw in the woods, though this one's rougher around the edges, its tattered sides bleeding into the air around it.

Well, what choice do I have, really? Whatever's through that portal can't be much worse than here. I'll just have to take the risk.

I walk toward the portal, my shoes sliding on the sand, and look down at the dandelion seed in my hand.

I should throw the vial away before I go through.

I should crush it under my shoe until it's ground into the sand.

But at the last minute, my fingers tighten around it.

There is great power in that small vial.

As I step through the shimmering portal over the sand, I slip my hand into my pocket and drop the seed inside.

CHAPTER EIGHT

As a Meter of Fact

AMAZINGLY, I MAKE IT back to the Echo Wood with no trouble at all, unless you count some minor nausea and chills from stepping through the portal. I shiver and double over until the feeling passes.

Behind me, the portal winks out of existence, and I'm left standing all alone in the dusk. For a moment I stare at the empty air where the doorway had been, wondering if it was all a dream. Darkness is falling, and the woods are murky and silent. The trees have gone quiet except for the occasional minor note.

Then I remember the vial.

Still rattling in my pocket, it's proof that moments ago, I was in the *Sahara Desert,* halfway around the world. All by myself. With a bunch of masked people who may or may not have been the most powerful group of musicians in the world. I have that—and I have the sand I can feel crunching in my shoes.

Clearly, there is only one thing to do now: what I *started* to do before the portal gulped me down like a cat swallowing a goldfish.

I run for Mrs. Le Roux's office.

The grounds are lit by the last, dull light of day; soon it'll be full dark, and time for dinner. But oddly, there's no one going into the cafeteria. The place is deserted when I run past.

Something's up.

By the time I reach Harmony Hall, I'm gasping for breath, clutching the vial in my pocket. I stumble through the front door—only to be grabbed by an incoherent Jingfei.

"Amelia!"

"Whoa!" I say. "What's up?"

"You *have* to believe me!" She grips my shoulders and shouts, her eyes wide and wild. "I *saw* them! Mermaids! In Orpheus Lake! I'm *not* crazy, Amelia, I'm not! Tell me you see them too."

She spins me around and points me toward the placid lake.

I blink, seeing nothing but the reflection of Harmony Hall's bright windows. "Uh . . ."

"Centipedes!" moans Collin Brunnings, who's leaning against the wall beside me like he's going to be sick. "Giant centipedes crawling out of the toilet . . . You saw them too, right? *Right?*"

"What is going on?" I ask, bewildered.

Looking around Harmony Hall's grand lobby, which doubles as a hangout area in the evenings, I see dozens of students of all grade levels stumbling around, shouting and whispering, gesturing frantically. A cozy fire crackles in the large hearth in the center of the room, and there stand Mrs. Le Roux and several other Maestros, looking exhausted as students mob them from all sides.

I spot Darby across the room and call her name. When things get weird, she's always the one who knows what to do.

But before I can get her attention, Mia slides between us, her expression steely. She gives me a small shake of her head, then pulls Darby out of sight.

I give a short, disbelieving laugh. Whatever that girl has against me, she is *committed.*

Then a hand grabs me, and I yelp.

"Jai!"

"Amelia! Quick! This way."

We hunker behind a potted fern and watch as kids run all around the grand lobby, shouting about mermaids and spiders, fires and circus clowns. Even a few Maestros and staff members look rattled; I overhear Miss Becker, head of the Percusso class, insisting that she saw an actual cow jumping over the moon.

I leave Mystwick for one hour, and everyone loses their *mind.*

"What happened?" I ask Jai.

He grins. "Someone played a white spell and screwed it up, big-time. Everyone who got caught in its radius started experiencing hallucinations."

An upper-class girl wanders past us, muttering about walruses in pirate costumes raiding the school kitchen.

"It's fantastic!" Jai chortles. "They have no idea who did it, and no one's confessing. I didn't get hit with the spell, so I'm just here for the show. Did you see Collin? He threw up all over the third-floor bathroom."

"Who could have—oh, never mind! Look, Jai, forget about them. The weirdest thing just happened to me."

He arches one dark eyebrow.

"Not a hallucination, Jai. I'm serious." I drop my voice to a whisper. "I went through a portal to the Sahara Desert and—"

"Oh, Amelia." He pats my shoulder. "I'd wondered if you got caught up in it too."

"Jai! I'm telling the truth! I went through a portal made out of piano keys in the woods and landed in the Sahara Desert, where this orchestra was playing, and they were like really super good . . ." My voice trails away. "Okay, I can hear how it sounds. But it was real! And it was all incredibly weird. They knew my *name,* and they knew about my black spell, and—"

"Yes, yes." He nods pityingly.

"This is *real,* Jai. The Midnight Orchestra is *real.*"

His smile drops, and I could swear his ears prick forward. "Did you just say *the Midnight Orchestra?*"

"Yeah. Why?"

"*The* Midnight Orchestra."

Relief floods through me. "You've heard of it? You believe me?"

Jai looks at me with a mixture of pity and amusement. "I'm sure *you* believe you saw the Midnight Orchestra."

"I got an invitation in the mail! I'll show you, it's . . ." It's not in my pocket. I must have dropped it in the woods or back in the desert.

But I do have something else.

I take out the vial with the dandelion seed inside and show it to him. "It's a memory, Jai. It's for Composing. Mr. Midnight gave it to me. He said he wanted to make me a great Composer. Not that I plan to use it, but still. It's *proof.*"

"Er . . . that's a dandelion seed, Amelia."

"No, you don't understand! I'm telling the *truth*. And I have to tell the headmaestro."

"And you really think she's going to believe you? Look around."

I do, and I realize he's right. With everyone else clambering to share their hallucinations . . . why would the Maestros believe *my* story?

Realization dawns on me. It feels exactly like the moment

when you reach the highest point on a roller coaster, just before you know you're about to drop.

"They did this," I murmur. "The Midnight Orchestra. Somehow they must have unleashed this spell on Mystwick, so nobody would believe me. They don't *want* me to tell the Maestros."

"Riiiiight. I see we're drifting out of hallucinations and into paranoia."

"Jai! There were people in masks, and horses made out of sand and . . . oh! Sand!"

"Er, Amelia? What are you doing?"

I kick off my shoes and dump them over, and sure enough, fine Saharan sand streams out onto the floor.

Jai stares, his jaw slowly falling open.

Then Collin Brunnings lumbers by, kicking through the piles and scattering sand everywhere. In a blink, it's completely gone, my only proof ground into the carpet.

"Ugh." I slap my face. "Seriously, Collin?"

"Centipedes," he moans.

But Jai saw it. He's staring at the floor so hard his eyeballs nearly fall out.

"Either *I'm* hallucinating now," he says, "or you're telling the truth."

"I told you I was!"

"You saw the Midnight Orchestra."

"I told you I did!"

"No. You don't understand. *You saw the Midnight Orchestra.*"

"Yes, I know! I mean . . ." I frown. "Wait, what do *you* mean?"

He's staring at me as if my hair has just caught fire.

"Amelia, come with me." Jai grabs my hand and yanks me up and out the doors, away from the crowd of hysterical students.

In the watery moonlight Jai races across the campus to the library, with me in tow, not stopping until we've climbed three flights of stairs to the computer lab.

There, panting, he slings himself into his favorite chair by the window and turns on the monitor. While the screen loads, the ticking metronome passing time, he drills his fingers on the table and refuses to answer any of my questions.

Finally, the internet pops open and he types in a website.

I read the title at the top of the page. "The Midnighters?"

"It's an old forum I used to be on, for people trying to track down the Midnight Orchestra." He scrolls through thousands of posts. "See? All these people around the world devote their *lives* trying to pinpoint the next location the orchestra will play at, how to get there, and who the guests are. Some people have claimed that they visited it, but even they can't tell where it'll appear next, or how to get an invitation. Apparently talking about it a lot gets you uninvited. Most people think the orchestra is just a myth, that the people who do admit to seeing it are making it up to get attention."

"It didn't look too mythical to me. And trust me—I don't want that kind of attention."

"I'm not saying I don't believe you. I do. It's just—how do you keep running into things that shouldn't exist? First ghosts, now this?"

"What do you know about the orchestra?"

"That the earliest mentions of it date around fifty years ago. That it appears only under a full moon and usually in some remote location. That you can only go to it if you're specially invited. That it's supposed to be the most powerful and amazing orchestra in the world, so amazing that once you start listening, you can never stop, and you get sucked into their instruments and eaten. Though, okay, that last one was a fringe theory that no real self-respecting Midnighter actually believes." Jai leans back in his chair, gazing at me with a look of wonder. "You really saw the Midnight Orchestra?"

My shoulders lift. "I guess so."

"And . . . What happened? You have to tell me everything. Slower this time, with more details."

"They played a cool spell. Well, more than cool. It was . . .

incredible. I wasn't the only person in the audience either. And they gave me this." I shake the vial with the dandelion seed. "They told me if I bite it, it'll give me some great Composing power or something."

"And you just *accepted* it?" Jai asks.

I look around to make sure we're being ignored; thankfully, most of the people in the computer lab are juniors and seniors, which means they pay more attention to the lint on the carpet than to us.

"I didn't mean to! He didn't give me much choice."

Of course, that isn't exactly true, is it? I could have dropped it back in the desert or in the Echo Wood. But I hadn't.

I'd kept it because a part of me couldn't quite let go.

"Are you going to use it?" asks Jai.

"Of course not!"

"Oh." He looks disappointed. "Not even if it might help us obliterate Souza in the Trials?"

"Not even for that."

"Not even if someone offered you a million dollars?"

"No, Jai."

"Not even if your life were in—"

"*No!* Look, apparently if I use it, this Mr. Midnight guy will come demanding some kind of payment. A favor for a favor, he called it."

He whistles. "Classic deal with a devil. Oh, Amelia. See, this is why you shouldn't go charging off into strange portals without your best friend, who *knows* how to watch out for this kind of thing. If I'd been there, I could have—"

"I didn't go charging off anywhere. That portal swallowed *me*."

"Right, well. What do you think this Midnight guy will want as payment for this seed thing?"

"Nothing, because I won't use it."

"If you say so. One thing's sure, though. You can't tell the Maestros about it."

"Of course I have to tell the Maestros about it!"

"And what will they do? Confiscate the thing, if they even believe you? Then what? Who will this guy hold responsible? Won't he want his payment then?"

I feel the blood drain from my face. "The . . . the Maestros won't let him or anyone come near me. Mystwick is protected."

"Like they stopped these people from scooping you up in the first place?" He shakes his head. "All right, Jones. New plan. Do you think you'll be invited back?"

"I think so. He said something about returning under the next full moon."

"Excellent! So, next month, if this portal pops up, you and

I go back, hand over the memory thingy with a polite thanks-but-no-thanks, no harm done."

"Better yet," I say, "if the portal pops up, we chuck the memory thingy through it and run the other way, really, really fast."

"Well . . . I might like *one teensy peek*—"

"Jai, we're staying far away from those people. Look what they did to Mystwick!" I point out the window toward Harmony Hall, where kids are still running around as if snakes are biting their ankles.

"Did they?" he asks, doubtful.

"Oh, c'mon. A hallucination spell playing *exactly* when I need to tell the Maestros about something that already sounds impossible? It's too big a coincidence."

"That's the thing, though," Jai says. "See, the Echo Wood doesn't just protect us from physical intruders. It's supposed to block *magical* interference as well. So how did the Midnight Orchestra open a portal here in the first place—much less play a hallucination spell?"

It's a good question, and not one I'm sure I want the answer to.

The less I know about the Midnight Orchestra, the better. And maybe that means leaving the Maestros out of it. After all, if they do somehow decide to believe me, wouldn't that mean a whole investigation—me recounting every detail of the night, them asking endless questions, maybe even trying to contact higher authorities? Not even two weeks after I unleashed a horde of ghosts on the school?

Maybe Jai's right about not telling the Maestros what happened.

Maybe I *don't* need that kind of scrutiny. All I want is to be a normal student with normal problems, like Composing a masterpiece to win the Orphean Trials.

"All right," I say reluctantly. "We'll try it your way. No involving the Maestros. And one month from now, if the portal shows up again, we'll toss the seed back and forget the whole thing happened."

"No harm done."

"No harm done."

CHAPTER NINE

An Awkward Composition

THE NEXT DAY, I meet Trevor, Rosa, Phoebe, and the rest of our Trials team for our first Composium practice. I arrive at the Shell yawning and red-eyed, having tossed and turned all night long. My head wouldn't stop replaying the Midnight Orchestra's music, and the few times I did doze off, my dreams filled with masked faces and towering sand dunes. But with the morning, the orchestra seems to fade away, unreal and dreamlike. It's hard to believe I ever left Mystwick at all.

I may be exhausted and completely unprepared for our first Composium practice, but at least it will be a reminder of normalcy.

Part of preparing for the Trials was recruiting Maestros to supervise each of the five events. Of course, my luck landed me with Mr. Pinwhistle in charge of the Composium.

Since arriving at Mystwick, I've learned that he's not as grumpy as he seems—in fact, there was a time when he was the only Maestro here who believed in me. I'd hoped afterward that he might be nicer, but if anything, he's only gotten crankier. It's like he knows I've seen how caring he *really* is, and now he's determined to make up for it by heaping on an extra dose of grouchiness.

As we settle into our seats, he looks over the students gathered before him and gives a weary sigh. "How did I get talked into this?"

Since the Composium requires the whole Trials team to participate, there are thirty-two of us altogether, representing the four classes—Aeros, Chordos, Vibratos, and Percussos. I sit in the front row between Jai and Victoria, and I'm as jittery as a frog in a pan.

Turning in my seat, I spot Darby in the back row. Mia sees me looking and leans over to whisper in Darby's ear. The girls laugh, and, my face warming, I turn around again.

I wonder what Darby would make of my trip to the Midnight Orchestra. If it weren't for Mia, I'd have told her about it already, but as it is . . . I'm not even sure I could get her on her own. Mia keeps her so close, it's like they're leashed together.

"Where is that woman?" growls Mr. Pinwhistle.

We're waiting for Miss Motte, who's supposed to be our other Maestro in charge.

She seems to make a habit of running behind. She turned up thirty minutes late to my last Composing class, fluttering and laughing as if nothing were wrong. I'd been too intimidated to point out the time, and we'd spent the next half hour stringing mood beads into necklaces (*monitoring emotive energy,* as she'd called it).

With a mutter, Mr. Pinwhistle gives up waiting, turns on the projector, and shines it on a screen that rolls down from the ceiling above the stage.

The video he plays shows a student chamber orchestra like ours. They're on an outdoor platform, set against a dramatic backdrop of snowcapped mountains. A banner over their heads reads THE ORPHEAN TRIALS.

"These are the Souza Musicraft Academy students," says Mr. Pinwhistle.

Immediately everyone starts booing.

He waits, pinching the bridge of his nose, until we quiet down again. "They are, of course, the winners of last year's Composium. And the year before that. And the year before . . . well, you get it. Now, until Miss Jones completes her Composition, we'll prepare by studying the spells of previous winners. Such as this one."

He steps back as the kids in the video begin playing.

The spell is beautiful and complex. It's a white spell, affecting only the mind, so I can't tell what it's doing, but when the camera pans to the audience, I see its results. There's not a dry eye in sight. Everyone is smiling and crying, holding their hands to their hearts or faces as if they're overwhelmed.

A cold sweat breaks out on my neck. How in the world am I supposed to top something like that?

"Here," says Mr. Pinwhistle, tapping the screen where a tall, dark-haired boy is playing piano, "is the Composer of this spell. Luca D'Alessio, who will be a senior this year, competing in the Composium for the fifth time . . . for his fifth win."

I lean forward to better study my competition.

Luca D'Alessio, a tall, tanned boy with black curly hair, smiles as he watches his fellow students perform his piece while he coaxes the melody from the piano. Ribbons of silvery-white magic flow from their instruments and curl like fog around the audience members.

"This was a memory recall spell," says Mr. Pinwhistle. "It summons the happiest memories in its listeners, as real as the day they happened. The spell created a unique experience for each listener, a very difficult trick to pull off. Compositions are judged for their musical technicality as well as their magical complexity and sophistication."

"So what's *our* spell going to be?" asks Kjersten.

Everyone looks at me.

My ears burn. "Um . . . I haven't really decided yet."

"But you've got something in mind?" says Kjersten.

"Sure. Yep." I clasp my hands in my lap, hoping they don't hear the tremble in my voice. "Working on it."

"Aw, don't worry about it," Jai says loudly, waving his hand.

"Amelia summoned an army of *ghosts.* Like, *from the dead.* She's got this in the bag. The other Composers will run scared."

The rest of the students laugh and add their agreement.

"Amelia's our secret weapon!" Trevor declares.

"Sure," calls Mia from the back. "Unless, of course, she's a one-hit wonder."

She's met with a stunned silence, and more than a few questioning looks turn my way. Clearly, most of them hadn't considered that possibility, but now they do.

Now *I* do.

I'm getting that queasy feeling again, as if I'm about to jump straight into the deep end of the pool without knowing how to swim, only now I know that the deep end is also full of sharks.

"My my my, what is going on in here?" rings out a sunny voice. "I *love* a party!"

Miss Motte has arrived, in grand fashion. She sweeps through the red curtain on the stage, wearing a rainbow assortment of draped, flowing clothes and one long, dangly feather earring. Her locks swing in a thick braid down her back.

"You're late," gripes Mr. Pinwhistle, his voice strained. Pausing the video, he stares hard at the clock on the back wall, not even looking at the other Maestro. "*Very* late."

"Why, Mr. Pinwhistle," Miss Motte says slowly as she descends the steps to the floor. "I suppose I am."

Mr. Pinwhistle waves a hand at us students. "Here's what we've got to work with. I'll make sure they're in tune, so long as *you* make sure there's an actual spell to play."

"I'm sure Amelia and I will be just fine," she says, coming over to wrap an arm around me. Her feather earring tickles my cheek. "But darling, you forgot your emotive energy necklace!"

"Oh," I say weakly.

She clasps my mood beads around my neck while, behind me, kids start laughing. Miss Motte doesn't seem to hear them, but she happily arranges the necklace until she's satisfied.

"Why, look at this!" She taps the beads, which turn dark green. "She's already burning with passion! Or perhaps—oh my!—romance?"

I'm burning all right, but not with passion. *Definitely* not with romance. While the others laugh, my cheeks are on fire. I eye Kjersten's euphonium and wonder if it's big enough for me to crawl into and hide.

"The important thing to remember," says Mr. Pinwhistle, "is that no matter what spell you play, you play *together*. You're an orchestra, and it'll take every one of you at your best to have even a chance. I mean, these guys are good." He points a thumb at the Souza kids, still frozen in place on the screen. "They're really, *really* good."

We wait, expecting him to add *but you're better*.

He never does.

After Mr. Pinwhistle makes us watch three more videos of Luca D'Alessio's past spells, the meeting ends and I leave the Shell in a daze. The other students file out behind me, chatting excitedly. The day is sunny and warmer than it's been all week, but I still feel cold.

"Don't look so scared," says Amari, clapping me on the back. "We totally got this."

"Yeah, I bet none of *those* Composers ever made a black spell," Victoria adds. "Amelia's gonna make toast of them."

I grimace; Composing a black spell isn't exactly something you brag about.

"Maybe," Mia says, leaning in the doorway. "But Luca's not just a good Composer. He's *brilliant.* I once saw him Compose a spell that convinced an entire roomful of people that they were peacocks. You should have seen how many of them tried to fly!" She looks directly at me and adds, "*His* specialty is white magic—the rarest kind. Except for, obviously, black spells."

"You know him?" asks Jai.

"Sure. We used to perform on the same tour circuit. He's almost as famous as I am."

"Well, Amelia opened a doorway to the afterworld," says Victoria. "I'm betting on her."

She pats my hand and smiles before rolling away, her guitar case slung over the back of her wheelchair. I smile gratefully after her.

Everyone heads off in different directions, to classes or study hall or free time. I wave to Jai and Darby, who have Musicraft history together across campus.

"When are you going to tell them?" Mia asks when it's just the two of us standing in front of the concert hall, Orpheus Lake glittering a short distance away.

"Tell them what?"

"That you can't do it. That you got lucky once, made up a spell you didn't even *know* you were Composing, and that you're leading them all down a dead-end road?"

My hand tightens on my backpack strap. I could just turn and walk away. I could ignore her.

Instead, I look her square in the eyes. "What's your problem with me?"

She scoffs. "Don't tell me you don't see it? How they all humor you just because you're like, an orphan or something?"

"I'm not actually—"

"Whatever. I don't care. Which is probably why I'm the only one around here who'll actually tell you the truth. Like how you're going to let everyone down at the Trials."

My teeth grinding together, I push past her and march

away, even though it's in the opposite direction of my next class. I just want to get away from her.

"Face it, Wondergirl!" Mia laughs. "You're in over your head!"

I don't give her the benefit of looking back.

But deep down, I'm scared she might be right.

CHAPTER TEN

Opus Pocus

"BREATHE, AMELIA JONES. INHALE and exhale. Take deep breaths and *relax*."

"I'm fine, Jai." We walk across campus, headed for Harmony Hall. Classes are over for the day, and despite my words, I feel like a giant alarm clock has been hung around my neck, counting down the days to the Composium.

Absently, my hand digs into my pocket to toy with the dandelion seed in the vial. I've gotten into the habit of carrying it around so Phoebe doesn't find it during her room checks. I'm just keeping it safe so I can be sure to give it back to Mr. Midnight, untouched, with no favors owed. I'm definitely not keeping it close because I'm tempted to use it.

At least that's what I keep telling myself.

"Are you really fine?" Jai lifts an eyebrow. "If I were you, I'd be screaming into a pillow. I'd be chewing my nails off while hiding under my bed. I'd be thinking I need to invent a bloody *magnum opus* so everyone at this school wouldn't hate my guts forever."

I glare at him. "Is this your idea of *relaxing?*"

"Just saying," he replies, pushing open the big wooden doors to Harmony Hall's common area. "I've got a bad feeling about this Luca D'Whatsisface, the prodigy Composer. I'm glad it's you going against him, not me."

Cringing, I recall the Souza kid's magic, how confident he looked leading his school's team. "What if I *did* make a huge mistake? I didn't even know I could Compose until a few weeks ago!"

"Hey, easy! There is one bright side. You've got *us*. Hey, Darby! Mia!" He waves at the girls, who are coming down the stairs from their afternoon language arts class.

I stop short.

"What's wrong?" Jai asks.

Right. I haven't told him the full extent of Mia's coldness toward me—or how she warned me to stay away from Darby.

Mia matches gazes with me and smiles. Only now I see the look *behind* her smile, the one no one else seems to see. It reminds me of the way some animals have bright colors . . . to warn you of the poison just beneath the surface.

I need to figure out how to deal with Mia. I can't seem to avoid her, not when we have classes and meals together and even share a bathroom. I have no idea how to win her over.

Maybe if I ignore her, she'll get bored and find someone else to torment.

"I was just telling Amelia we've got her back in the Composium," Jai says, giving them meaningful looks.

"Of course we do," Darby says, clutching a copy of *The Phantom of the Orchestra*. "If we fail, we fail together."

I give her a grateful smile even as my stomach sinks. That wasn't exactly the vote of confidence I was hoping for.

"Yeah," says Mia. "And I'm sure the whole school won't blame her for blowing their chance at redemption. They'll all totally move on, like she didn't just embarrass them in front of the entire world. C'mon, Darby, let's go."

"You're not going to embarrass anyone," Darby tells me.

Mia scowls. "I said, come *on,* before someone else claims the showers!"

She drags Darby out by her elbow, and my former roommate casts an apologetic look my way. Honestly, why does she let Mia push her around like that? I've seen Darby put kids twice her size in their place. So what mysterious power does Mia hold over her? Does she not *see* how controlling and mean that girl is?

"Don't let her get to you," Jai says. "She's probably just jealous of the attention."

"It'd be easier if everyone at this school *stopped* looking at me like they thought I could peel the moon out of the sky." When Jai lifts a questioning finger, I add, "And no, I can't actually do that, so don't ask."

He pats my shoulder. "Chin up, Jones. We can figure this out. How far along is your spell? What will it do? Can I hear a few measures?"

I just look at him, until realization dawns on his face.

"Oh," he says. "You . . . haven't even started on it."

"I want to, but all Miss Motte has me do in our classes is write down my feelings and make mood jewelry that doesn't even work." I hold up the beads, which are now registering *relaxed* blue. "Half the time I don't know if I'm in Composing class or art lessons."

"What you need is inspiration." Jai begins pacing in front of the grand fireplace, his hands clasped behind his back, as if he were solving a crime. I sling myself sideways into an armchair and watch him. "What inspires Amelia Jones? Hmm. I *have* seen you look at a bowl of ice cream with something like *passion*."

"I think this is going to take more than an Ode to Moose Tracks."

"True, sadly." He pats his stomach. "Well, when you Composed that black spell, you thought of your mum, right?"

"Yeah . . ." I sit up. "You know, I found the notebook where she recorded *her* Compositions when she was a student here. I wonder if she wrote down the spell she created for the Trials."

"That's it!" cries Jai. "Inspiration! Where's the notebook?"

I sigh. "Too late. Someone stole her spells. The pages are torn out."

"Show me anyway. Maybe there's something you missed."

Doubtful, I lead him upstairs to the attic classroom. This is the first time I've showed it to anyone, and I feel a little embarrassed when he sees how shabby and dusty it is.

"I don't think Miss Motte really notices things like cobwebs," I say, brushing one off my sleeve. "And the maintenance workers seem to have forgotten about this place."

"This is *fantastic!*" Jai turns a full rotation, taking it all in. "It's like a secret club!"

"Yep, a jolly old club of one." I take down my mother's notebook and open it. "See? Her spells are all gone."

"Weird." Jai runs his finger over the torn edges. "Who'd steal your mum's spells? And why?"

"Maybe she took them when she graduated."

"Then why not take the whole notebook? It was hers, after all. No. Somebody tore them out so they'd get away with it. A missing notebook might've drawn more attention, but a few pages? Not so much."

"I guess this is a dead end."

A voice sounds from the doorway. "What's a dead end?"

Jai and I turn to see Darby there, leaning on the frame.

"What are you doing here?" I ask.

"I left my homework in Aeros class, but then I saw you two . . ." She pushes off the wall. "It looked like you were onto something. Thought maybe I could help."

And if Mia catches us hanging out? I wonder inwardly.

But you know what?

Who *cares* what Mia thinks?

I'm tired of her pushing me around, and even tireder of her pushing *Darby* around. Darby deserves better friends than that.

"Come see," I say. I show her the notebook and explain my mom's missing spells, how they might have helped me Compose.

"So . . . you wanna know who took the spells?"

"I mean, I don't know how—"

She groans. "Amelia! You're a musician! Start thinking *magically*. If you want to know who stole your mom's spells, just *find out*."

"How?"

Darby picks up my flute case and pushes it into my hands. "A little thing called *magic*. Ever heard of it?"

"You know a spell to find them?"

"I know a hundred finding spells, but that won't work here. If they're not on school property, the trail could lead a thousand miles away. Just figure out *who* took them and go from there."

"And . . . you know a spell for *that?*"

She looks away thoughtfully, then shakes her head. "That's trickier. But I bet some kind of time spell would help." Looking at my expectant expression, she adds, "And no, I don't know any time spells. Which is why you'll have to Compose one."

"What?" I gasp.

"Wait," Jai says. "No. No no no. Sorry. Gotta draw the line there, ladies. This is the worst idea. Haven't you heard the old saying? Time is the *strongest* magic. Very, very dangerous. Probably as dangerous as black spells."

"It's purple magic," Darby points out. "Which is really just a subset of blue spells. And those get played all the time."

"There's a reason you have to have a license to play teleportation spells," I say. "And time magic is even more dangerous."

"Which is why"—Darby grins—"it'd be *especially* impressive to perform a time spell at the Composium. Nothing too fancy. Just open a little window to the past and take a peek."

There's the Darby I'm used to seeing—full of bold plans

and ideas, even if those ideas sound terrifying and borderline illegal. It feels like old times, when we were running around Mystwick trying to capture ghosts or kidnap Mrs. Le Roux's musicat.

It figures that the real Darby would make an appearance only when Mia's on the other side of campus.

Jai opens his mouth to argue with her, then stops and cocks his head. "You know, that's actually not a bad idea."

I fling up my hand. "You literally *just said* this is the worst idea."

"Which is probably why Mr. Luca Whatever His Name Is from the Souza Fancybutt Academy would never even think of it. He Composed a spell to let you remember your best memory. So? *You* can Compose a spell that lets you actually look back through time and *see* it. Talk about a magnum opus!" He grins. "Go on, Amelia. Try it."

I look from Jai to Darby, speechless, waiting for someone to interject sense into all this.

But no one does, and I suppose that in the end, I'm just desperate enough to try.

I think briefly of the dandelion seed hidden in my pocket and feel a moment's temptation . . . but no. Maybe they're right. Maybe a time spell *could* win this thing, and maybe I can Compose one—all on my own, no favors from mysterious orchestras needed.

"Stand back." I sigh, opening my flute case. "Like, *really* back."

Right.

A window to the past.

That sounds totally doable, right? I mean, if I can open the wall between life and death, why not between past and present?

Still, doubt makes my flute feel twice as heavy as I raise it to my lips.

After calming my breath and doing my best to clear my head, I begin playing. The notes are tentative at first, as I feel my way into a melody. It's like stepping onto a tightrope, my balance all over the place, my stomach wobbling like Gran's Jell-O casserole.

I harness my thoughts to the notebook in front of me. *Who did this? Who stole the spells?* My question becomes my music, the notes low and eerie. I pick out a minor key, each note bound to a word. *Who? Who was here? Who opened this book? Who tore out its pages? Show me. Show me. Show me.*

"Is it working?" asks Jai in a hush. "Where's the magic?"

My hands grow sweaty, but I can't stop playing long enough to wipe them. This hasn't happened before—when I Composed in the past, the magic started flowing right away. So what am I doing wrong?

I frantically think of Miss Motte's lessons, if you can call them that. *Emotion* is key, she'd said. So I try to reach for some. I think of the B I got on my World Musicraft test this morning, how relieved and happy I'd been, given that I'd kinda sorta forgotten about it completely and had to wing it with no studying.

Just like that, a shining droplet of light forms at the end of the flute and then drops.

The droplet splashes on the creaky old floorboards and sends shimmering purple ripples flowing outward. Across the attic, Jai and Darby step closer. Ignoring them, pouring all my focus into my flute, I repeat the melody over and over, staring hard at the notebook.

Who are you? Who did this? Who stole the spells that should have been mine? Who took what didn't belong to them?

More magic shimmers from my flute—branches of violet light that grow outward and bend and twist, forming a kind of glowing picture frame in midair, not unlike the portal that took me to the Midnight Orchestra, only smaller. The magic smells strongly of melting plastic.

Let me see what happened.

Show me who was here.

And just like that, the air inside the magic frame shines white. I blink hard, blinded, and feel the others creeping up behind me, too curious to stay back any longer.

"It's working," breathes Darby.

The white light gradually fades, replaced by . . . the attic. My heart almost falls, until I realize that the attic I'm gazing at through the magic frame is *clean*. No dust or cobwebs here. The walls and ceiling gleam as if freshly polished. And there's more light, from actual lamps, not just candles. The frame shows the shelf with the notebooks on it, and I see my mother's there, looking newer than it does now.

My heart begins to race.

It's working.

I play on, forcing my fingers to maintain an even tempo. Rushing now, no matter how excited I am, could botch the spell. But the longer I play, the stranger I start to feel. My body gets shaky all over, my stomach clenching like I'm going to throw up. I blink hard, trying to banish the wave of dizziness in my head.

What's happening to me?

My breath catches when a shadow flickers across the scene in the magic frame. Someone's moving around, just out of sight. My spell is focused on the shelf with the notebooks, but I wonder if . . .

Very carefully, I shift my body, turning to face the attic door.

The spell moves with me, the frame sliding across the room and showing other parts of the attic. I turn, turn, turn . . . There!

Someone is searching another shelf behind me, hunched

over and in shadow. It's a man, wearing a wide-brimmed hat that hides his face. He searches methodically, then moves on to the desks, his heavy boots making the floor creak. His long black coat is damp on the shoulders, as if he's walked through rain or snow to get here.

Battling a surge of exhaustion and weakness, I play on, determined to see the spell through.

When he doesn't find what he's looking for in the desks, he pounds a fist in frustration, then catches sight of the last shelf—where my mother's notebook is. He walks quickly toward it, moving so fast I lose sight of him. I have to slowly turn around again before I find him once more, running his gloved hands over the notebooks.

When he finds my mother's, he freezes a moment, his finger resting on the spine.

Then he pulls it down and tears it open, flipping pages frantically. I can see the sweat on the back of his neck.

Sweat is also running down *my* neck, my body feeling like its shrinking. The nausea in my belly rises to my throat. What is happening to me?

Suddenly a thunk sounds, and I jump, thinking someone's at the door. But the man in the past reacts too, and I realize the sound came from *his* time, not mine.

He looks toward the door, then back at the notebook. In one swift, angry motion, he rips out all the spells.

"You can't be here!" a voice shouts.

The man turns. "Get back!" he snarls. "I'll only warn you once!"

In that moment, the light hits his face.

And the flute drops from my hands.

CHAPTER ELEVEN

Rockabye Jai

When my flute crashes to the floor, the spell goes haywire. The time window explodes and out-of-control magic zings all over the attic. I dive for the ground, my hands over my head, the drill the Maestros taught us for just such a disaster. Bolts of purple magic smash into the walls, floor, and furniture, leaving smoking scorch marks. The candles all blow out, and the attic is lit only by searing violet light.

"Stay down!" I yell.

A glass pen jar on Miss Motte's desk shatters. A buzzing ball of magic burrows into the shelves of Composition books like a snuffing dog, knocking notebooks and papers everywhere. With a crash, one of the desks flips over and skids to the wall, as if there's an invisible elephant throwing a temper tantrum, tossing and smashing whatever it can reach.

When everything finally settles, the magic's energy spent, I slowly lift my head and groan at the mess. Darby stamps out a flame that had spread from a fallen candle to the scattered papers. Only one candle remains lit, its flame safe inside a glass lantern.

"Well," says Darby, brushing a singed spot on her sleeve. "That went swimmingly. What happened?"

I don't dare tell them the real reason I dropped my flute.

Or who I saw through the time window.

"I . . . lost control of the spell. It's like it was draining me." That's true, at least. I put a hand to my head, still feeling an ache. "Have either of you ever played a spell that made you feel sick? Jai? Wait. *Where's Jai?*"

Darby is still standing over the mess of burned papers. But there's no Jai anywhere.

"Jai?" I whisper.

A moment of silence is the only answer I get, followed by a soft, gurgling "*Coo.*"

"Huh? Did you hear that?"

Darby nods, her eyes round. She points wordlessly to something behind the upside-down desk.

I dart over and spot a pile of clothes—*Jai's* clothes—puddled on the floorboards.

My heart stops.

Did I disintegrate my best friend?

I fall to my knees, crawl to the pile of clothing, and reach for it, tears starting to burn in my eyes.

But then a tiny hand reaches up from the folds of Jai's Mystwick sweater.

"Oh," says Darby. "Oh oh oh oh *oh*. We are in *so* much trouble."

I carefully push aside the clothes to reveal . . . well, *Jai*.

There's no mistaking those large ears.

Even when they're attached to a *baby*.

The chubby brown-skinned little guy couldn't be more than a year old. He lies on his back, gurgling, and grips my finger in one tiny hand. His bottom half is covered by Jai's pants . . . now roughly a hundred sizes too big.

Horror spreads through my body.

"H-how?" I whisper.

"Time magic," Darby says, as if that explains everything.

"What do we do? How do we turn him back? Jai, can you understand me? Can you talk? Wave your hand if you understand."

He blinks, his tiny, adorable mouth forming a perfect *O*. Then he blows an enormous spit bubble. It drips down his double chins.

I start to pick him up, then shriek and drop the sweater over him, my cheeks going hot. "He's . . . um, kind of naked."

Ohhhh no.

There are some things a girl just cannot unsee.

Darby tentatively reaches out to poke Baby Jai's cheek, as

if to prove to herself he's real. "Time magic is unpredictable, and *uncontrolled* time magic even more so, I guess," she says. "He must have got hit by a stray blast, and it zapped him back to his past self."

"But we can undo it, right? Will it wear off? Is there some kind of counterspell?"

She shrugs. "I've never heard of something like this before."

"This is bad," I moan. "This is really, really bad. We need to take him to the Maestros."

Baby Jai starts squirming, then throws his head back and wails.

"What did you do to it?" cries Darby, clapping her hands over her ears.

"Nothing! I—" The baby's screams drown me out. His little mouth is wide open, displaying soft pink gums. Frantically, I wrap him in the cardigan and pick him up. "Darby! Help!"

"No way." Darby raises her hands above her head. "I don't do babies. Don't hold, don't touch, don't babysit."

Jai screams so hard his face turns red.

Darby points. "He's, um . . . leaking."

Sure enough, something wet and definitely not-just-water is trickling from under the cardigan.

Ugh.

"Miss Motte!" I say. "We'll take him to Miss Motte. She's the Composing Maestro, right? She has to know what to do."

"Yeah. She'll make sure we spend the rest of the year in detention."

I think a moment, then shake my head. "I'm not so sure. I have an idea. But we need to get Jai to her *now,* without anyone seeing him."

Darby reluctantly agrees. She collects Jai's clothes, and I wrap him snugly in his sweater.

"Where is this Maestro of yours anyway?"

"She's staying in the headmaestro's cottage. They're sisters."

"Oh." Darby slings Jai's backpack onto her shoulder. "So we just have to cross the *entire campus* with a screaming baby, no big deal."

"He's quiet now." I peel back the sweater to peek at Baby Jai. He burbles at me happily, snot dripping from his nose. "But let's hurry."

We race down the stairs as fast as I dare while carrying my little bundle of boy. Jai bounces in my arms, chortling, totally ignoring my desperate shushes.

"Hey!" call Amari and Jamal from the common area, where they're playing checkers. "How's our spell coming along, Jones?"

"Uh, fine! Splendid! Just peaches!" I yell over my shoulder.

Darby pushes open the doors, and we spill outside.

"Rats," she says, scouting the grounds. "Bad time. Everyone's out of class."

"We don't have a choice." It's a cloudy day, but there are kids everywhere, walking, sitting by the lake, bundled in winter coats. The air smells of coming snow.

This will be like smuggling a pound of bacon through a dog park.

"All right," Darby says. "Just stay cool and keep that thing quiet."

"He's not a *thing*." I follow her down the steps, trying to look casual, knowing there's a river of sweat pouring down my face. "Please, Jai, just work with us here, or you might end up as the first baby in history to get detention."

He blows bubbles and laughs.

We make it only as far as the statue of Beethoven before Claudia comes running over.

"Darby!" She waves, and Darby lets out a sigh.

"She's been all over me and Mia," she mutters. "I think she stole one of Mia's socks and tried to sell it on the internet, and I'm pretty sure she's trying to get her hands on the other one."

"What are you two doing?" Claudia says when she reaches us. "Where's Mia? I heard about the Trials. Hey, do you think you could get me invited on the team too? They probably just forgot to—"

"We're kind of in the middle of something," Darby says.

"What?"

"It's time-sensitive, okay? *Bye,* Claudia."

Seeing Claudia's face fall, I start to feel bad. "Maybe we can hang out later," I say. "We could play badminton in the gym."

"Oh, get over yourself, Jones," Claudia says. "Unlike the rest of these morons, I have no doubt that you're going to totally flub this Composting thing."

My goodwill toward her evaporates. "It's called a *Composium.*"

She smacks her gum, eyes narrowing. "What are you holding, anyway?"

"Nothing!"

"*Goodbye,* Claudia," Darby says, louder.

"Hey! It's moving!" Jumping in front of me, so I'm forced to stop, Claudia starts to grab at the bundled Jai. I yelp and lurch away.

"It's a puppy!" I shout, panicking.

Darby groans and slaps her face. "Great."

Claudia's eyes grow huge. She raises her hands to her cheeks. "A PUPPY?"

All around us, every kid in earshot stops what they're doing and stares at us.

"Amelia's got a PUPPY!" Claudia shouts, reaching for Jai again.

I break into a quick walk, bolting past her. Darby hurries

alongside me. Kids move toward us like packs of zombies, calling out "Puppy? *Puppy?* Where's the puppy?"

"Hang in there, little guy," I whisper to Jai, who's jouncing around in my arms, his expression turning to one of supreme displeasure. "Oh no, oh no, he's gonna—"

Jai rips an earsplitting scream. At that moment, so does Darby. She shoots me a frantic look, shakes her head, and keeps singing like an opera star. As long as she belts out note after note, Jai's voice is drowned out.

"Laaaaa la la la *laaaaaaaa, how much longer do I have to keep this up laaaaaaaaa!*"

"What the heck?" calls Claudia, who's steps behind us. "Why are you singing? What's going on? Is that really a puppy?"

"Puppy?" shouts an older girl, coming from the left, arms outstretched. "Can I see? Can I hold it?"

"Get away!" I yell. "It's, um—sick! Very fragile! Probably about to die!"

The crowd of students lets out a collective gasp of horror.

"Just when I thought this couldn't get worse," Darby hisses, "you make it worse!"

"Have you got a better idea?"

"Yes," says Darby. *"Run!"*

CHAPTER TWELVE

Staccato in the Middle

WE SPRINT ACROSS THE school grounds, leading a pack of confused, horrified, puppy-craving students behind us. The Maestros' dorm, Clarion House, isn't far now, and behind it waits Mrs. Le Roux's cottage. I hope the headmaestro isn't home; if she answers the door, we are well and truly doomed.

"Don't stop," Darby gasps out. "Don't look back!"

We round the Maestros' dorm and go full tilt toward the Echo trees. Just inside the forest's bounds sits a little yellow cottage with blue shutters, as pretty as a fairy tale. Darby reaches the door first and pounds on it. A wind chime made of metal music notes tinkles by the front window.

Many of the students have given up and turned back, but Claudia and a dozen others close in, looking determined.

"C'mon, Miss Motte," I mutter. "Be home, *please!*"

"Amelia Jones!" Claudia shouts. "Let us see that puppy!"

At that moment, the cottage door opens and Miss Motte blinks at us. "What the—"

"Help!" I cry.

Bewildered, Miss Motte steps back, holding the door open, and Darby and I jump inside. Claudia steps away when Miss Motte blocks her.

"Sorry, um . . . private meeting," she says, then shuts the door.

Darby and I stand panting and red-faced in her living room. Out of nowhere, a ball of white fuzz comes streaking across the floor. It launches itself at me, yipping, and I shriek and clutch Jai.

"Janet!" Miss Motte grabs the fuzz ball and snuggles it. "Down, girl. What have I told you about manners?"

The squirming, wiry-haired thing turns out to be an *actual* puppy, or rather a dog. It pants happily in Miss Motte's arms, its eyes hidden behind a fluff of hair.

"Janet, calm down! Girls, what on earth brings you here?"

The cottage interior certainly has Mrs. Le Roux's style. Portraits of famous historical Maestros hang on the wall, and the furniture is all immaculate velvet and polished dark wood. A record player in the corner sings out the resonant trumpeting notes of Louis Armstrong, one of the great jazz Maestros. I know this one—it's an elemental spell that conjures clouds, though the recording itself emits no magic, of course. An upright piano is decorated with pictures of Mrs. Le Roux and her late husband at their wedding, and a few with her and

Miss Motte when they were little, dressed in matching overalls and braided pigtails. Atop a fringed ottoman, Mrs. Le Roux's musicat Wynk watches the dog with a look of loathing, her fur bristling.

But there are signs of Miss Motte around too, like a tie-dyed tapestry and jasmine incense held by a bronze monkey figurine. The smell fills the cottage, sweet and a little heady. And of course, there's Janet, who jumps down and starts scratching her ear. In response, Wynk leaps to a shelf, hissing indignantly.

"Well, Amelia?" Miss Motte asks, looking amused. "Will I get an explanation?"

"First," I say, still breathless, "I want to ask if you meant what you said at our first lesson, about how there are no rules in Composing class."

She tilts her head, the beads in her hair clinking. "Is that how I worded it?"

"Did you mean it?"

"I never say what I don't mean, Amelia. But—"

"Okay. Good. Just . . . remember that, please. Because we, um, well . . ." Unsure how to explain, I give up and open the sweater in my arms, revealing Jai in all his cherubic glory.

"Ah," she says, seemingly robbed of words. "Ah-*ha*. Oh my. My my *my*."

"Remember! No rules in Composing—so technically we didn't break any!" I push Baby Jai into her arms. "Please say you can fix him!"

"It wasn't my fault!" Darby adds.

And then we're both talking at once, spilling out the tale in jumbled bits.

"I was just trying to—"

"—and then *boom!* Magic everywhere!"

"And he *peed!*"

"—don't know what went wrong."

"Both of you just take a breath," says Miss Motte, putting the baby to her shoulder and patting his bum. He grabs one of her beaded dreadlocks and giggles. On the floor, Janet wiggles in an obvious fit of jealousy. "There, there, little one. I have to admit, I didn't think this would be in my job description. Amelia, what happened?"

I tell her about our idea to do a time spell at the Composium, how I wanted to find the person who stole my mom's spells, and how it all went sideways fast. She nods as she listens, studying my face carefully as if looking for any secrets I might be holding back.

"What do we do now?" I ask helplessly.

"Well," she replies, "we wait."

I flinch. "For him to grow up?"

"Dear me, no. It's not transformation magic, which is permanent, but time magic, which usually fades on its own. If we wait a bit, then *poof!* Jai will be himself once more. A pity really, hmm? What cheeks!" She pinches his wobbly jowls. Baby Jai jibber-jabbers back, staring at her adoringly.

"So what you're saying is . . ." Darby frowns. "We *can't* sell Amelia's spell as a kind of immortality magic and become mega-zillionaires?"

I stare incredulously at her. "*That's* what you're worried about?"

"It crossed my mind."

"No one will be selling any spells," Miss Motte says. "Why don't you girls sit in here while we wait for the magic to wear off? My sister is away for meetings all day, and this little handsome man needs some cleaning up, don't you, my squishy-bum? My googly-goo? What a good boy!"

Darby makes a gagging sound, and I laugh weakly, imagining how we'll explain this to Jai later. Miss Motte disappears with the baby into another room, Janet tailing her.

Cool, sweet relief floods my body as I realize he'll be okay.

Only to be followed by the vivid memory of what I saw through my time spell.

Shuddering, I pick up a book of Musicraft history from

the coffee table and focus my attention on the pictures inside. But after a moment, I set it down again.

"You know, despite Jai turning into a baby and us almost getting blasted by magic . . . that was kinda fun," I say.

"Yeah." Darby laughs. "Like old times."

Before Mia, I think.

An awkward silence falls. I know she must be thinking the same thing.

"Look, Amelia—"

"The thing is," I say at the same time, "I don't get why she's so possessive of you. I mean, I know you're best friends, and I don't want to come between you two, but what's she so scared of?"

Darby's forehead creases as she picks at a thread on her skirt. "I don't know. She's been acting weird ever since she showed up. Almost like . . . she's hiding something. You know, she never talks about the shipwreck, or the island, or her mom. I suggested that she see the school counselor, and she practically went nuclear on me." She lifts her gaze to mine. "But she's not a bad person, Amelia. I think she's just got a lot of stress and trauma under the surface."

I nod, knowing she's right. What Mia went through is probably beyond anything I could imagine.

But still . . .

"Is it something *I* did?" I ask. "Because it feels like this is personal. Like it's mainly me she's angry at."

Darby shrugs. "I don't know. I hate being stuck in the middle of you two, believe me. I think maybe—"

But I never find out what Darby thinks, because at that moment, Mia herself appears—knocking sharply on the window, her face livid. A gentle snow has started falling outside, dusting her fuzzy pink coat and bare head.

Darby and I jump.

"What do we do?" I gasp.

"You stay here. I'll talk to her." With a grimace, Darby stands and goes to the door, unbolts it, and steps outside.

I sit rigidly on the sofa, pretending to be absorbed in the history book, but I don't even have to strain to overhear their conversation.

"I told you to stay away from her!" Mia says.

"Amelia's my friend. You should take it easy on—"

"I don't *care,* Darby. I don't want you hanging out with her, or talking to her, or even waving in the hallways!"

"But *why?*"

"Because . . . because she's not good enough for you, Darbs!"

Not good enough?

Heat rushes over my skin. I sit up taller, my hands clenched on the book in my lap.

Not good enough?

"And she's shady," Mia continues. "You yourself told me about her *black spell.*"

"Mia . . . you and I both know you've played one too."

"That was eons ago! And it was to save my poor Sir Fluffington, you know that! This is different. That girl is not like us. She's from a different kind of world. I heard she's even here as some kind of charity case."

How in the world would she know about my scholarship? That was just between Mrs. Le Roux and Gran! And since when does being poor make me a bad friend?

Darby must realize that they're too loud, because she pulls Mia away and their voices fade. Does she stand up for me? If so, I never hear it.

The rest of the next hour passes numbly. I lie back on Mrs. Le Roux's fancy velvet sofa and try hard not to let the tears in my eyes fall. Wynk hops up with me and curls against my chest, and I stroke his soft fur, making him purr—only to remember just in time that his purring has the power to make people fall asleep. I settle for hugging him instead, and amazingly, he lets me.

Just when I'd thought maybe things could be normal again, that Darby and I could be friends and work things out with Mia . . . it has all fallen to pieces.

At least I find the perfect distraction when Jai returns.

Awkwardly, I try to stare at anything but my rumpled, slightly dazed friend leaning on Miss Motte. He's his normal size and age again, but he has a haunted look in his eyes, and he keeps twitching, as if to be sure he's all there.

"Where's your friend?" asks Miss Motte.

"Oh, she had a . . . thing. Is Jai all better?"

"We don't talk about this," he says hoarsely. "Ever ever ever. *Ever.*"

Miss Motte's eyes are amused, even though her lips are set in a firm line that makes her look a lot like her sister.

"Do you remember anything?" I ask. "Like how you—"

"I said no talking about it!" shouts Jai, his ears on fire. "And I remember . . . bits and pieces. Like a really, *really* bad dream. Was Claudia there at some point?"

"Oh, right." I give a sheepish grin. "If anyone asks, tell them the puppy's fine and on his way to a nice farm in the country."

"There was a puppy?" Jai's eyebrows draw together. "And I *missed* it?"

Miserably, he pops his thumb into his mouth, then freezes, his expression turning to one of horror. He slowly extracts his thumb and stares at it.

"Ah, yes . . ." Miss Motte says. "There may be some lingering effects for the next few days. You might find yourself mashing your peas before you eat them. And, uh, craving milk more than usual."

Jai's eyes bulge.

"Well, I do believe it's dinnertime!" Miss Motte claps her hands. "Off with you, sonny. Amelia? Stay where you are. We need to talk."

CHAPTER THIRTEEN

Truth and Consonances

OUTSIDE, THE LIGHT SNOW dusts the trees and ground. Mrs. Le Roux's birdhouses look like they're made of gingerbread, with sugary rooftops. The rich tones of Louis Armstrong's trumpet coil through the cottage, and Wynk hops down from my lap and curls up on a cushion in the window.

I wait on the edge of the sofa, unsure whether I'm about to get a lecture from Miss Motte or a recipe for banana bread. I've given up trying to predict what she'll do next.

"You know," she says, "when my sister asked if I'd come to Mystwick to tutor a young Composer, I told her no at first. I was in Papua New Guinea, documenting indigenous spells. It's a passion of mine, studying magic from different cultures and discovering links between them. But then she told me more about you, and I realized I couldn't go another day without meeting this Amelia Jones, whose love was so powerful she pulled her mother's spirit right from the dead."

She goes into the kitchen and puts a kettle on the stove,

then gestures for me to sit in the breakfast nook. I slide onto the upholstered bench under a window that looks out to the Echo trees. Janet jumps up and rests her head on my knee. I pet her fuzzy head while Miss Motte sits opposite me.

"So. What happened in that attic?" she asks.

"Like I said, I Composed a spell to create a time window to find out who stole my mom's spells, but I lost control of the magic." Sighing, I add, "I know what you're going to say. I should never have messed with time magic in the first place."

She seems to ponder that a moment, then rises to open a cabinet and take out two teacups. Their handles are shaped like treble clefs, and they have little matching saucers stamped with staff lines and music notes. As she spoons loose leaf tea into a teapot, she says, "You didn't *take* anything, did you?"

"Take anything?"

"You didn't stick an arm through your time window, grab hold of, I don't know, a book or pen or something, pull it through to *our* time?"

I blink. "You . . . can do that?"

"Well, you shouldn't. There are some laws even we Composers dare not trespass. One of them is the Law of Equal Consequence." She gives a little laugh. "Gracious, I sound like your Mr. Pinwhistle, don't I? So serious!"

"What's the Law of Equal Consequence?"

"It states that if you move something from one time line

to another, you must replace it with something of as equal consequence as possible. Swap an apple for an orange, for example, but better yet, an apple for an apple. Bonus points if they're the same color. In essence, something that will affect that time line much the same way it would affect this one. The more ways it matches—size, color, chemical makeup—the better." She points a spoon at me. "You're *sure* you didn't take anything?"

"Honestly, no!"

"Good. Because if you had, and you didn't leave behind something of equal consequence, it could leave *holes* in the fabric of space-time. Basically it would cause a great deal of chaos and the unwinding of events that would unravel our own time lines and . . . well, basically it'd be a catastrophe. It's happened before, once or twice. Took a massive amount of magic to set it right again, and I believe it also carries a hefty criminal sentence. But if you didn't take anything—or *leave* anything—then there's no problem." She gives a cheery smile. "So, time magic aside, what do *you* think went wrong?"

I fiddle with Janet's soft ears. "I don't know. It was going so well to start with. Then . . . I guess I lost my concentration. My mind slipped."

She sets the empty teacups on the table. "What have I told you fuels a Composition?"

"Emotion." If there's one thing I've learned from her, it's that.

"And what emotion did you use to fuel your time spell?"

"A . . . grade of B on my World Musicraft test." Even as I say it, I feel embarrassed. It sounds so small and silly in light of the kind of magic I was attempting.

"Ah." She studies me closer, then nods to herself. "Let me guess. You got dizzy and nauseated, didn't you? Felt like your strength was draining out through your fingertips?"

I sit up straighter. "Well, yeah, actually. What happened?"

She sighs. "A Composition is like a long road trip. You have to make sure there's enough fuel in the tank or you'll never make it the whole way there. Otherwise, the spell will start feeding on *you*. Magic cannot come from nothing, Amelia. It requires sufficient energy. If you don't feed it properly, it will consume you."

"And it's emotion that the magic wants to eat?"

"Exactly." Behind her, the kettle starts whistling. She stands up and pours tea. "And the bigger and more complex your Composition, the more emotional fuel it'll take. While I congratulate you on your noteworthy test score, I fear that it elicited too weak an emotion given the ambition of your spell. If you hadn't broken off your music when you did, it might have taken a lot more energy from you. Of course, setting off an explosion of uncontrolled magic isn't ideal, either. You were lucky it only resulted in a temporary rearrangement of your friend's cells. You or he could have suffered much worse. That spell might have drained you entirely."

I shudder. "Meaning . . ."

She gives me a serious look. "Meaning exactly what it sounds like, Amelia. It could have drained you to a husk. And there's no coming back from that."

I look down at my flute case, queasy again for a whole different reason. My hand slips into my pocket, curling around the vial with the dandelion seed.

There is great power in that small vial.

Whatever memory is trapped in the seed, it must be an incredibly emotional one, if it really is as powerful as Mr. Midnight promised.

Miss Motte sets the teacup in front of me and I yank my hand from my pocket.

"Which brings me to another matter," she says, stirring her own cup. "What did you see, through your time spell?"

"The attic," I say. "But in the past."

"And your mother's spells?"

I look down at my tea. "They were stolen."

"You saw someone take them?"

I nod. The steam rises from the hot liquid in gray wisps, like white magic.

"And? Did you recognize the thief?"

I look past her to the cuckoo clock hanging over the kitchen doorway. It's almost six o'clock, and I'm going to miss my study session with Jingfei and Victoria in the library if I don't leave soon.

"Amelia?"

"I just remembered that I have a history report due tomorrow," I mumble. "I should probably go write that."

"Amelia." Miss Motte puts her hand on the table between us. "Who did you see?"

My chest tightens till I can't breathe. She waits, unmoving, as our tea cools and the cuckoo clock ticks along.

"I saw my dad," I whisper at last. "He took the spells."

She sits back, letting out a long breath. I look out the window, where the snow is now thicker. It's already formed a thin layer on the ground, sparkling white, covering the dead leaves and rotting logs.

Miss Motte asks, "How long has it been since he left?"

I pick up my teacup and tilt it, watching the dregs swirl. "It doesn't matter. He's gone, and that's that."

"He's never written or called?"

"I don't care!" I set my cup down too hard, and tea spills across the table. With a yelp, Janet leaps down and scurries out of sight.

Standing up, I clutch my flute case and glare at the puddle.

"I don't want to talk about him, okay? He's a loser. He ran away from everything important. He's gone, and that's better for everyone. Now I need to go to study hall."

I take a step to the door, but Miss Motte catches my arm.

"Amelia, *look*."

She points at my shirt. I look down and suck in a breath.

The mood beads around my neck glow bright red. I touch them lightly, half expecting them to burn my skin.

"Anger," whispers Miss Motte. "Remember how Compositions are fueled by emotion? Well, Amelia, it seems you've found a mighty source of fuel."

Of course I'm angry! I'm angry at her for asking questions she has no business asking, and angry at Darby for recommending the time spell, and angry at myself for going along with it all.

"What do you mean?" I ask.

"I mean, with strength like that"—she taps the fiery beads around my neck—"you might Compose a spell to stop time itself. But if you bottle up emotions that are this powerful, they eat you up from the inside."

My heart thumps in my chest. "I don't know what you're talking about. I'm not bottling up anything."

"Amelia, your feelings about your dad, that anger and pain, they need to be set free—safely. *With this.*" She pats my flute case. "Composers are lucky, you know, to be able to weave their emotion into sound. Use your anger before it uses you."

"Lucky? You think I'm *lucky?*" Blinking back tears, I pull my flute away and step past her. "I'm not talking about this anymore. He's not—he's not a part of me, and I won't let him be!"

"Amelia!"

Rushing out the front door, I nearly slip on the slick snow, but I catch myself and plunge on. Miss Motte doesn't follow. By the time I leave the woods and look back, the cottage is hidden by a veil of drifting snow.

CHAPTER FOURTEEN

A Tough Note to Crack

I **CHEW ON MY PENCIL** eraser and stare at the blank page, as if words might appear any minute, but the Composition notebook remains stubbornly blank. Empty staff lines stripe the paper, waiting for me to fill in the notes.

But what notes? What notes?

It's like a puzzle I can't crack.

With a groan I look up from the page and gaze at the cavernous auditorium of the Shell. Seated in the front of the balcony, I have a view of the rows and rows of blue velvet chairs, the big empty stage, the heavy red curtains drawn shut. It's the quietest place on campus if you get there at the right time of day. Something about the stage and the dimly glowing footlights usually inspires me, but right now, nothing seems to be working.

A spell, a spell, I just need one spell! One amazing spell that will win the Trials and prove to everyone I'm not a one-hit wonder. I'd like to hear Mia Jones say I'm *not good enough* when I bring that Crystal Lyre back to Mystwick.

To create that spell, however, I need three things, the three components of an original Composition: an emotion, a melody, and an intention.

Intention was the subject of my last (and surprisingly helpful) lesson with Miss Motte. It's how I focus my thoughts on the task I want the magic to perform—like *reshelve these library books* or *turn that pencil into an earthworm* or *open a time window to the past.* All musicians should concentrate when they play a spell, but for Composers, it's especially important. She'd described it as the difference between following a trail through the woods and forging one. The latter requires a lot more attention and work.

But there's no use in trying to think up intentions if I don't have a melody to play, and there's no way I can start a melody without the proper emotion to fuel it. The last thing I want is to start a spell that feeds on *me* the way the time window spell had.

Yesterday I did some research on my own and discovered more than a few stories of Composers who were killed by their own spells draining them dry.

I didn't get much sleep after that.

Instead, I wound up on the floor of my dorm room, studying the dandelion seed in its glass vial, wondering how a memory ended up trapped in it. My research into *that* hadn't yielded anything. Mr. Midnight had told me that all great Composers borrow memories for their spells, but if that's true, they're very good at hiding it.

I ended up shutting the seed away in my desk drawer.

Or at least . . . I thought I'd put it in the drawer.

But now, when I slip my hand into my pocket, it's there, cold to the touch.

With a shudder, I pull my hand out and study my notes so far, written in the margins of the notebook.

COMPOSITIONS NEED FUEL.

Emotion = Fuel

No Fuel = BAD THINGS HAPPEN,

such as I die. Expire. Bloop from existence.

Sighing, I doodle a question mark on the page, with smaller question marks jumping all around it.

I don't want you to write down music, Miss Motte had said when she'd given me the notebook. *Record your emotions.*

I press my pencil tip to the page again.

CONFUSED.

FRUSTRATED.

NERVOUS.
ANGRY.

I freeze after that last word. It seems to pulse on the page with its own horrible heartbeat.

Amelia, it seems you've found a mighty source of fuel.

No no no no *NO.*

I won't think of my dad. I won't let him in my head. Not as I'd seen him through the time window, frantic and shadowy. Not as he'd looked in that photo of the last Mystwick Trials team, with his cocky smile and his arm around my mom's shoulders. And not as I remember him from when I was little. Those memories are too faded and jumbled to be much use anyway.

"Amelia Jones! What are you up to?"

I jump, nearly stabbing my own eye with the pencil. "Jai! Where did you come from?"

He leaps over the seats to sit beside me, propping his feet on a little sign on the railing that says NO SHOES ON THE RAILING! His violin case is slung over his shoulder.

"Ah, yes, that story begins long ago," he says, "and it starts out a bit messy, but all right, if you insist. You see, in a hospital in London nearly thirteen years past, on a sparkling summer morning, the beautiful and renowned cellist Elleni Kapoor was about to give birth—"

"*Why* are you here?"

"I'm avoiding George." Jai shudders. "He wants to show me his earwax collection."

"His . . . *Ew!*"

"That's what *I* said! Anyway, I saw you heading off with a face like a constipated troll and thought, every time Amelia Jones gets that look, something interesting usually happens."

"Yes. Welcome to the thrilling world of my homework."

He notices the notebook in my hands. "You're Composing?"

"Well. Trying to." I turn my notebook around to show him my progress.

"Lucky for you, I'm here now. But this time, let's *not* dabble in the fabric of—what? Why are you looking at me like that?"

"You're, um, drooling."

His eyes widen, and he quickly wipes his sleeve across his chin.

"Sorry," I say. "Again."

"We're *not* talking about it, remember?" Jai shudders. "Back to the *real* problem: your brain. So. How did you Compose before? You've done it three times, right?"

"Four," I say. "The spell I played that made it snow, the one that called up my mom's ghost, the one I used on my Echo tree for the Maestros . . . I shouldn't count the time spell, though. I didn't exactly finish it."

"The point is, you *have* Composed before." He spreads his

hands. "Just do whatever you did *then,* again. Should be easy, right?"

"Except it's *not.* All those times, I knew what to play without thinking about it. The music was in my head long before I ever let it out. It's like . . . the difference between writing down a poem you've memorized and one you have to make up from scratch." I rub my eyes in frustration. "It was easy to Compose when no one was watching. Now that everyone *is,* it's like all I can think about is the pressure of their expectations."

"Okay, so *don't* think about it."

"Huh?"

"You just said that before, you knew what to play without thinking about it. So stop thinking. Start *feeling.*"

"You sound like Miss Motte."

But maybe he has a point.

I've been trying to think my way into a melody when I should be feeling my way in. Looking at the page, I realize I've even been overthinking my feelings. Before, I didn't approach Composing like a formula—*emotion, melody, intention.* Those things always happened together, naturally, without my even trying.

I shut my eyes and let out a long breath, reaching inward. Listening. Searching for the music within.

"Yes. Yessssss, Amelia, become one with the wind . . . let the earth breathe through you—"

"JAI."

"Sorry. Shutting up."

After shooting him a look, I lean back and stare up at the ceiling of the Shell. It's painted dark blue, with tiny golden music notes scattered across, glowing faintly like stars. The longer I stare, the more my eyes pick out shapes and lines, musical constellations that glitter and gleam, as if full of secret spells. If I stare long enough, maybe I'll decipher the music they hide.

Slowly, I breathe in and out until the world fades around me. All that fills my head are those glowing stars. The silence of the Shell sinks into my bones.

Then, somewhere deep, deep inside me . . . I hear a note.

Soft and resonant and trembling, it flickers in the back of my mind. I shut my eyes and focus on it, the way you watch a very faint star, because you know the moment you look away, it will vanish.

The golden music notes on the ceiling seem to shimmer on the insides of my eyelids, and as I watch them, one peels free and glows right at my fingertips. Then another slips loose, and another and another, notes bright and resonant. I hear each one as sharp as a bell in my mind. My hands twitch, feeling the fingering as if I were holding my flute. More and more notes fall from the ceiling to gleam before me, taking their places in a marching row, my own constellation of sound.

Measure by measure, a melody takes shape, like a shadow coming into focus . . .

Then I see *him,* turning away from the Composition notebooks in the attic classroom, a sudden slant of light illuminating his face.

Dad.

The notes dance all around him, their light sharpening his features, forcing me to remember.

Anger shoots through my body, curls my fingers into fists, burns in my cheeks. The music keeps playing, getting faster and more frantic, furious staccato notes that hiss and scorch in my mind. The melody entwines with the memory until I can't tell one from the other.

NO!

I wrench my mind away, shutting out the sound, sending the glowing music notes scattering in all directions. They fade in the darkness like dying sparks.

With a gasp, I open my eyes and shove away my notebook. It falls with a rustle to the floor.

"Amelia? Are you all right?"

I crush the heels of my hands into my eyes, trying to push the melody out of my head.

"Amelia!" Jai sounds alarmed.

"I'm fine," I whisper. "It didn't work, that's all."

"Oh."

I can tell he doesn't believe me, but I don't offer more explanation. I'm not ready to tell him that it's a lie, that it did work, that I *did* find music waiting inside me.

It's just not music I ever want to let out.

CHAPTER FIFTEEN

Achy, Breaky Harp

I'M SITTING ON THE stairs leading to the Composing classroom when Miss Motte arrives. Jumping up, I meet her halfway down.

"Hey, Miss Motte! I wondered if maybe we could have class outside today?"

She blinks. "It's *sleeting*."

"The library, then? I found a whole section of Composers' biographies that—"

"Yesterday we met in the cafeteria because you said you were hungry. The day before that, we met on the dock because you said fresh air might make you more inspired. While I wholeheartedly applaud learning *en plein air,* we haven't set foot in our classroom for a week, Amelia."

"Yes . . . well . . ." I struggle to think of a convincing excuse.

"I think I know what this is about." She steps past me and opens the attic door. "Coming?"

Deflated, I follow her up, my stomach twisting. This is the

first time I've stepped into the attic classroom since my time spell went all wibbly-wobbly. The place is still a wreck. I guess the custodians don't come up here . . . or maybe they were so offended by the terrific mess I made, they decided to leave it to me to clean up. I can't say I'd blame them.

Desks are overturned, pencils and papers are scattered everywhere, and bits of glass and broken ceramic crunch under my shoes. My eyes scan the mess but stop just short of the bookshelf full of Composition notebooks.

The place where I'd seen *him.*

"My, my," says Miss Motte, looking around. "You really did a number on this place."

I sigh. "I'll go get a broom."

"Broom? Tsk! This is a Composing class, isn't it?" She gives me a light nudge with her elbow. "Maybe it's time we actually do some Composing and add a cleaning spell to your repertoire."

I look down at my flute case. "I . . . could try, I guess."

Reluctantly, I assemble my flute and stand in the center of the room. Anything to avoid the looming bookshelf, or the memory of who I saw there.

He stood *here,* in this classroom. Maybe in this very spot.

The idea feels slimy. I wrench my mind away.

"Now slow down just a minute," says Miss Motte. "While I

admire a can-do attitude, you can't grow flowers unless you've tilled the soil."

"Huh?"

"What I mean is, let's do this properly." She sits on the teacher's desk, spreads her hands, and shuts her eyes. When I say nothing, she cracks one eye open and cocks her eyebrow. "You gonna join me or stand there gawping like a fish on a platter?"

"Oh, um . . ." I shut my eyes.

"Good. Yes. Remember what we talked about. Emotion is the fuel your magic needs. So let's dig some up." She takes a few deep breaths, then murmurs, "You perch on a rocky cliff above a turquoise lagoon. Your heart flutters with anticipation. Then you *leap* into the unknown, enter the water with hardly a splash, dive deep, deep, deep . . ."

I breathe in and out, searching for the calm places inside me, but I can feel a presence in the room, a shadow in the corner of my mind. No matter which way I turn my head, I can still sense it pressing on me.

I can feel *him*.

"Breathe deep, Amelia. Now . . . plunge your hands into the muck and pull out the oysters of memory there. Yes, yes. What will we find today? Joy? Sorrow? Love? What will we spin into sound? What shape will your magic take?"

Cold sweat runs down the back of my neck.

My dad's not here, obviously. That time window showed him years in the past. He's long gone, just like he's always been.

So why does it feel like he's standing right behind me?

"Amelia? Got your oyster yet?"

"Working on it," I mumble.

Fighting to clear my head, I rummage for some memory to use. A happy one. The day I got my Mystwick acceptance letter?

"Okay," I say tentatively.

"Good," says Miss Motte. "Now crack that memory open and find the pearl of emotion inside. That's it—that's your fuel. Let it run through you. Feel it all over again, from your head to your toes. Let it whisper its melody in your ear. All great emotions have music hidden within them. All you have to do is *listen*."

I try to remember everything about that day—the letter in Gran's hand, the glittering ink, the crinkle of the paper in my hands. It's still fresh and vivid in my mind, and I feel the joy and amazement I'd felt when I realized . . .

Smooth and silky, notes slither through my thoughts.

But it's no happy melody.

It's *back*. That dark, angry music I heard in the Shell just won't go away, no matter how hard I try to ignore it. It weaves through the memory I'd chosen, turning it sour. My joy withers, turning to dread. Those awful notes wind through me like a snake, tightening around that happy day and squeezing all the light out of it.

My eyes crack open to see Miss Motte watching me.

Suppressing a shiver, I set my flute back in its case. "I—I think I'll just go get that broom from the closet downstairs. I guess I'm feeling a little off today."

"Mm-hmm," says Miss Motte, never taking her eyes off me.

I take my time finding a broom, walking slow and pressing a hand to my chest, as if searching for the mute button that'll silence the music pounding in my skull. Prickly, hot anger burns on my skin like a rash.

What's *wrong* with me?

Why can't I Compose?

It's as if that time spell has broken me somehow.

When I return a few minutes later, armed with everything I could carry from the custodial closet, I find Miss Motte still sitting on the desk. But she's got a yellow folder in her hands that I hadn't seen before.

"Did you know your dad attended Mystwick?" she asks, as if she were commenting on the color of the walls and not opening the earth beneath my feet.

The broom slips from my hands with a clatter; the dustpan,

spray bottles, cloths, and sponges go next as I frantically try to grab all of it but end up catching nothing. The stuff clatters on the floor, making a tremendous racket.

"Yeah," I mutter when its quiet again. "Of course I knew that."

"I found his old student file," Miss Motte says, ignoring the cleaning supplies I just dumped all over the floor. She sets the file on my desk. "My sister says it's technically against policy to share it, but she agrees that in this case . . . the benefit might outweigh the red tape."

Without looking at the folder, I pick up the broom and start sweeping broken pottery. "I don't know why I need to look at that."

"You don't have to look at it today," she says, her tone still mild. "Or tomorrow. You just wait till you're ready. Just remember: to be free of this anger, you must first understand it."

Without answering her, I keep sweeping. I'm uselessly moving broken pieces around on the floor, like an idiot, but I can't think straight enough to figure out what to do with them. The hair on my arms has gone all prickly. I just want her to say class is over so I can leave.

Instead, Miss Motte reaches behind her desk and pulls up a pretty little Celtic harp. Smaller than the great concert harps

I've seen some students playing, its frame is carved with beautiful whorls and knots and creatures. I let out a soft breath; it's the most beautiful instrument I've ever seen. The wood is so sleek and warm, it's as if it's breathing with life.

"I was thinking," she says. "This *is* a Composing class, right? Maybe it's time I learned a little something myself."

Miss Motte lifts the harp and sits atop one of the empty desks, the instrument propped against her thigh. She closes her eyes, and for several long moments she doesn't move or speak. I wait, my pulse racing. This is the first time I'll see her—or *anyone*—Compose. Not daring to speak, I wait and sit very still.

Finally Miss Motte opens her eyes, lets out a little sigh, and places her hands on the strings. Another breath, and she begins to play.

Miss Motte's fingers move delicately over the strings. Like bright birds, notes take to the air one by one, a steady trickle, then all at once in a tumbling flock. Her tempo quickens to a frenzy, fingers raining along the strings in a blur, then slows again to a gentle murmur.

She moves with the music, leaning into and away from the harp, her eyes closed again. Her lips press together, her brow furrows, as if every note carries some special, hidden meaning to her. I find myself watching her face more than her hands.

Gradually the strings of the harp begin to glisten with sunny yellow magic.

"Did you know, Amelia," she says softly over the music, "I was engaged once."

I slide into a chair, my hands folded atop the desk, watching her with wide eyes.

"He was a good man," she continues, her eyes still shut. Her strong fingers pull and dance over the strings, and her golden magic shines on the mahogany of her skin. "A man I loved."

Magic flows away from her, curling through the air in the shapes of shimmering vines. It collects broken pieces, fallen chairs and books, and begins putting them back in their places.

"The day of our wedding," she says, "I realized I couldn't make that commitment. I still had too much wander in me. He wouldn't deserve that . . . me always gone, chasing every whim, him chasing after me. He called it my *butterfly heart*."

A tear runs down her cheek even though she's smiling. Riveted in place, I hardly dare breathe. All around me, her magic restores the room back to order, shelving books, stacking loose spell sheets.

"I don't regret leaving, you know. I have to be honest about that. But I do regret not telling him I would. I left without a word, you see. Not even a note. I think he knew why I left, but still, I should have had the courage to say it aloud. But I didn't. And that's the one thing in my life I wish I could do over again—simply *facing* the truth of my feelings."

I lower my eyes a little, not wanting to see the tears on her face. Even though she's telling me this story, it still feels like something too private, especially for a teacher to say to a student. Teachers are supposed to be . . . I don't know. All rules and assignments and red pens. I don't think I've ever seen a teacher *cry* before. Awkwardly, I stare at my hands.

"Guilt, Amelia," she says. "That's a powerful emotion. Putting that guilt into music doesn't erase the pain it causes me, but it does ease the burden. It helps me understand it better, and to forgive myself a little more."

I glance at the folder on my desk, but then my eyes slide away again.

Finally she finishes her spell. The harp's notes trickle sweetly into silence, and the magic fades from the air. The classroom is sparkling; even the dust and cobwebs from the highest beams have been magicked away.

Miss Motte smiles, looking pleased. "Well, that did the trick, didn't it?"

"Aren't you going to write down your spell?" I ask. "Before you forget it?"

She runs her fingers over the carvings on her harp. "No, I

don't think I will. We are Composers, Amelia, but that doesn't mean everything we create has to be given away. Some music is just for us."

That's all well and good, as Gran would say, but none of this is helping me with my *real* problem: Composing a spell for the Trials.

"Miss Motte, what happens when a Composer . . . *can't* Compose?"

She nods slowly, thoughtful. "You're talking about Composer's block."

"It's a thing?"

"It's a thing, all right. Rachmaninoff had it for four whole years."

"Four *years?*" I moan. "What causes it?"

"Oh, could be anything. Maybe some folks say mean things about your music and it throws you into a funk—like what happened to poor old Rachmaninoff. Maybe you work too hard for too long and burn yourself out. Maybe you're too scared of messing up that you never start." She turns up a hand. "But it's no joke. Once you're funkified, it's not easy to get defunked."

Great. So here I am, in a funk, with three weeks left to Compose a masterpiece or I'll let down the entire school *and* prove Mia right: that I'm a one-hit wonder on a dead-end road. Worse than a has-been: a *might-have-been. Too bad about that*

Amelia Jones. She showed a lot of promise. Might have been something special . . . if it weren't for that slump she got herself into. Guess we were wrong about her.

Maybe she's not Mystwick material after all.

Maybe she doesn't belong here, period.

With a groan, I plant my face on the desk—only to realize that my dad's student file is still lying there.

I jerk away as if stung, rising to my feet and reaching for my flute case.

"Is that all for today, Miss Motte?" I ask stiffly.

She studies me a moment longer, her expression unreadable. Then she says "Yes, Amelia. That's all for today."

I tuck my case under my arm and walk quickly to the door, leaving the yellow folder on the desk, untouched.

CHAPTER SIXTEEN

A Different Point of Fugue

THAT EVENING, AFTER DINNER, the Trials team meets again to practice for the Composium.

The dandelion seed is in my pocket with my Composing notebook, which is full of mindless scribbles and frustrated, dead-end melodies. I rub it between my fingers as I slog through the freshly fallen snow. A few flurries still drift lazily down from the clouds.

I have absolutely nothing to show for all my efforts over the past three weeks.

It's not for lack of trying. The problem is, every time I *do* try to Compose, all I can hear are those angry, stinging notes that swirl around the memory of my dad. They block everything else, like wasps buzzing in my ears. It's getting so I hear them even when I'm *not* reaching for the music inside. The melody threads through my dreams. If I'm not careful, I find myself tapping my desk in time with it.

Yesterday Jai caught me *humming* it.

I mumbled something about it being an old tune I heard in church.

I think of Rachmaninoff. I read up on him after my last Composing lesson. For four years he moped around Europe, out of money and out of ideas. And he was one of the greatest Composers ever! If he couldn't shake his slump, how can I?

I slink into the Shell and take a seat in the back, wearing a coat over my Mystwick sweater, the hood pulled over my head. It's too much to hope that no one will notice me, given I'm sort of the main event when it comes to the Composium, but I hunker down anyway.

Once we're all assembled, Mr. Pinwhistle announces that he has acquired a copy of Luca D'Alessio's winning spell.

"Mia Jones has agreed to play it for us," he says.

Mia swans up to the stage and takes the sheet music Mr. Pinwhistle hands her. With a flick of her hair, she sits at the piano.

Everyone else sits up a bit straighter, eyes widening, including me. I can't remember hearing Mia play once since she got here.

"Amelia," Miss Motte calls out to me. She beckons with one finger.

Uncertainly, I stand and go sit next to her in the front row.

"What's going on?" I ask her.

"It's important that you study the music like a Composer," she replies. "Listen and try to understand what Luca wanted to *say* with this spell."

I'm pretty sure Luca was trying to say *I'm awesome and the competition can suck it,* but I'm guessing Miss Motte wouldn't agree.

When Mia begins to play, I shut my eyes, trying to concentrate. I feel a tingle of curiosity; the spell is supposed to conjure a person's happiest memory. I wonder what it'll make *me* see. The day I became a full-fledged Mystwick student? The day I met my mom's ghost?

It's hard to think at all with Mia's music.

Mother of Beethoven, the girl is *good.*

Cracking an eye, I peek at her as she leans into the piano, swaying with the tempo. Her face is transformed when she plays, her expression intense and focused, as if she's pouring her entire being into the spell, as if she's forgotten everyone else in the concert hall. The other students watch, captivated, as Mia's fingers perform a mesmerizing dance over the keys, sometimes so quickly they blur. The notes crash and then soften, *forte* to *pianissimo,* lifting and falling.

Mia half rises on the bench, completely absorbed in Luca's piece. His music is good, but her skill takes it to an entirely different level. It isn't long before foggy plumes of white magic begin to pour from the piano and spread across the stage.

I may not like Mia much, but I'm still awed by her talent.

"No, no," Miss Motte says. "Just *feel* the spell, Amelia. Close your eyes and listen with your heart."

On the other side of me, Mr. Pinwhistle gives a snort.

I do as Miss Motte says. Leaning back in my chair, I feel myself start to relax, not from the magic so much as from the beauty of the sound. Mia's music is a rushing river, and I float, helplessly caught in its current.

A desire for sleep settles over me, and I start to lose the feeling in my body. I can't sense the chair I'm sitting on or feel the slight chill in the air.

Instead, I feel the tickle of grass against my bare ankles. I smell the sweetness of roses.

My eyes open, and I see blue sky over green, green grass, and a patchwork quilt spread out with a picnic on it. I'm much smaller, wearing a yellow polka-dot dress and no shoes, and Mom sits on the blanket, laughing under the brim of her wide sun hat.

This must be my happiest memory, but it's not one I've thought about for a long time.

We've just finished a day at the zoo, I recall. I skip around Mom and hum the spell the zookeepers played to call the elephants. Mom's flute rests on the blanket.

"Let me play it!" I say, winding my fingers in her hair. "Please, Mama? I'll call an elephant, and we can ride it home!"

"We're not going home, silly. Remember? Tonight is our big camping trip!"

"*Please,* Mama?"

She laughs again and hands me the flute. I blow into it, but the sounds that come out are random squeaks. I'm nowhere near skilled enough yet to produce any magic.

Then, suddenly, someone picks me up and swings me in a circle. Mom grabs the flute before I drop it, and I fling my arms out and throw my head back as I spin around, around, around, dizzy with happiness.

But then unease stirs in my belly. I'm still being spun around, but when I look down, all I see are two strong hands around my waist. The person holding me is out of sight. I could see their face if I just tilted my head back a little more.

I don't. I already know who's there.

Suddenly the memory *changes,* in ways I know aren't true. The blue sky disappears behind fitful dark clouds. The grass withers, brown and dry. It's like someone's messing with the memory, getting the details wrong.

And still I'm spinning around, my arms and legs pushed outward by centrifugal force, my messy curls spilling over my face.

"You can have the moon if you want it, baby girl," says a deep voice behind me. "I'll lasso it for you, and you can eat it like a cookie."

"Don't steal the moon, Dad," I hear myself say. "Then the sun would be lonely."

He laughs, but the sound is drowned out by a crack of thunder.

With a jagged gasp, I open my eyes and jump up from my seat, back in the Shell. I have to blink a few times before the memory fully leaves my vision. For a moment it seems as if all the other students are sitting in that brown field under that angry dark sky, their eyes shut as they relive memories of their own. Foggy white magic seeps across the floor and hangs like heavy mist in the air.

"Amelia?" Miss Motte stands up behind me. "What's wrong?"

I'm breathing hard, my throat knotted. I bend over and put my hands on my knees. I can feel Luca D'Alessio's spell, thick and silvery and cloying, stealing into my mind, trying to tug me back under its power. I resist it with all my might.

Finally, Mia brings the spell to a close, holding the last note as she turns to look at me. A smirk flashes across her face.

That's when I realize that my eyes are dripping with tears.

I run my hands over my cheeks, trying to wipe them away, but more keep coming.

"What's wrong with her?" someone calls out.

Miss Motte tries to put her hand on my shoulder, but I turn from her and run down the aisle. Students turn to watch me go, some of them laughing. I can't get far enough away.

I can still feel his hands on my waist, his laughter in my ear. I turn around, half expecting to see him standing there.

That music is back.

Those awful notes are clanging in my head, singing their spell of anger and pain. I try to crush them, but they only get louder.

Miss Motte finds me in the lobby bathroom a few minutes later. I sit on the floor in the corner, knees drawn up, eyes finally dry.

"Amelia, I'm so sorry," she says. She sits beside me, her face crinkled with concern. "I should have guessed what would happen. I just didn't know how bad it was."

"You don't even know what I saw," I whisper.

She gives me a funny look. "You kept saying *'Dad'* over and over, honey."

"I . . . did?"

Miss Motte gently pushes my hair out of my face, tucking it behind my ear.

"I should never have let you endure that. If I'd realized how deep this wound is . . . Amelia, I think it's best if you drop out of the Trials."

I look up at her. "*You* were the one who wanted me to use memories of my dad to Compose. You said it was fuel."

"This pain is deep, Amelia. Composing means opening yourself up to those feelings, which can be good and helpful, but it's also hard. And it takes *time*. You don't need to rush this just to win a competition."

"I'm not dropping out of the Trials. If I do, nobody gets to go. They need me."

"And *you* need to heal. When somebody hurts you that deep, the hurt turns into poison, poison that seeps into happy memories and twists them into painful ones. That's what happened back there, isn't it? A happy memory turned rotten." She waits a moment, then adds, "Sooner or later, Amelia, you're going to have to let that poison out."

I think of the memory of the picnic, but when I get close to recalling my dad again, my soul flinches away, as if the memory is barbed wire.

"You bottle up feelings this big and they just get stronger, until eventually they burst out on their own. It's starting to bubble up out of you, isn't it? That anger is getting too strong." She puts her fingertips to the mood beads around my neck.

They're fiery red again.

"There's music inside you, Amelia Jones, that's aching to be let out."

Deep within me, the notes clamor and scurry, spiders in a bucket.

My eyes start tearing up again. Angrily, I ball my fists and wipe them away.

"No. This is *your* fault!" Rising to my feet, I glare at her. Something sharp and nasty twists inside of me, operating me like a puppeteer. "I was doing just fine till you started digging into things that aren't any of your business. I *can* Compose, and I don't need your phony beads to do it."

I yank the necklace off, and the string breaks. Beads scatter all over the floor.

Someone knocks hard on the bathroom door.

"Amelia?" Mr. Pinwhistle's voice is even more gruff than usual, as if he's panicked. "Mathilde? Everything all right?"

My vision blurring with more tears, I push open the door, slipping past Mr. Pinwhistle. He takes one look at my tear-streaked face, and his eyebrows shoot up to his hairline. Then, with a thunderous expression, he turns to Miss Motte.

"This is your doing! I *knew* your touchy-feely methods would make trouble!"

Miss Motte rises to her feet and follows me into the lobby. "Fred, this is none of your concern."

"Amelia is my student too. She is most certainly my concern! And now look—*you've* gone and broken her!"

"I am NOT broken!" I yell, and they both turn to stare at me in surprise.

Kids are piling into the lobby, gaping at the argument, so

I run the other way and leave through the front doors of the Shell. I already can't stand to have Miss Motte prying into me. It's even worse when Mr. Pinwhistle starts too.

The night is cold and quiet, the only light coming from the gleaming windows of the school. I run across the grass to the one place I've always run to when I'm overwhelmed: the forest.

The Echo Wood is silent beneath the snow. I miss its usual sound, when the wind rustles the branches and the trees hum their soft musical tones.

Tonight, all seems frozen.

The fresh, unbroken snow seems to call to me, and I wander along until I come to the row of Echo tree saplings planted along the forest's edge. They're taller than they were a few months ago, when the other seventh-graders and I planted them there and became official students of Mystwick. The branches are bare, of course, so they look like little more than sticks jutting out of the snow. Mine is easily the most recognizable, bent at an awkward angle. I'd straightened it, thinking it needed to look as perfect as everyone else's trees, but then I realized that it was more important for it to be itself. So I'd Composed a spell to bend it back to its original shape.

Why had my Composing worked then, with hardly an effort?

Crouching down, I touch a tiny bud on the sapling, where a new branch is starting to grow, and think of that day.

Every Composition requires a powerful emotion to fuel it.

I know what I felt the day I played over my Echo tree: *confident.* Not just in my strengths, but in my imperfections too. I was proud to be every inch myself.

And that was just a few weeks ago. So where did my confidence go? Why did I get everything I wanted, only to find myself right back where I started?

Well, I know why.

Because of him.

My loser dad.

The moment I saw him through my time spell is when everything started to fall apart, and a door deep inside me—a door I'd forgotten was there—opened wide.

I'd lied to Miss Motte. I'm not fine. There *is* music inside me aching to get out. But it's angry, clashing music, discordant notes, and jumbled dissonance. It's no symphony—it's a cacophony.

If I let it out, it might burn me up.

CHAPTER SEVENTEEN

When Presto Comes to Shove

"**Hi, Amelia. Do you,** um, have a minute?"

As soon as I hear Trevor Thompson's voice in the dinner line behind me, my stomach sinks to my shoes. I know exactly what he wants to talk about. I've been avoiding him—and every other member of the Trials team—since last night, when I ran out of the Composium practice like my tail was on fire.

I turn around slowly, staring at him over my tray of steaming chicken potpie.

He's not alone. Kjersten, Phoebe, and Rosa are with him.

"The Trials are in three weeks," he says gently. "We should have started practicing for the Composium days ago. I don't want to stress you out or anything, but . . . you told us you could do this."

"And I can. I will. I mean—I'm working on it."

"Right. Well." He exchanges looks with the girls. "Thing is, if we don't have a spell by tomorrow, Amelia, we might need to think about withdrawing from the trials altogether."

I feel the blood drain from my face. "Seriously?"

"Look, we all want this to work out, but if you can't pull it off, it's only fair that you tell us now, before we waste any more time on—on practicing."

Had he been about to say *before we waste more time on* you?

Trevor walks away, shaking his head. Kjersten and Phoebe both give me disappointed looks, while Rosa just nods sourly to herself, as if this is how she always knew it would turn out.

Wilting, I go to my usual table with Jai, Jingfei, and Victoria, but find my seat filled by Claudia. She watches me smugly, waiting for me to say something.

"I told her to shove off," Jai says. "She won't budge."

The other kids look from Claudia to me with obvious anticipation, waiting to see what I'll do.

This is a clearly a trap, and I've walked right into it.

Reaching down deep, I try to find the *bigger person.*

"I see you're sitting where I usually sit, Claudia." I'm actually proud of how calm my voice is. "That's okay. I can sit over there."

At the next table, Collin and George look up with bugging eyes; everyone knows that sitting with them makes you a prime target for stray spitwads and flicks of gravy. Nobody sits with them voluntarily.

But I go to do just that, head held high—until Claudia says, "Are you sure, Amelia? You won't cry about that too?"

I stop cold as snickers sound behind me.

"Shut up, Claudia!" Jai growls. "You don't know what you're talking about."

"Oh, please. Everyone heard about Amelia running away from class yesterday, sobbing for her daddy. She's cracking under the pressure of the Trials, and we all know it."

"I'm not cracking," I whisper.

"What's that?" she says.

"I said I'M NOT CRACKING!"

The cafeteria goes totally silent.

Everyone's watching me, eyes wide, forks frozen. A piece of chicken slides off George's fork and lands with a splat on the floor.

Jai stands up. "Amelia—"

"I'm fine. I just need some space." I leave my untouched dinner on the dish room counter and walk stiffly out of the cafeteria before I embarrass myself even more.

Mortified, I crouch in the snow against the outside wall, my arms wrapped around my knees and my face down. I should have seen this coming. I guess what happened yesterday was never going to stay a secret, not when everyone on the Trials team saw my meltdown. No wonder Trevor was talking to me like he was afraid of setting off a bomb.

"Well, well. This is just sad, Wondergirl."

I look up to see Mia standing in front of me.

Great. Of course she'd show up now.

I look around for Darby, but we're the only ones out here. Mia's steps crunch as she walks over the snow toward me.

"I mean, I knew you'd fall apart eventually. I just thought you might actually make it to the Trials before that happened."

"What is *wrong* with you?" I whisper.

"Sorry. Should I be more careful of your feelings? Everyone else around here is, I know. Poor Amelia Jones—the *other* Amelia Jones—from the back end of nowhere, with no parents to speak of, no money, accepted to Mystwick out of pity. You find out you're a Composer and think maybe you'll finally *be* somebody, but alas. Here you end up, sniveling in the cold, all alone."

"You want to play *that* game?" I stand up, my hands shaking until I curl them into fists. Furious notes pop in my mind; my angry music sings through me.

"You're the one people treat like glass," I say. "Mia Jones, the poor shipwrecked prodigy whose mom got lost at sea. But weirdly, you don't even seem to care. From the way you act, it's like she could be off on vacation."

Mia slaps me.

Shocked, I lurch back, a hand pressed to my burning cheek.

Mia's eyes are open wide, her skin flushing scarlet. She

takes a few short, sharp breaths, her chin lifting higher with each one. It's like she transforms into a whole other person right in front of me, full of rage and venom.

It's one of the most terrifying things I have ever seen.

"You," she whispers, her voice as tight as piano wire, "*you* do not get to bring up my mother. *You* do not get to question *me!* YOU are the one who—" She pauses to breathe, and for a second she seems on the verge of passing out from sheer fury. "You're a *failure,* a rotten little copycat! Slinking into this school under *my* name, stealing *my* best friend, making yourself out to be some great, all-powerful Composer when you can't even grind out a single original note! You're *nothing,* and I cannot begin to understand what they see in you! I heard your little sob story from Darby. No wonder your dad ran out on you. He probably saw what *I* see—that you're more trouble than your worth. I bet his leaving was *your fault.*"

I gasp.

Tears sting my eyes, from her words even more than her slap. I turn my face away as she walks past me, her hair rippling in the cold wind.

His leaving was your fault.

The melody inside me roars, putting out claws. It rips at the inside of my head, hungry and furious and sharp.

Your fault.

Your fault.

If I don't do something, that music will tear me in half.

Crack!

The glass vial breaks when I smash it against the brick wall, and I catch the dandelion seed before it can blow away.

"I *am* a Composer," I say.

Mia stops, her hand on the cafeteria door.

"I am, and I can prove it."

She doesn't see me put the dandelion seed on my tongue.

But she does see me turn around, my face twisted with anger and determination. She sees my flute case fall open and the joints sliding together in my hands.

Her eyes widen slightly, and she lets go of the door.

Raising my mother's flute to my chin, I lock eyes with Mia Jones and, with the smallest of movements, crunch the dandelion seed between my teeth.

CHAPTER EIGHTEEN

Great Bars of Fire

A COLD, SHARP WIND BLOWS through me, turning my blood to ice. Head spinning, I stumble back, barely catching myself before I fall. My tongue tingles from the seed—or rather, the memory it contained.

Instinctively I lift my flute, and my fingers take position as around me the world turns gray and full of static, like one of Gran's old TV shows. I glance at Mia, who stands in front of me in shades of black and white, her eyes narrowed. Then I look away as a flash of movement catches my eye.

A girl, in full color, runs in slow motion to my left. She's a little older than I am, with short blond hair and a blue nightgown. Slowly, walls take shape around her, then furniture: a bed, a dresser, a chair. She seems to be running from something, because she looks over her shoulder, eyes wide and afraid.

Then I see it.

Fire spreads across the floor and the walls, consuming everything in its path.

The girl opens a door, and the memory pans like a camera, following her as she bursts into another bedroom. She pulls a young boy out of a bed and drags him out. They run in slow motion down a hallway as behind them, the fire grows.

In a wave, the girl's emotions wash over me. I feel her horror, her fear, her shame.

I did this, she is thinking. *I did this. Mom told me no candles in my room . . . I didn't listen . . . fell asleep . . .*

Rooted in place, I am forced to watch the terrible memory play out. I see the girl wake her parents, and together they flee outside. They stand on the grass right next to me, and we all watch their house burn to the ground. And that's the moment the girl realizes.

We forgot Bonnie.

She bolts forward, but her father grabs her around the waist and hauls her back. She screams for her dog, her precious yellow dog with the blue collar, but there's nothing she can do now. I feel her love, her sorrow, her searing guilt, as sharp as if they were my own.

The house is gone, and everything inside.

I can smell the smoke and feel the heat of the flames on my face. I feel the girl's tears on *my* cheeks. Her shame burns in my belly, as hot as the inferno destroying her home.

That shame flows through me, pulsing and insistent. It builds up like pressure inside my chest, pushing against my ribs, searching for a way out.

I know that this is the time to play.

Raising my flute, I press it to my chin, but another force seems to take control of my fingers. I can only stand there, helpless, as my hands begin to play and my lips blow into the flute. Notes take flight, strong and resonant.

The memory fades then; it had all happened in less than an instant, no longer than it took me to bite down on the dandelion seed. Then it's gone, but the girl's emotion remains. Tears on my cheeks, I pour the girl's shame into my flute, transforming it into sound.

Mia crosses her arms, watching me with an expression of contempt as the spell takes shape. Does she know what just happened? Does she suspect that this magic is not truly my own?

I couldn't stop it now if I tried. The memory has taken possession of my hands. The melody I play sounds strange in my own ears, like I'm moving my lips but hearing someone else's voice. The way the notes are strung together, the turns and trills, the sad melody in a soulful minor key . . . none of it comes from me. It's all born from the girl's memory of the fire. This magic is *her* magic, whoever she was.

It leaps from my flute, curling tongues of blue flame.

Elemental magic, I think, panicking. I have no idea what it will do. It's completely out of my control. I'm no more in charge of the spell's course than my flute is. We're just the powerless vessels through which the music plays out.

A few kids step out of the cafeteria then, see me playing my flute, and start shouting. Soon, more students follow, then a whole flood of them. Mia vanishes into the crowd, and I'm left standing alone with my flute and this strange, unrelenting spell.

"Amelia!"

I glance at Jai helplessly; I can't unglue my fingers from the keys. Already I regret what I've done, the rotten choice I made, but it's too late.

The magic must play out.

The spell must run its course.

As the crowd of students grows and a few Maestros join them, I play on. Cerulean magic flows in banners, spiraling around me and all across the grass.

Then, one by one, strange fires spark, burning on the snow with no fuel or smoke.

Shouts of alarm rise from the students watching. They back away while the Maestros present move to the front. I see Miss Noorani, Miss Becker, and Mr. Walters there, as well as Coach Phil and Miss March. They usher the students back, well away from the little fires blazing all around me.

The spell isn't finished yet.

The magic begins knitting the fires together. Blue light weaves with red flames, growing brighter and brighter, forming the shape of a . . .

"Dragon!" shouts Jai.

Two fiery wings unfurl, one stretching to Harmony Hall, the other over the roof of the cafeteria. Its skin is layered in scales of flame, and its claws and teeth burn white-hot. When it opens its mouth, blue fire shoots out.

Everyone gasps as it swoops toward us, then arcs upward, flying in a loop around the school. The sound of crackling flames fills the sky, and its fiery reflection shimmers on the windows.

I keep playing, my flute like a spool of string, the dragon my burning, roaring kite. The melody is as vicious as the dragon, sharp and high. Dragged along by the melody, I can do nothing but hope it will end soon—without setting anything or anyone on fire. As the second rule of Musicraft states, *Lest you be doomed by your own art, always finish what you start.* Breaking off the music now would cause an explosion like the one that turned Jai into a baby—only this time, a lot more people could get hurt. I have to finish the piece, whatever happens.

High above our heads, the dragon loops and rolls, then swoops straight toward us. Screams rise behind me. Kids dive into the snow and the bushes. Eyes widening, I force myself to keep playing, to not drop my flute and run—if I do, all that magic in the air will go haywire, and I could end up burning down Mystwick altogether.

"It's going to eat us!" screams Claudia. She faceplants into the snow.

The dragon soars just above my head, its flaming body illuminating the ground and all the students cowering there. Its heat washes over my face.

Then, trailing sparks like glitter, the dragon twists upward, high into the sky. It lets out a roar of flame that scorches the roof of Harmony Hall before it dives again—straight into Orpheus Lake.

With a resounding hiss, a massive wall of steam rises up as the dragon is extinguished, and the sky goes dark again. A long minute passes as we wait to see what will happen, but the dragon doesn't reappear.

Everyone lets out relieved breaths behind me and climbs to their feet.

Dizzy from playing so long, I feel a cool rush of relief as the spell finally draws to an end and I can lower my flute. My arms are shaking, my legs are jelly, and I don't have a breath left in my body. I sway a little, exhausted.

Then everyone starts applauding.

"Amelia Jones!" Trevor Thompson swoops in and nearly hugs me, but he backs off at the last second and turns it into an awkward shoulder pat. "Please tell me you just Composed that."

Unable to find my voice, I can only nod.

He whoops, then claps his hands together. "Okay, okay! We can work with this. Phoebe, did you get it all?"

"Most of it!" My dorm captain walks up with a handheld recorder. "We can get the whole thing transcribed, arrange it for the orchestra, and start practicing tomorrow night!"

"Sweet!" Trevor looks ready to cry himself. "We got it! We got our spell for the Composium! Amelia Jones, you're *magnificent!*"

It's as if my breakdown yesterday is entirely forgotten. Everyone's buzzing about the fire spell. Dazed, I exchange high fives with dozens of students before I find myself face-to-face with Mia.

"Well, well, Wondergirl," she says wryly. "I guess you showed me, huh?"

"I'm sorry for what I said about your mom," I say quietly. "You're allowed to deal with it however you want. I shouldn't have—"

"Oh, please." She waves away my apology. "As if your opinion mattered to me."

She stalks away again, but throws me one last look, her expression a strange mix of disgust and . . . *smugness?*

I shrug it off. I've given up trying to understand that girl.

"Well, Amelia," says Mrs. Le Roux, making me jump. I hadn't even known she was watching. "I see your lessons have been paying off, though next time, I'd prefer it if you cleared your Composing sessions with us Maestros first." She eyes the roof of Harmony Hall and the rather large scorch mark there.

I wince. "Sorry."

Mrs. Le Roux turns to her sister, who's standing quietly by, watching me with a thoughtful expression. "Mathilde, you must explain to me how our young Composer has grown so much under your tutelage."

"Yes . . . It's very interesting, isn't it? Quite a show you put on, Amelia. Quite a show."

The sisters regard me a moment longer before moving away. Nervous, I watch them go, wondering if they saw right through me to my cheating heart.

I can't stop thinking about the girl whose memory I just lived. Who was she? How long ago did the fire happen? Can she remember anything about it, or is that night a void in her mind now? Did she give the memory up voluntarily?

"Amelia!"

I jump as Jai grabs my arm and shoves his face into mine.

"Jai! What are you doing?"

His gaze narrows as he studies me closer. "That dragon . . . very cool, Amelia. Very cool. *Too* cool."

"What?"

He steps back, folding his arms. "In all our brainstorming sessions, you *never* suggested a fire spell."

I lower my gaze.

"In fact, I believe I *did* suggest a fire spell, and you said something like, 'No way, I'm not nearly fun and cool enough to do a fire spell.'"

"Actually," I mumble, "I said if I tried it, I'd probably set something on fire."

He flaps his hand. "Point is, I know you, Amelia. And that magic wasn't your style."

Swallowing, I look around to be sure no one is listening in. "Jai . . ."

"You used it." He looks around too, then whispers, "You know, the *thing* from the *guy* at the *place*."

I shut my eyes for a moment, knowing there's no point in lying. I'm terrible at it anyway. "I didn't know what else to do. Mia cornered me, and it was like . . . I lost control of myself. I just wanted to show her—to show *everyone*—that I'm not a failure."

Things only get worse a few hours later when I finally make it back to my dorm room.

Waiting on my pillow is a black note card with gold lettering.

Amelia Jones,

I see you've learned your first lesson. Now it's your turn to do me a favor.
I'll expect you beneath the next full moon.

—Mr. M.

CHAPTER NINETEEN

Preventive Measures

TAP TAP!

It's dark outside, the world heavy with sleep, when I hear the noise at my window.

At first I freeze, my pulse jumping.

Tonight is the full moon. It's been two weeks since I used the memory seed to Compose the dragon spell, and all day I've been keyed up, waiting for Mr. Midnight to make his move.

Tap tap tap!

Whoever's there, they're getting impatient.

I pull back the curtain to find Jai's face pressed against the glass, his hair and shoulders dusty with snow. He smiles enormously and motions for me to open the window.

It takes some effort; it's probably been years since anyone opened it. But finally the latch gives and I lift it enough to let in a thread of freezing air.

"What are you doing?" I whisper. "It's almost eleven o'clock! You're insufferable, you know that?"

He just waves his hand, wanting the window open more. "Please? My butt's freezing off!"

Sighing, I shove the window up all the way and step back while Jai crams himself through. He falls in a heap on my floor but bounds up quickly, leaving a puddle of melting snow on the carpet.

He looks around at the bare walls and the dusty, empty shelves. "Gosh, I knew you'd got a room to yourself, but this is just *gloomy*."

"Shhh! If you get caught in here, you could be expelled."

"There are worse things. Like my best friend getting kidnapped by creepy orchestras."

We both turn to stare out the window at the full moon.

Since I Composed the dragon spell, the Trials team has spent every spare moment practicing, polishing my spell until it shines. With the power of a full orchestra, we've managed to multiply my one dragon into a whole flock; when we practice, we light up the campus and even the surrounding mountains. In one week, we'll leave for the Trials and perform the spell in front of the entire world.

But it's hard to think about that when my mind is occupied, worrying over what might happen tonight. Since I have no idea *where* the Midnight Orchestra will perform, or in what time zone, I've spent the whole day jumping at every movement, unsure when the portal might appear—if at all.

"Maybe he won't demand payment for the memory," I say. "Maybe he'll wait months or *years.* Maybe he'll forget about me altogether."

Jai lifts one eyebrow. We both hear how weak that sounds.

"Right." He lifts his chin. "Let's get going."

"Going? *Where?*"

"Somewhere unpredictable. Somewhere nobody'd think to look for you."

"Why? What are we doing?"

"Oh, Amelia." He spreads his hands wide and grins. "We're going full werewolf prevention mode."

"Uh, excuse me?"

"C'mon! Don't you watch any good movies? When there's a full moon and your best friend's a werewolf, you do what you must: lock them in a silver cage so they don't become a danger to themself or others. Then you sit up all night and keep watch over them till morning."

"I'm pretty sure I'm not a werewolf."

"It's a metaphor! Anyway, that's not the point. Neither is the fact that we don't have a silver cage, or that in the movies this plan almost *never* works. The point *is,* I'm going to stick it out with you till morning and we know you're safe."

"Jai . . ." I press a hand to my chest, touched. "You'd really do that for me?"

He rolls his eyes. "Well, not if you're going to get mushy about it!"

"I don't want you to get into trouble on my account."

"Amelia." He folds his arms, tilting his head to one side. "Remember the day we met? *How* we met?"

"I . . . had just set my clothes on fire and you put them out."

He nods magnanimously. "Do you really think I didn't know exactly what I was doing that day? You had *trouble* written all over you, but I still decided to be your best friend, didn't I?"

Somehow, that's the nicest thing anyone's ever said to me.

"All right," I say. "What's your plan?"

His grin returns. "I'm *so* glad you asked."

"Now *this,*" Jai proclaims, "is what I call *kidnap proof.*"

"I can't move my anything." I stare at him pleadingly. "This is a bit much, Jai! And since when does Mystwick have a *weight room?* Who even uses it?"

I'm currently lying on the floor of that weight room, unable to even scratch my nose. Using athletic tape, Jai has secured each of my limbs to the heaviest weights he could find. Well, the heaviest weights he could lift. Which, let's be honest, aren't exactly *heavy*. But he made up for it in quantity, and altogether, I've got to be tethered to at least two hundred pounds of barbells and steel.

"Jai, this is ridiculous. I can't sleep like this."

"You were planning on *sleeping?* Tonight of all nights?"

I shrug—or would, if my arms weren't taped to dumbbells. "I really don't think anything is going to happen."

"Classic Amelia."

"What's that supposed to mean?"

"Just that you've got a certain *modus operandi,* which is to say, you pretend things are fine until it's absolutely too late."

"I do not!"

"Case in point: if Mia hadn't gotten under your skin a couple of weeks back, you'd never have opened that vial and Composed a spell for the Trials. You'd have procrastinated and pretended things were fine all the way up until the *actual* Trials."

Yeah, probably. Not that I'll give him the satisfaction of admitting it aloud.

"If I hadn't opened that vial," I counter, "I wouldn't currently look like I'm auditioning to be a cruise ship anchor."

"Well, excuse me for trying to help."

Thunk!

"Was that a door?" I ask, wriggling in vain. "Jai! If we're caught—"

"No worries," he says. "That's just our backup."

"Our what? Jai! Who did you—"

My eyes widen as Darby steps into the weight room. She stares at me for a long moment, seemingly unable to find words. Then she stares at Jai. Then at me again.

"Okay," she says at last. "Whatever you two idiots are up to this time—and I am not at all sure I want to know what that is—it definitely does not qualify as a *life or death emergency*."

"You got my note!" Jai smiles.

"You mean this?" Darby holds up a crumpled piece of paper. She unfolds it and reads, "'Life or death emergency, come with haste and urgency, to the room where weak gets strong, two strikes before midnight's gong, or risk impending grisly end, of a young and tragic friend.'"

"Tragic friend?" I glare at Jai. "Really?"

"I had to make it sound dire," Jai explains, "or Darby wouldn't have come. The rhyming's good, though, right? Everything sounds more serious when it rhymes."

"I'm going back to bed," says Darby, and she starts to turn around.

"No! Wait!" Jai moves between her and the door and looks at me pleadingly. "Amelia, we need her. Obviously, I'm the brains here, which makes Darby our brawn."

"*You're* the brains?" Darby snorts.

"What does that make me?" I ask.

They glance at each other.

"The . . ." Jai spreads his hand. "Damsel in distress?"

"Hey!"

"Oh, go on, tell Darby what happened and about the mess you've got yourself into."

Her brow furrowing, Darby looks back at me. "Another mess? Does this have something to do with your fire dragon spell?"

My jaw falls open. "Why would you guess that?"

"Because, Amelia. It just wasn't your style."

"That's what *I* said!" Jai claps his hands together, delighted. "See? We're a trio. We *have* to do this together."

"Do *what?*" asks Darby, sounding annoyed.

"Won't Mia realize you're gone?" I ask her.

She shrugs. "She said she was going to phone her dad and it would take a while. Now. *What mess?*"

Jai raises a finger. "If you won't tell her, Amelia, I will."

"Tell me *what?*"

But neither of us gets to tell her anything, because at that moment we're interrupted by a searing cascade of notes rolling in from all directions like a thunderclap. Where it's coming from, I have no idea, but sound pours in and fills the room. Billowing purple clouds of smoky magic flow in from the hallway and windows and vents.

"The orchestra!" I gasp. "Jai—it's happening again!"

"Oh no, it's not!" roars Jai. "Darby, quick! Help me hold her down!"

"Hold her down? Why? What's that music? *What is going on?*"

"The Midnight Orchestra!" Jai dives, valiantly taking hold of my arm and pinning it to the floor. "They're trying to kidnap Amelia because she made a deal with them—"

"I didn't make a deal!" I protest. "I was *tricked!*"

"—and that's how she made up the fire dragon spell, only now they want payment—"

"And I don't have anything to give them! I have like, a dollar and forty-three cents left from my allowance!"

"So we went full werewolf method!"

"Werewolves?" Darby's voice sounds strangled. "There are *werewolves?*"

"It's a *metaphor!*" shouts Jai.

It's getting hard to hear over the avalanche of notes thundering through the room. Purple magic hisses all around us until we're practically choking on it. I gasp as a string of piano keys snakes through the air, then begins to spin, just like last time.

"There!" I yell.

The portal opens in the air above, spinning horizontally, like a monstrous eye staring straight at me.

"Shoo!" Jai says. "Get away!"

"It's not a fly!" I say. "You can't just *shoo* it off!"

"Holy mother of Beethoven, Amelia," Darby gasps. "What sort of werewolves did you tick off?"

"IT'S A METAPHOR!" yells Jai.

An icy wind rushes out of the portal, along with gusts of snow. The temperature in the weight room plunges like someone opened an enormous refrigerator door.

"Don't worry!" Jai shouts in my ear. "My plan will work! *Darby!*"

Darby grabs my other arm and holds it down, her face as white as a sheet.

All three of us lie on the floor and stare up at the spinning portal. It descends nearer and nearer, a glittering sheet of rippling purple interdimensional silk. The piano keys look like teeth, as if they were a giant mouth intent on gulping me down.

To my right and left, Darby and Jai scream.

I scream.

We scream until the music crashes so loudly it swallows our voices.

Then the portal swallows *us*.

CHAPTER TWENTY

Give the Devil His Duet

I LAND WITH A CRUNCH, and at first I think I must have broken at least three bones.

Then I realize it's snow crunching beneath me, not broken limbs, but I don't breathe any easier. Jai and Darby land on either side; they must have gotten caught in the portal too. The weights didn't seem to have followed us. The portal must have somehow sucked me up despite them holding me down.

With a groan, I push myself to my knees and look around.

This place is *cold.* We're not in the desert where I landed last time, but on a wide, flat plain of hard-packed snow. In the distance, jagged peaks rise from the frozen earth, and above us, the dark sky is mostly blocked by a huge mountain of ice.

Darby jumps up first. She stares, wide-eyed, and takes several short, panicked breaths. "Where—where—*how?*"

"The Midnight Orchestra." I sigh, heaving myself to my feet. "Everything Jai said is true. Except for the werewolf part."

"So far," Jai mutters. He brushes off some snow. "Well, that was a spectacular failure."

"Thanks for trying," I say earnestly.

He gives me a weak smile.

"Well," I say, "I guess we might as well see this through. Who knows? Maybe Mr. Midnight will ask for a tie-dye bandana or an origami swan. I've got plenty of those."

"Mr. Who?" Darby asks.

"Welcome back to the Midnight Orchestra, Miss Jones," says a smooth voice, and we turn to see Mr. Stewart bowing to us. Tonight he's wearing a puffy red coat, ski pants, and a red mask, with his bagpipes in hand. "It is an honor to have you return, and I see you've brought guests. What a lovely surprise."

Darby stares. "Tell me that's not Santa Claus."

I sigh. "That's not Santa Claus." Though between the beard and the red outfit, he does fit the bill.

"And *where* are we?"

"Well, if it's midnight Mystwick time," Jai says, "that makes this Canada, I'm guessing."

"Quite astute," says Mr. Stewart. "If you would follow me, please?"

"C'mon, Darby," I say. "I'll fill you in while we walk."

I tell her everything as we follow Mr. Stewart down a trail made of tamped-down snow, the hard crust supporting our weight. Along either side of the path, lamps made of ice hold glowing balls of blue light. Whether that's magic or just stage tricks, I don't know, but it creates an eerie mood.

"So, to recap," Darby says, "you made a deal with this Midnight guy, no questions asked, and—"

"I didn't *make* a deal. It just sort of happened. And I planned to return the memory seed."

"Except you didn't."

I wince. "I didn't."

"So now you owe this guy some kind of favor."

"Yep."

"Any idea what he'll ask for?"

"Nope."

"Or what he'll do if you don't give him what he wants?"

"Not a clue."

Darby shivers. I'm not sure I've ever seen her truly *scared,* not even when a horde of ghosts was attacking our school. "I always thought the Midnight Orchestra was a myth."

"A common misconception," says Mr. Stewart, making us all jump. I didn't think he could hear our whispers. "Tell me, honored guests. Have you ever been to a glacier?"

All three of us shake our heads.

He smiles and sweeps an arm. "Then I'm guessing you've never been *inside* one either."

Darby's eyes grow wide. "What?"

Mr. Stewart has led us to a sort of cave, but it's like no cave I've ever seen. This one is a rough opening into the snow itself—a cave made entirely of undulating ice.

"Whoa," I say, putting a gloved hand to the wall. "Is it safe?"

"Perfectly," Mr. Stewart assures us. "Proceed inside and follow the lamps."

He leaves us then, and Jai eagerly takes the lead. Despite everything, he seems to be falling for the orchestra's showmanship. Darby and I follow with more caution.

Even with dread churning in my belly, I can see how beautiful the place is. The walls shine like blue glass, smooth in some parts, jagged in others. Our shadows ripple wildly in the light of the blue lamps, making it seem as if there are monsters creeping inside the translucent walls, following us. The ground is a mixture of slick ice and smooth gray rocks. We follow twisting tunnels past glittering columns of ice. I shiver, glad I don't suffer from claustrophobia. Some of these tunnels are so narrow we have to walk single file.

Just like last time, the lady in the lace mask waits beside her stall. She smiles in greeting and opens the red curtain.

"Just go with it," I tell Jai and Darby.

I take the same fox mask as last time, while Darby picks out a painted cat face and Jai selects a half mask covered in glittering diamonds, with tall silver feathers springing out of the side and crystals dangling from the bottom.

"What?" he says as Darby and I give him looks. "It spoke to me."

He fixes the mask on his face and smiles, looking like a walking disco ball.

"Enjoy the performance," says the mask lady.

Finally, we come to a large cavern beneath a great dome of ice. Here we find the audience gathering.

Instead of a sunken amphitheater, this time the stage is a raised, circular platform with rings of plush chairs all around it, draped in furs. Fantastic ice sculptures are frozen in a circle around the stage—fairy-tale animals like unicorns, satyrs, and griffins. They shine in the light of the blue lamps that glow all around the cavern. Above the stage hangs a great chandelier of ice spheres. I shudder to think what would happen if one of these fragile pieces snapped off.

Unlike the last time, the orchestra is visible, but encased in a wall of crystal clear ice that surrounds the stage. They sit perfectly still inside, as if frozen themselves.

"Fantastic," Jai murmurs. "Wonder what spell they'll play?"

"We're not here for the show," I remind him.

He shrugs. "Well, now that we *are* here, might as well make the most of it, don't you think?"

"Who are all these people?" asks Darby. She looks around at the masked guests.

"If we knew the answer to that," I say, "I think we'd be in even deeper trouble than we already are."

As if to drive home how deep that trouble is, the lady in the lace mask appears at my elbow.

"Miss Jones. I must steal you away for a bit, I'm afraid."

"Um . . ."

"Mr. Midnight would like to see you."

"Oh, uh, do I have to?" I ask in a small voice.

"We're coming with her," says Jai, sticking out his chest.

"I think not." She gives him a tight smile. "Mr. Midnight prefers to conduct his business . . . privately."

"You're not taking Amelia!" Darby tenses, her hands raising into one of her self-defense poses.

"It's all right." I sigh. "I'll be back soon. Just lie low till then, please?"

They exchange looks, and I add again, "*Please.* I've already dragged you this far into my mess. Just let me finish this so we can go home. Lie low and stay out of trouble."

"You're one to talk," Darby points out.

But they relent, and I follow the lady.

She leads me away from the orchestra toward a small doorway in the ice wall. It leads to a steep stairwell cut into the glacier.

The steps zigzag back and forth, the ice steps overlaid with rubber mats so they aren't slippery. But there's no safety handrail, and I'm left grasping the cold walls for balance. I ask the masked lady how far we're going, but she doesn't seem to hear me. Finally, after a short climb, we emerge atop a wide, snowy plateau.

"Oh," I breathe.

Dancing across the stars are the northern lights.

Green banners with streaks of purple and pink curl silkily overhead. The edges stretch and warp, winding like a river through the dark navy sky. The aurora's colorful shine reflects on the mirrored surface of the glacial ice, making me feel like I'm standing at the bottom of the sea, looking up through glowing, rippling water. Beyond the colors, the stars gleam by the thousands.

All the spells I've ever played could not compare to that magic sky. It's as if the stars are playing a symphony all their own, their spell ancient and strange and endless.

"This way, señorita," says the masked lady, making me jump. I'd got so caught up staring at that sky I'd almost completely forgotten she was there.

She leads me over the hard crust of snow to a small table setting. A plush rug is laid on the snow, with a table and two armchairs. A collection of white candles burns on the table, along with little plates of strawberries, chocolates, and madeleines. In the center of the table is a white vase full of roses—*dead* roses, their petals shriveled and dry, some already littering the tablecloth.

"Uh . . ." I look around. "Is there supposed to be someone here?"

"Mr. Midnight will be along shortly."

"Won't he be in the orchestra?"

"For distinguished patrons like you, he will make time."

"Oh. I dunno if I'm as important as all that . . ."

Her smile drops as she gives me a deep, probing look. "Miss Jones, I assure you. When you have Mr. Midnight's attention, you become the most important person in the world."

I sit there nervously. A white fur blanket is draped on the back of the chair, and the lady removes it and offers it to me, her flawless smile back in place.

"I'll send cocoa," she says, going back down the steps into the heart of the glacier.

Shivering, I wrap the blanket around me and look up at the aurora borealis. The night seems to be getting colder. The food on the table looks delicious, but I'm scared to touch it. It might be enchanted, like the food in a fairy tale.

I wonder if the orchestra has begun playing. I can't hear anything, but that's no surprise given the thick layers of ice between me and the music. Are Jai and Darby okay? I hope they're staying quiet and out of the way like I told them to. I wish I'd never told Jai about any of this. I won't be able to breathe properly until they're both safe at Mystwick again.

What will Mr. Midnight ask for? Will I be able to afford it? He told me he never demands payment that a person can't afford, but what can he ask of someone who has practically *nothing?*

"Cold, Miss Jones?"

I suck in a breath and turn to see Mr. Midnight walking toward me, his steps silent on the snow.

"Um, a little," I say. My heart thumps like it's leading a drumline.

"Allow me," he says, lifting his violin to his chin.

He plays a solemn tune, the notes as sweet as chocolate in the air. As he plays, he walks slowly around the table, just out of the candlelight, little more than a shadow. In the sky, the northern lights seem to dance in rhythm with his lovely, sad music.

Sparks of blue light drift from the violin to burn all around me, making the air shimmer with heat, like a cloud of stars. I feel warmer at once—but no less nervous.

Mr. Stewart appears with a silver tray of hot cocoa and a small bowl of marshmallows. He sets them down with a smile, nods to Mr. Midnight, and then retreats.

I might be able to resist the food, but that steaming-hot mug is too much.

I wrap my hands around it and sip, not surprised to find it's the most delicious cocoa I've ever tasted, as warm and smooth as Mr. Midnight's music. I almost don't care if it *is* enchanted.

"Thanks," I say. "That's much better already. And, um, thanks for meeting me."

I figure the more polite I am, the better my chances of leaving this place in one piece.

He gives a small nod, still playing. Feeling more than a little awkward, I wait for the spell to finish, my hands clenched tightly on my lap.

At last the finale note shivers off the strings. He lowers the violin.

"Welcome back, Miss Jones."

"Th-thank you. I know what this is about, sir. I used the memory you gave me. I didn't mean to, not really, but . . ."

Still in shadow, he looks at me a moment, and my voice scurries down my throat to hide between my lungs.

Then, slowly, he steps into the light and sits in the chair opposite me. His black mask conceals everything but his eyes, which are the same cold blue as the glacier. The mask is sculpted into an expressionless face, with sharp, ridged cheekbones and temples, but there's no nose or mouth—just smooth, shiny porcelain down to a square chin. Unnerved by it, I look down at my cocoa instead.

"Let me guess," I say. "You want payment, don't you?"

"Great magic comes at a cost," he acknowledges softly.

"I don't have any money," I say. "Or much of anything of value."

The most expensive thing I own is my mother's flute, and there's no way I'm giving that up.

"On the contrary, Miss Jones, you have something of priceless value. You possess the ability to create *new* magic—something many musicians would kill for."

The way he says that makes me shiver all over again.

"What I desire," he says, leaning forward, his violin resting on his knee, "is a spell for a spell. An equal exchange."

"A . . . spell," I repeat. "What sort of spell?"

He smiles, then takes one of the dead roses out of the vase and sets it on the table before me.

"Miss Jones, you will Compose for me a spell to raise the dead."

CHAPTER TWENTY-ONE

Either Rhythm . . . Or Against Him

My mouth drops open, but I can't manage a single word in reply. My insides constrict like there's a boa wrapped around my middle.

"It should be no trouble," Mr. Midnight says. "After all, you have some experience in this area. Few musicians have the ability to Compose, but even fewer also possess a natural talent for . . . let's call it the *darker side of music*."

"That—that was different," I gasp. "That was *ghosts*. Not resurrection. What you're talking about . . . that's impossible. Not to mention illegal. And really, *really* dangerous."

"Few people in the world can Compose spells like the one you did," he replies. "I have searched long and hard for someone of your unique ability. Many others have tried, yes, and failed. But we are musicians, my dear Miss Jones. We do not deal in *impossibilities*."

He's right, in a way. It's not impossible to raise the dead.

I'm living proof of that.

But I also know the cost of my life. Eight years ago, when I drowned in a flash flood, my mother brought me back by Composing a resurrection spell. But the magic was so big, so hungry, it destroyed her.

I stand shakily, nearly knocking over my steaming cocoa. "So that's what this is all about? From the start, you only ever invited me here because you want me to Compose a resurrection spell for you?"

Tears of shame and anger prick my eyes. I brush them away with my hands. But if he thought I was just a dumb little girl who would Compose one of the most forbidden spells in the world for him, he's in for a nasty shock.

"It has to be you," he says. "I've tried so many other musicians, so many spells . . . But I think they went wrong for a reason. I think this magic must come from *you,* Miss Jones. It was always you."

"My mother *died* Composing a resurrection spell," I say. "And I made her a promise that I would never, ever attempt one. It's the most important promise I've ever made in my life."

His eyes darken as the aurora flares over his head.

Slowly, he sets the violin on the table, then rises to his feet. Now he towers over me, and the warmth of his earlier spell vanishes.

"You took the memory seed," he says. "You are indebted

to me now. If you do not pay what you owe, there *will* be consequences." He points to the dead rose. "I'm not asking for much. Simply bring this rose back to life, and your debt will be settled. My orchestra will take care of the rest. You needn't be involved any further. Unless . . . you want to be?"

"What?" I breathe.

"I already told you I could make you the greatest Composer in the world. The offer still stands, Miss Jones. I could teach you what no one else can. Magic without limits. Magic without *rules.*"

As he leans over the table between us, the candlelight illuminates his mask and the sharp line of his clean-shaven jaw. Something drips from his left ear and lands on the white tablecloth.

Blood.

I glance at his ear and see something glint along his lobe—a narrow metal bar. There's one on the other ear too, along with a trickle of dark blood.

He's Barred.

My breath turns to ice in my throat.

I've never seen a Barred musician outside of movies, but everyone knows what those dull metal earrings mean. Mr. Midnight must have once been convicted of a terrible magical crime, something so awful he was struck with the most severe punishment for any musician. The Bars are supposed to set off a high ringing tone in the ear of the person wearing them whenever they get too close to someone playing music—or try to play themselves. According to the stories I've heard, the tone is supposed to be so painful it can even knock a person out.

But I just watched Mr. Midnight play the violin, and clearly, the Bars on his ears are working, because his ears are *bleeding.*

He played through his spell anyway, despite the pain he must have been in.

Just to make me a little warmer.

"Miss Jones."

With a start, I realize that he asked me a question, but I have no idea what he said, because I'm still reeling.

This is a dangerous man.

Something tickles deep in my mind. I focus on it, knowing it's important, that there's more to what I've just seen than I know. My subconscious is trying to tell me something.

"I said," snaps Mr. Midnight, "are you truly willing to risk everything in order to deny me?"

For emphasis, he slaps the table, making the plates and candles rattle.

My heart's pounding against my ice-cold ribs, every instinct screaming *Run!*

Not wanting to look as terrified as I actually am, I stand up and march over the snow to the icy staircase, forcing myself not to look back. My legs shake so much I don't know how I make it down the steps in one piece. Once he's out of sight behind me, I break into a run, slipping and sliding down the tunnels in the glacier.

At some point I must take a wrong turn, because I definitely do *not* remember a spiraling staircase of pure ice. Too scared to turn back, I rush on and find myself bursting into some kind of storage room. There are a lot of empty instrument cases—the orchestra's, I guess—along with crates and bins and sound equipment.

And . . . the lady in the lace mask, sitting next to a plate piled with crawling beetles.

What on earth?

She sees me at once, but merely smiles her bland, empty smile before reaching onto the plate, lifting an entire handful of wriggling beetles—and then stuffing them into her mouth.

I scream, stumbling backwards, but slipping on the ice.

Instead of wiping out completely, I find myself gripped by strong hands on my arms, which push me upright again.

"You shouldn't run through ice tunnels alone," says Mr. Midnight, still holding my arms. "It's dangerous."

"Let go of me!" I say, pulling free and stumbling into

the room. The lady is still smiling, but this time it's around a mouthful of mashed beetles.

"As I told you," says Mr. Midnight, "many others have attempted resurrection spells for me and failed. You can see, now, that the results were disappointing. I tried to save Rosario, for example, but she didn't come back quite . . . *right.*"

The lady, Rosario, chews a few times, then smiles again. I look away from the ghastly sight.

"Sh—she was dead?" I whisper.

"Was, and essentially still is," explains Mr. Midnight. "She can't remember anything of her past, can barely remember anything since she was resurrected, and oh, yes, she came with a regrettable appetite for *insects.* We can't really explain that one, but we spend a fortune each month on fresh entomological buffets."

The room spins around me. I put out a hand to brace myself against the wall, but Mr. Midnight reaches out to steady me—or is it to capture me? I don't want to find out.

Ducking under his arm, I bolt out the door and run back the way I came. This beautiful glacier has become a haunted house of mirrors, with my own distorted, terrified face shining back at me from every gleaming ice wall.

I soon hear the distant sound of the Midnight Orchestra warping through the ice, seeming to come from all directions.

Their music is frantic and fast, notes chasing me like a flock of screaming bats.

Spotting a fork in the tunnels, I take one at random and end up regretting it instantly, as the floor suddenly drops away and I find myself sliding along a curving icy channel, screaming the whole way. My head slams against the wall when the chute turns sharply, leaving me dazed, and then all at once I spill out into open air.

With a wild cry, I land hard on the floor of the main cavern, where the Midnight Orchestra is in the midst of a rolling symphony. But no one seems to notice my sudden and noisy entrance. Everyone is up and dancing, as if caught in a frenzy spell.

The ice sculptures around the stage are now moving as fluidly as living creatures, pulling the audience members into their dance. It's like some dreamy fairyland scene, with cords of golden magic twisting through the air. The symphony is lively and quick, a waltz with an infectious tempo. But just like last time, the orchestra members are playing with stony expressions, sitting as still as statues.

Are they resurrections too?

I spot Jai and Darby standing awkwardly in the crowd while an ice satyr prances around them, trying to cajole them into dancing.

Then the hair on the back of my neck prickles. I turn and see Mr. Midnight coming down the stairs.

Bursting into a run, I dart through the crowd, nearly getting trampled by an ice unicorn.

"Jai, Darby!" I say. "We have to go!"

"There you are!" Jai says. "What happened?"

I look over my shoulder; Mr. Midnight stands by the wall, watching me motionlessly. The mask is worse than any face. It leaves far too much to my imagination.

"We have to *go,*" I say, grabbing Darby's arm. "Now."

She glances at Mr. Midnight, then at me. "What's going on?"

"And what did you *do?*" Jai asks.

"I'll tell you back at Mystwick!"

We hurry down the ice tunnels, chased by our own shadows. Our steps crunch on the pebbled ground, and the sound of the orchestra fades behind us at last.

"Where are we going?" Jai shouts. "And how do we get back to school?"

"I have no idea! Just don't stop!"

We burst out of the glacier and onto the open snow, where it's harder to run. But I slog on anyway, Darby and Jai steps behind me. The snow is above my ankles, and the night is getting colder by the minute. With the full moon glowing overhead, reflecting on the white snow, it's almost as bright as daylight.

"Now what?" pants Jai. "We're stuck here!"

Suddenly I hear the sharp wheeze of bagpipes, and I look up and see Mr. Stewart standing ahead of us, playing open a portal for some guests who are leaving early.

My throat tightens.

Is *he* undead too? Is everyone here the subject of one of Mr. Midnight's resurrection spells?

There's no time to worry about that. This might be the only shot we get at escaping.

"We have to reach that portal!" I say.

Darby shakes her head. "We don't know where it leads!"

"It's a something-directional interdimensional . . . uh . . . It takes you where you want to go. So just run through it and think about the Mystwick weight room!"

"Are you sure?"

"No. But trust me—anywhere is better than here!"

We run toward the portal as it yawns wider, crackling with purple magic that branches outward like threads of lightning. The other guests walk toward it, unaware of the three of us pelting at full speed toward their exit. Mr. Stewart's playing is so loud, it covers the sound of our crunching footsteps.

"Go go *go!*"

We race past Mr. Stewart and dive for the portal. The guests scatter like bowling pins, gasping in surprise.

Abruptly, Mr. Stewart breaks off playing long enough to growl, "Miss Jones!"

"Jump through and think of Mystwick!" I shout. *"Now!"*

As we leap into the shimmering purple doorway, Mr. Stewart roars in a strange, raspy voice, "You cannot run far, Miss Jones! Mr. Midnight *always* gets his due!"

CHAPTER TWENTY-TWO

Fear and Tremolo

We land in a flailing pile of arms and legs on the weight room floor, breathless and soaked through from melting snow. It takes a minute to sort out whose limbs are whose, and then we sit and stare at each other, shocked and dizzied from the tumble through the portal.

"What," Jai gasps, *"was that?"*

"Yes." Darby crosses her arms. "Time for some explanation."

"And what was with the old guy with the bagpipes?" adds Jai. "*Mr. Midnight always gets his due.* He sounded like a creepy zombie when he said it."

Maybe because Mr. Stewart is exactly that. But I'm still processing it all, hoping I overreacted, desperate to poke holes in my own theory.

But I know what I saw, and there's no way around it.

"Amelia?" Jai waves his hand in front of my wide-eyed stare. "Hello? We're waiting. What happened back there? Did the guy ask for payment?"

"Yeah, so . . ." I inhale shakily. "He wanted me to Compose a resurrection spell."

Shocked silence. Jai's eyes nearly swallow his face.

"I guess he somehow heard about my ghost spell," I say. "He thinks I have . . . well . . ."

"A talent for Composing black spells," murmurs Darby.

"I told him no, obviously. I'm not doing that stuff again, and this is way worse than even the ghost-summoning spell."

"Not to mention more dangerous," says Darby. "Didn't your mom—"

I nod. She and Jai know the real reason my mom died, and how the resurrection spell she Composed to save me ended up claiming her life instead.

"You can't Compose that spell for him," Jai says firmly.

"I agree. Which is why I said no way. He got mad and said there would be *consequences*. That I owe him the spell in exchange for using the memory seed."

"What kind of consequences?" asks Darby.

I shrug.

Jai lifts a finger. "Why does this guy even want a resurrection spell?"

"I don't know that either. Also . . . he played his violin in front of me, and then later, I noticed something on his ears." I draw a deep breath, then whisper, "Mr. Midnight is *Barred*."

"Barred," Jai repeats, as if he didn't hear me right. "As in,

he's a criminal who was banned from all Musicraft? Are you sure? But you said he played the violin."

I nod. "I'm sure. His ears were, um, bleeding."

"Gross," says Darby.

"Yeah, and that's not all." I tell them what happened next: about the masked lady and the beetles, and Mr. Midnight claiming she was a failed result of a bad resurrection spell. How I suspect that the entire Midnight Orchestra and Mr. Stewart and all the vendors in the market might be messed-up resurrections too.

In my own head, it had sounded insane.

But as I lay out my suspicions before my friends, I can hear the pieces clicking together, forming a complete picture. A terrible, gut-wrenching picture—but a true one.

"So what you are saying," Darby replies when I'm done, "is that Mr. Midnight is a Barred musician who leads an entire horde of"—her voice wobbles—"of *zombies*."

"First ghosts," says Jai. "Now zombies. Great. Of course. I mean, why not? Why stop there? Why not have a whole party—vampires, werewolves, vampire-werewolves—" He stops, his face transforming into a mask of pure horror. "Wait a minute. Mr. Midnight is a Barred musician who leads a horde of zombies."

"That's what I just said," Darby points out.

"No, no no. You don't get it." Jai shakes his head, the blood draining from his face. "Mr. Midnight is a *Barred* musician who leads a horde of *zombies*."

"Yes," says Darby. "We get it. The dude's a real creep job."

"You still aren't hearing me." Jai begins pacing, rubbing his hands over his face. "Think about it. Haven't we heard stories about a Barred man who plays music anyway, whose trademark is his bloody ears? A man who's supposed to exist only in rumors and ghost stories? Who leads an army of the dead? A man so terrible, kids speak his name in a whisper?"

Again, I feel that tickle in the back of my mind. It's the same feeling I got when I first saw the Bars in Mr. Midnight's ears, as if my subconscious was trying to tell me something.

"Jai, no," says Darby, looking a bit green. "That's impossible. That's just a story."

"So were ghosts, until they're weren't," he points out. "So was the Midnight Orchestra, until it wasn't. C'mon, you know I'm right on this. Our masked friend back there . . . he's got another name. A name everyone already knows."

I gasp.

There's a kid, George, in my Aeros class, who has a real talent for telling scary stories. The drama club has already recruited him for their spring performance of *Macbeth*.

But there's one story he loves telling more than any other, about a Barred man and his zombie followers.

Jai must see me come to the same conclusion, because he

points at me and nods. "Exactly. You see it now? Your Mr. Midnight has another name." He drops to a theatrical whisper, raising his hands for emphasis. *"The Necromuse."*

"The Necromuse isn't real," says Darby, but she says it like she's trying to convince herself.

"Oh, he's real," says Jai. "And he's after Amelia."

We all sit with that for a minute. My stomach sinks lower and lower.

"Well, I'm not Composing anything for him."

"Of course you're not," says Jai. "We won't let you."

I give him a grateful look. But I feel queasy. I should have asked for some specifics regarding the "consequences" the Necromuse promised, but all I could think about at the time was getting as far away from him as possible. It's like my subconscious knew who he really was before I did.

"I think it's pretty fantastic, you having a nemesis." Jai pulls up his jacket over his face like a vampire cloak, wiggling his eyebrows at me. *"You vill never defeat me, puny girl!"*

"What kind of accent is *that?* He's not Dracula." I hesitate, then add, "Maybe we should tell the—"

"We are *not* telling the Maestros," says Darby. "Breaking the school rules is one thing. But if people find out you've been making deals with the Necromuse? This is bigger than detention, or even getting expelled. Like . . . that's the kind of thing people get *Barred* for, Amelia."

I stare at her, my heart in my throat.

"Let's just wait it out," she suggests. "He might have been bluffing."

"Sure. Fine." I am almost certain he was not bluffing. They weren't there. They didn't hear the winter in his voice or feel the chill in the air like an oncoming blizzard.

CHAPTER TWENTY-THREE

Etude, Brute?

BE COOL, AMELIA, BE COOL.

I chant the words under my breath as I leave breakfast the next morning and head to the Shell. The Sparring team is practicing today for the Trials, and I told Jai I'd cheer him on.

That was *before* I realized I'd made a deal with the actual Necromuse, who is now determined to collect payment.

All night, I dreamed about zombies chasing me around Mystwick, the Necromuse's masked face jumping out of the shadows. When I looked in the mirror this morning, my eyes were bloodshot.

I stumble into the Shell with a huge yawn and sit near the back, slumping down in the seat.

Somehow Jai managed to squirrel his way onto Kjersten's squad, despite being a head shorter than any of the other students. He waves at me from the stage, where he's lined up for the first round of matches.

How does he manage to look so chipper? I'm sweating up a monsoon beneath my coat, worried that someone will look at me and see the whole truth written across my face.

Amelia Jones made a deal with the Necromuse!

It doesn't help that Mrs. Le Roux herself is here to oversee Sparring practice. Apparently she was once a world-class champion. Dressed in a blue pantsuit and matching turban, she sits on the stage, her cello primly propped beside her.

Because there's an uneven number on the team, Kjersten recruited Darby to help out in practices. She stands opposite Jai, tapping her oboe. As if she can feel me watching, she glances into the audience and gives me a little smile.

I smile back.

Maybe Jai shouldn't have dragged Darby into my problems, especially without asking me first, but I have to admit it's nice having her as part of the team again. She's braver and smarter than I am. Just knowing she's on my side makes me feel like things might turn out okay after all. Of course, there's the problem of Mia, but . . .

As if summoned by my thoughts, a voice whispers from the row behind me, "I know where you went last night, Wondergirl."

My spine goes stiff. It takes everything in me not to bolt out of my seat. But that would only get everyone else's attention, including Mrs. Le Roux's.

"Mia," I murmur. "What are you talking about? I didn't go—"

"Cut the innocent act. Darby told me *everything*."

My neck flushes with heat as, on the stage, Miss Noorani calls Jai and Darby to Spar.

My voice is a faint flutter. "I don't know what you mean."

"The portal, Wondergirl. The Midnight Orchestra. The deal you made."

I grip the seat in front of me. Completely unaware of Mia and me, Darby and Jai begin their Sparring match, with Mrs. Le Roux nearby as referee. Magic springs from their instruments and forms two tigers of glowing light that stalk around each other, fangs bared.

"She told you all that?" I finally manage to say.

Mia leans forward, her arms folded over the back of my chair and her chin practically resting on my shoulder. "Oh, yes. She told me what a naive baby you are, and how you ran from this Mr. Midnight, and how you're sure to end up Barred, or worse, before this is over." She leans even closer. I can feel the warmth of her breath in my ear. "We sat up all night, laughing about it."

I can't move. My heart pounds against my ribs. I watch Darby, her focus absorbed in her spell, her fingers dancing over her oboe's keys. Her shimmering blue tiger leaps and pins Jai's red one on the stage floor.

"Laughing?" I whisper.

Is it true?

Have I been this wrong about Darby all along?

Deep inside me, the angry, wounded melody begins to sing once more. The notes skitter through me like scorpions.

"Do you really think Darby's your friend?" Mia asks. "You're stupider than I thought."

My knuckles turn white from gripping the seat in front of me.

Onstage, Jai's tiger twists away and runs for Darby, but she responds with a delicate shift in tempo, and her tiger recovers to block the attack. The kids watching cheer, and I can see Jai's frustration on his face.

"Oh, Wondergirl," Mia sighs. "I hate to be the one to tell you this, but Darby was never your friend. You think I didn't know about the note Jai sent her? You think I didn't *send* her to check up on you so we could laugh about it later? You're just a joke to her, like you're a joke to this school."

I would press my hands over my ears if it would do any good blocking out the roaring music pounding in my head.

Don't let it out, I tell myself. *Don't let it out.*

Finally, I twist around to look at her. "I told you I was sorry for taking your spot at Mystwick, not that it stopped you from getting in anyway. I gave up my bed, my room, I've given you space. What more do you want from me? Why do you hate me so much?"

"I want you to stay *away,*" she says. "If I see you talking to Darby again, I'll tell everyone that you Composed your fire dragon spell with a stolen memory. Yes, Darby told me about that too. Then they'll all know you're worse than a failure. You're a cheater. Mystwick will be disqualified from the Trials, and it will be all your fault. This is the last time I'll say it: *stay away from her.*"

And with that, she stands and walks up the aisle toward the doors.

I slump in my seat, feeling a hole in my chest, tears stinging my eyes, angry notes sparking in my brain.

Gasps rise all around me as Darby's tiger finally triumphs, breaking past Jai's and paralyzing his fingers long enough to break off his music. In triumph, Darby concludes the spell for both of them with a haunting note from her oboe.

Not wanting Jai to see me like this, I rush out of the Shell—and straight into Miss Motte.

"Heavens, Amelia!" She steadies me. "Where are you . . ."

Her voice trails away as she takes in my crumpled face. She has Janet on a leash, and the dog sits and cocks her furry head at me, as if copying Miss Motte's expression.

"Do you want to talk about it?" she asks gently.

"No."

I brace myself, ready for her to suggest that I sculpt my feelings with clay or write a poem or something.

Instead, she smiles, hands me Janet's leash, and says, "Very well, then perhaps you can exercise this fluffy fool for me. She just won't settle down, and I've got a drum circle club to lead! Sometimes, a good walk settles the most restless of spirits, don't you think?"

"Oh. Um, sure. Wait—there's a drum circle club?"

"There is now!" She laughs.

I take the leash and watch Miss Motte float off, humming to herself. Then I look down at Janet.

"Guess it's you and me, huh?"

At least this is an excuse to get away from everyone for a while.

I've never really taken care of a dog before. Gran is allergic to most breeds. But Janet seems content to take the lead, and we go on a stroll along the edge of the forest. She dives into every snow pile she sees, snuffs a bit, then carries on, her tail raised like a flag. The Echo trees are restless today, sighing and singing their gentle music. I watch the shadows anxiously, in case any portals appear—or, worse, the Necromuse or one of his minions. But before long, my heart stops thumping so much and the heat cools in my cheeks. I sit to rest on a log near the amphitheater, where we find Miss Motte and a few Percusso kids in their drum circle.

Their magic rises in bright bursts of green that pop into smoky clouds overhead, magic smelling of evergreen forests. The bushes around them shiver in response to their music, leaves dancing in time.

I wave down another Percusso on his way to join them, a bongo under his arm. "What spell are they playing?"

"Spell?" He lifts his eyebrows. "No spells in drum circle club. Just *vibes*."

"Huh?"

"We don't play to do fancy magic. Just to feel the beat, you know?" He shrugs. "We're Percussos."

As if that explains everything.

He joins the circle and is soon drumming away with the rest of them. I tap my foot to their tempo, scratching Janet's ears.

"How could Darby do this to me?" I ask the dog.

She stares at me with her big black eyes, wagging her tail.

"I don't get it, Janet. I thought we were becoming friends. I thought I could trust her. And she goes and tells all my secrets to the one girl who hates me most? *Why?*"

Was Darby really just playing me the whole time? If so, I am definitely the clueless, naive dummy Mia said I am. It's far too easy to picture them sitting in their room, laughing at stupid Amelia.

It just doesn't make *sense.*

I squeeze my eyes shut, listening to the endlessly repeating notes circling in my brain, my terrible, furious refrain.

But when I hear a sudden *crack,* I look up into the Echo Wood.

That didn't sound like a drum.

Then comes another crack, along with snaps and crunches and groans, like something's out there chewing up the trees.

What in the world?

The drum circle plays on, oblivious, their ears filled with the beat of their bongos and snares as the cracking sounds get louder. I stand up, and Janet begins barking, her ears pricked forward.

Miss Motte looks up then, frowning.

"Janet?" she calls. "What—"

Before she can finish, something white and misty comes *rushing* out of the forest, creeping along the ground at a rapid pace. At first it looks like a flood of water, but the drummers begin shouting as it sweeps over their feet. One girl stands up, only to slip and crash to the ground, her drum rolling away.

It's *ice.*

Another kid yelps as the spreading ice washes over his shoes, freezing him in place. It flows up and over the amphitheater steps, the bushes, the lampposts, completely freezing everything in its path with a layer of ice several inches thick.

Behind me, screams start to rise from Mystwick.

I spin around and see ice overtaking the campus from all sides, flowing out of the Echo Wood and pouring over the grounds, consuming everything it touches like a living, ravenous monster. The terrible sounds it makes—groans and pops and splintering cracks—fill the air.

"Amelia!" Miss Motte shouts. She's stuck to her seat, ice creeping up her skirt. "Get the headmaestro! RUN!"

CHAPTER TWENTY-FOUR

A Show of Forza

SCOOPING JANET INTO MY arms, I run at full pelt for Harmony Hall, barely keeping ahead of the wave of ice. Behind me, the entire drum circle club is frozen up to their waists.

"Get help!" they yell. "HURRY!"

Trees and bushes are swallowed by the icy wave, crackling as they freeze into spidery shapes, bent from the weight. Curlicues of frost wind up the walls of the cafeteria. The ice is flowing in from all directions, and I see students running ahead of me, only to be overtaken. They freeze in mid-step, trapped in pillars of ice. Collin Brunnings trips, lands on his knees, and is quickly frozen up to his neck, one hand outstretched, his scream pitched to an impressive *E#*.

"Mrs. Le Roux!" I shout. "Mr. Pinwhistle!"

A wave of ice rushes toward me from my left. With a yelp, I alter my course, now hemmed in on two sides. Janet bounces against my chest, whimpering.

I run past the Shell just as the Sparring team is letting out. Kjersten leads the group, while Jai and Darby bring up the rear.

"Run!" I yell.

In response, I get a lot of stares and not nearly enough terrified sprinting.

"I SAID RUN!" I point behind me.

Kjersten sees it first. She gasps and pushes the others back inside.

"No!" I wave wildly at them. "You have to *run!*"

Only Jai and Darby listen, sprinting after me. I glance back to see the ice rush into the Shell and over the lobby floor. The windows go white with frost, and ice crawls up the outer walls of the building, swallowing it whole. Glittering icicles spring from the eaves, their dangerous points flashing in the sunlight. Screams rise from inside the concert hall, where I have a feeling that the Spar team has been trapped.

"What happened?" Jai gasps.

"I don't know. Just get to Mrs. Le Roux's office!"

Together, we run uphill toward Harmony Hall. Jai shrieks as the ice freezes the heel of his shoe. He yanks it loose before it can swallow the rest of his foot.

"We can't outrun it!" Darby says.

"Then what do we do?"

There's no outclimbing it; we already saw it engulf entire

trees. The concert hall is locked in ice all the way to its high, armadillo-shell roof, so it resembles a small iceberg. I spot Trevor Thompson halfway up a lamppost, his hands and legs frozen solid against the metal.

Darby, who's taken the lead, suddenly slows.

"What are you doing?" I ask.

She turns around, looks at the ice through narrow eyes, then says, "Trying something."

I shout as she runs past me, takes a wild leap—and lands atop the ice, skating on her shoes. Her arms pinwheel until she finds her balance.

"Come on!" she shouts, grinning at us. "It's safe on top! Just don't let the edges touch you."

"Why do these things always happen to us?" groans Jai. "Here goes!"

He turns and runs at the ice, jumping high over the edge and landing in a heap. But he seems safe, spinning away in a tangle of arms and legs.

"Amelia!" Darby shouts. "Stop running!"

I tuck Janet under my arm like a football. Poor thing, she looks seasick. But Miss Motte trusted her to me, and I'm not going to let her become a furry Popsicle.

I run straight toward the ice's rippling edge, leap, and land on both feet. Shrieking, I hold Janet tight as I slip and slide toward Darby. We crash into each other and land hard, Darby on top of me, Janet yipping wildly.

We skid into the plinth of Beethoven's statue; the old Composer has disappeared beneath several inches of ice, his bright pink hat barely visible.

"Careful!" Darby says, hobbling to her feet. "Have you ever ice-skated?"

"No, and I don't need your help!" I say, pushing her hand away. I make it to my feet, only to slip and fall hard on my butt. Janet yelps, and I barely keep my arms around her.

"What's your deal?" Darby asks. "Let me help you!"

"I know what you did, Darby!"

"What? What did I do?"

I shake my head; this isn't the time to get into it.

"This is awesome!" yells Jai, who goes gliding past on his shoes. He turns and skates backward, then pirouettes.

"Jai!" I point to Harmony Hall. "Skate up there and get the headmaestro!"

"Too late," he says.

The ice has reached the building and is quickly climbing the walls, sealing the windows and doors. Victoria is trapped on the front ramp, her wheelchair encrusted with ice, and behind her, Mr. Pinwhistle is frozen in mid-step, his face purple with anger.

"WHO DID THIS?" he roars as ice climbs up to his waist.

He struggles to open his trumpet case, but the ice swallows it before he can, freezing his hand to the latch.

Jamal and Amari, who must have also figured out how to avoid getting iced over, skate up to Jai, their eyes wide.

"What's happening?" Amari asks, her voice shrill with alarm as she wobbles along. "And how do we stop it?"

"No idea," Jai answers. "But whatever it is, I think it already *won.*"

I look around and see every inch of Mystwick encased in ice. Every surface gleams and shines, and it would look beautiful if it weren't totally terrifying. It doesn't even look like our school. It looks like some icy, alien planet. Only the mountains in the far distance are untouched. And all over campus, kids, staff, and Maestros are frozen in place, squirming and shouting.

What now?

"Does anyone have an instrument they can use?" Mr. Pinwhistle yells.

I left my flute back by the drum circle. Jai dropped his violin case; now it's frozen over on the ground. Jamal and Amari don't have their instruments either.

"I do!" Darby shouts.

Cheers rise all around.

"Darby, very good!" Mr. Pinwhistle says. "Very carefully take it out and assemble it."

She takes out her oboe, but just when she finishes assembling it, she slips and falls, and the oboe goes spinning away across the ice. Panicking, Darby goes sliding after it, but ends up crashing into a frozen bush while her oboe rolls off toward the Shell with a clatter.

I groan into Janet's fur.

Mr. Pinwhistle rubs his free hand over his face.

"Everyone just chill!" Jai says. Then he giggles. "Chill. Get it?"

"Shut up, Jai!" snaps Jingfei, who's frozen against the door into the girls' dorm.

"Amari and I can try to reach the headmaestro," Jamal says, and the twins skate off toward Harmony Hall. But Harmony Hall is uphill, and no amount of skill will propel them up the frozen slope. They end up in a pile back where they started, yelling at each other.

"There!" Darby shouts, pointing toward the girls' dorm. "Rosa!"

Rosa Guerrera stands in an open window, ice up to her waist, holding her electric guitar. She looks rattled, but when she sees us all looking, she scowls.

"Whoever did this will face my wrath when this is over!" she warns.

"Just play that thing and get us out of here!" Jingfei calls back.

"If I could do that, do you think I'd be standing here talking to *you?*" She nods at her other hand, which is frozen to the windowsill. "I'm a bit shorthanded at the moment!"

"I can do it," Jai says softly.

I'm the only one who hears him. "What?"

He lifts his head, his eyes wide.

"I said I can do it!" he shouts at Rosa. "Throw me the guitar!"

"There is absolutely no way—"

"Let him play it!" Amari shouts.

More voices join in.

"Let him play!"

"Just get us out of this!"

"Give him the instrument, Miss Guerrera!" bellows Mr. Pinwhistle.

Growling under her breath, Rosa lowers the guitar by the cord. Jai takes it reverently.

"Hey! Gentle!" Rosa slams an amp onto the windowsill. "Put a scratch on her, and I'll destroy you and every person you love, Kapoor! Do you even know how to play it?"

"Yeah . . . Er, what should I play?" he asks, still gazing at the guitar in wonder.

Rosa rolls her eyes.

"Some kind of heat spell!" Darby shouts. "That should do the trick, if Rosa cranks that thing up."

Jai nods, thoughtful, probably transposing notes in his head. "I can do that."

Rosa twists the knob on her amp to maximum, and all of us within earshot hold our breath.

Jai holds the guitar for a long moment. I've never seen him concentrate so hard. His fingers move slowly over the frets, his lips moving slightly as he talks to himself.

Then, tentatively, he strums the first four notes, which echo across the campus.

Jai pauses, takes a deep breath, then plays on.

His long brown fingers curl over the neck of the guitar, picking out the chords, unsure at first. But then the tempo gets faster and faster as he finds the melody. He begins swaying with the instrument, his fingers blurring over the strings.

"Oh, dang!" says Amari, still spread-eagled on the ice. "Jai can shred!"

And shred Jai does.

He converts the music into electric fire. Notes sizzle from the strings, blasted out by Rosa's amp all across Mystwick. Blue elemental magic smokes from the guitar, swirling and popping, and gradually, the ice around Jai begins to melt. Heat spreads in a shimmering blanket.

From the eaves and walls, the branches and statues, water begins to drip, then trickle, then pour. The blast of sound from the guitar washes over me like a summer day.

Rosa is the first to be freed. She vanishes into her room, then appears with another amp. Plugging it in, she doubles the strength of Jai's sound.

He plays on, curled over the guitar, as if no one else were around. And all across Mystwick, ice melts away. Trees straighten, students scramble free, and doors open. Within minutes, the ice has receded to the woods.

Jai finishes the spell in a daze, then looks up to see students gathered all around, watching him. He lifts the guitar, and everyone cheers.

"Mr. Kapoor!" Mrs. Le Roux claps, and everyone falls silent. "Brilliantly done."

"Yeah, it was, wasn't it?" He grins.

"I *will* check for scratches!" Rosa shouts, stepping out of the door. She snatches her guitar, then gives Jai a considering look. "Not too terrible, Kapoor. Not too good, either, but not too terrible. Shame you skipped out on that rock class."

She stalks off, and Jai bows before his adoring new fans. I run to him and give him a high five.

"Did you see me, Amelia Jones! Was I not fantastic? Was I not *on fire?*"

"You were amazing, Jai!"

"I know! I was!" He whoops. "Did you hear Rosa? *Not too terrible!*"

Miss Motte appears, the drum circle team running breathlessly behind her, and scoops Janet from my arms. "Good girl, Janet! Oh, who's my best, most wonderful girl? Did Amelia keep you oh so safe? Did she, my snooky-poo?"

"Is anyone going to ask *what just happened?*" asks Phoebe. "Where did that ice come from?"

I swallow hard, feeling a murmur of unease in my gut.

"A very good question," Mrs. Le Roux says, walking up. Students part for her, and she looks around at us all with thinly veiled suspicion. "A very good question indeed."

She arches an eyebrow at Phoebe.

Phoebe waves her hands. "Wasn't me! The ice sculpting club finished practice two hours ago!"

"It must have been Souza!" says Trevor Thompson.

Mrs. Le Roux arches her eyebrows. "I beg your pardon?"

"Isn't it obvious? Souza's messing with us again! They did this!"

The headmaestro presses her lips together. "Hmm."

I don't think she's convinced, but everyone else is.

"All right, team!" shouts Collin Brunnings. "We gotta get revenge on these jerk faces! Who's with me? Who's got ideas?"

"You're not even on the Trials team, Collin," Victoria points out.

"Nobody is getting revenge," says Mrs. Le Roux sternly. "Nobody is doing *anything* except moving along to their next class. Leave this to your Maestros. There is likely a very natural explanation . . ."

But she doesn't seem to know what that explanation might be. She stares pensively at the lake and says no more.

It isn't until later, when I go to my room to change my soaking clothes, that I find it.

Resting on my pillow is a dead, shriveled rose atop a slim black card.

My body goes cold. I run into the hallway and look up and down, but I'm the only person in sight.

There isn't a doubt in my mind what the rose means or who left it there. Was he *here,* in my room? Is he hiding on the campus? Or did he somehow put the rose there by magic?

I pick up the card and find silver letters inked on it in beautiful, flowing handwriting.

> *You owe me a spell, Amelia Jones. The next consequence won't be so harmless.*

Shuddering, I grab the rose and rip it apart, then do the same with the card, throwing the pieces in my trash can.

The icy spell was the work of the Necromuse, just as I'd feared.

It was his first consequence.

He's toying with me, letting me know he can reach me even at Mystwick, and that everyone around me is also at risk. He wants me to see that he can do anything he wants, despite the protective forest around the school.

And whatever's coming next, it will be worse.

CHAPTER TWENTY-FIVE

The Early Bird Gets the Earworm

I WAKE UP THE NEXT morning with a pit of dread still in my belly. Rolling out of bed, I'm met by my own reflection in the mirror. Messy red hair, tired eyes, rumpled shirt and jeans because I didn't change clothes last night, just tumbled into bed, exhausted. Jai might have melted all the ice on campus, but it had left everything soaked through, including our beds and clothes and the carpet. Luckily, everyone's instruments were protected by moisture-repellant wards. Every musician I know, myself included, is paranoid about damage, so we all routinely refresh the protective wards every time we clean our instruments. A few simple spells is all it takes to guard them from most types of damage for a few weeks. But there was still a ton of work to do to clean up. I'd spent hours playing drying spells alongside the other seventh-grade girls, slowly leeching the water from the first floor of the dorm.

The going theory among the students is that Souza somehow orchestrated the ice spell, literally. Trevor led a whole group on a hike through the Echo Wood to try to find evidence, but nothing turned up.

Of course, I know the answer, and so does Jai. I told him everything, including how Mia now knows about our trip to the Midnight Orchestra, the Necromuse . . . all of it.

"I can't believe Darby turned on us like that," he said at dinner last night when I told him everything. "This is my fault. I trusted her."

"We both did."

"If the Necromuse really did freeze over Mystwick, what do you think he'll do next?"

I have no idea, and it's all I can think about. How long will he wait before he strikes again? Even walking from one class to the next, I paused at every corner, scared of what might be hiding around it.

This morning is no different. It's after seven, but the hallway is quiet. Usually girls are lining up for showers by now, yelling up and down the dorm.

Weird. Where is everyone?

My stomach sinking, I go from door to door, peeking in. All the rooms are empty, beds messy and unmade. Phoebe will have a fit when she sees.

The last room I come to is Darby and Mia's. I pause a minute in the doorway and stare at the pictures they've hung on strings across the walls—lots of shots of the two of them, going all the way back to preschool.

What must it be like to have a friend so close you're like sisters through all those years? Someone you can trust to always have your back, always keep your secrets? Someone you'd betray everyone else for?

Feeling guilty for snooping, I start to back away—but then I realize that Darby's bed is unmade. Well, they both are, but it's Darby's that strikes me as weird. She's the neatest person I know. Her bed is perfectly remade almost even before she rolls out of it in the morning.

Darby would never leave her room like this unless something was very wrong.

I run back down the hallway and burst through the outside door. The morning air is frigid, and fog wraps around the buildings and trees. It looks like a hazy dreamworld.

And in that fog, *shadows* move around.

Teeth clenched, I creep closer. My skin crawls with the sense of wrongness permeating the air.

The first shadow turns out to be Phoebe.

"Hey!" I shout, breaking into a run. "Phoebe, what's going on? Why . . ."

My voice dies when I see the shovel in Phoebe's hand. There's a groundskeeping shed next to the dorm, and the door hangs open, tools scattered around like someone's been digging through them in a frenzy.

Phoebe's digging a hole in the hard, frozen dirt, her lips blue from the cold but her face and shirt damp with sweat. She's still in her pajamas. And judging by the size of the hole, she's been at this for hours.

Horror drags at my stomach when I see the shape of the hole she's dug: a rectangle, about eight feet long and two feet wide.

A grave.

"Phoebe? Phoebe, what are you doing?"

She doesn't answer or even look at me. I don't think she can hear me. Her eyes are glazed, and she doesn't stop digging.

I run past her to the next shadow—Claudia. Behind her are Jingfei and Darby. They're all digging. Claudia and Jingfei have small gardening trowels, and their holes are not nearly as deep as Phoebe's, but they're still undeniably grave-shaped. Darby has a pickax and is driving it so hard into the dirt her hands are blistered. I try to wrestle the pickax away, but without saying a word or even looking at me, she shoves me so hard I fall onto the wet soil. Her next swing of the ax comes straight for my head.

I scream and roll aside just before the sharp blade buries into the soil.

"Stop! Darby! Can you hear me?"

Blank-faced, she hacks at the soil again.

I run on, past more girls digging with anything they could get their hands on. A few are even using metal spoons, their holes little more than an inch deep, but they scrape away at the dirt determinedly, moving it teaspoon by teaspoon. From her muddy wheelchair, Victoria swings a sharp hoe, slamming it into the ground and sending sprays of dirt flying. Like everyone else, her face is completely blank.

What is going on?

It's like walking through a nightmare. I wander all over the school grounds, and everywhere I go, I find more students digging holes. The boys are out here too, having raided another one of the groundskeeping sheds or using kitchen utensils.

Nauseated and shaking, I make my way uphill to Clarion House, where the Maestros, teachers, and staff live. And sure enough, all the adults are outside too, digging away in their pajamas and housecoats and slippers. I run to Miss Noorani, Mr. Pinwhistle, even Miss Motte—but none stir from their trances, not even when I shake them. They just push me away and keep digging.

Whatever spell has trapped the entire student body and faculty, it's a powerful one. But the weird thing is, I don't hear any music. I haven't heard a single strain of melody since I woke up. And to be under such a strong enchantment, a person has to be able to *hear* the spell being played. It's as if everyone is listening to music that I alone can't hear. But that makes no sense.

"Mrs. Le Roux!" I spot the headmaestro beneath a large maple tree, digging with a trowel. She ignores me and chops at a root with the blade.

Jai. I have to find Jai.

Running back down the hill, I search the crowd of boys until I find him. He's by the lake, up to his knees in mud. He's digging with a pitchfork, which I eye nervously as I edge closer.

"Jai?" I approach him as if he's an angry cobra. "Nod your head or blink or *something* to show you can hear me."

He slings a pile of dirt that spatters my pajamas. Spitting out a clod, I draw a deep breath, bounce on my feet a moment —and then I dart in and seize the pitchfork. Yanking it out of his hands, I hurl it into the lake with a big splash.

Jai immediately bends over and starts digging with his fingernails.

"Stop it! Stop stop *stop!*"

With a wild yell, I tackle him to the ground and pin him. He struggles wordlessly, his eyes still glazed, trying to scratch at the soil.

"Jai, wake up! Please, please, just *snap out of it!*"

I can barely breathe for the terror filling my lungs.

"Who did this to you? *How* did they do this to you?"

And then I see it—a faint glow deep inside his ear.

What on earth?

He twists, trying to throw me off, and I have to grab his hair to keep him from headbutting me.

"Keep still, Jai! There's something in your . . . *oh my gosh.*"

A skinny, squirmy *thing* reaches out of his ear, like an eel in a coral reef. I nearly puke all over Jai then and there.

It's a worm, pale white and wriggling. And it is glowing, clearly the source of whatever magic has Jai entranced.

Which means I've got to pull it out.

"Ugh. *Gross gross gross gross!*"

I grab the worm, trying not to hurl when I feel its slimy body wriggling in protest. Then, carefully, I begin pulling it out.

It's nearly as long as my index finger, and about half as thick. It resists me, trying to burrow back into Jai's ear.

Gagging, I have to give it a sharp little tug to finally detach it from his ear canal. Then it slithers out all at once, writhing between my fingertips.

Disgusted, I hold it up to my face until I can hear the faintest thread of sound coming from its body, like the chirp of a cricket, but more musical. At once, fog starts to collect in my brain, the magic at work.

Jumping away from Jai, I hurl the worm to the ground and crush it with my shoe. Then, for good measure, I grab a rock and smash it until it's pulverized.

Breathing hard, I look back at Jai and see him blinking away the haze in his eyes. He sits up, stares at me, at the fresh grave he's lying in, at the mud on his clothes—and he *screams.*

"It's okay!" I toss the rock away. "It's okay, Jai. You're safe now."

He sucks in breaths like he's been underwater too long. "What's happening? Where am I? Is this a . . . grave?" His horrified eyes fix on me. "Amelia. Did I *die?*"

"No, but *I* nearly did trying to save you." I brush dirt off my hands and help him up. "You were under a spell. Everyone is!"

I gesture at the other students around us, still digging away.

Jai stares for a long moment, taking it in. "What? But . . . how?"

I point to the smashed worm. "This was in your ear. And I pulled it out. With my *bare fingers.*"

He crouches down and squints at the worm, then shudders. "Well, that's positively horrifying."

"You don't have to tell *me.* Do you know what it is?"

He nods. "It's an earworm. They're incredibly rare."

"Earworm?"

"They're sort of like humfrogs in that they can repeat simple melodies."

"So if you put them in someone's ear, say, while they're sleeping . . ."

"They can control the person for as long as they are in there. *Blegh!*" He stands up and kicks dirt over the worm, then looks around at the other students. "Now what?"

"That's a lot of earworms."

"I got it!" He snaps his fingers. "I remember watching a documentary about these things when I was little. Apparently, the whole colony is controlled by one worm—the queen worm. Kinda like bees or ants. She transmits the melody the other worms repeat. So if we find her and smush her . . ."

"The whole spell breaks!"

He nods.

"Except we have no idea where she is," I point out. "And it's just a matter of time before one of these kids really gets hurt." My stomach turns over as I realize what we have to do next.

He seems to have the same thought, and he grimaces. "So it's gotta be the hard way, then. Better suck it up and get it over with."

We split up and go to the nearest students. Before we can pull out the earworms, we have to wrestle them to the ground, take away their digging tools, and get them still enough to reach into their ears. I hear Jai moaning and retching as he extracts his first one, freeing George from the spell. I take care of Collin Brunnings, quickly tell him what happened, and while he's still reeling in bewilderment, push him toward an upperclassman at the next grave.

In this way, we slowly free the students, each newly wakened one stumbling off to help someone else. Screams of horror sound all over the campus with each newly freed person, along with gagging from the students trying to extract the worms from their classmates' ears.

In front of Harmony Hall, Jai and I run into Darby and Mia, newly freed from the spell. Both girls are covered in dirt, their faces pale.

For a moment, we just stare at one another, Mia glaring, Jai glaring back, Darby looking dazed. Then Mia pushes Darby along, muttering in her ear.

Someone must have started rescuing the Maestros, because the adults now flood the campus, trying to get control of the situation. Miss Motte approaches the four of us.

"Everyone okay?" she asks, looking frazzled. Her silk pajamas are ruined by the mud, and her black hair is in a tangle. "Back to your dorms to shower and change, then meet in the Shell for an emergency assembly." She starts walking away, then pauses and glances back. "Amelia. You don't know anything about this, do you?"

I freeze. She couldn't possibly be suspicious, could she?

Guilt floods through me. I can't keep hiding this. I *have* to tell the truth before someone gets seriously hurt.

But before I can say anything, Mia interrupts.

"This is outrageous!" she says. "My lawyers will hear all about this!"

Miss Motte sighs, a hand to her temple. "Mercy, child. Let's just get through the day, please, before we start filing lawsuits. Go back to your dorm, students, and clean up while we sort this out."

"C'mon," Jai says, tugging my sleeve. He whispers, "Consequence number two, you think?"

"It has to be. Why else would I be the only person not affected? This is a message for me."

"Couldn't he have just written in blood on your mirror or left a dead rat on your pillow like a *normal* bad guy?" grumbles Jai. "You really know how to pick your enemies, Amelia Jones."

I sigh.

We split up at the top of the hill to head to our own dorms. Most everyone's awake now, stumbling around with horrified expressions. A few kids are crying loudly, and Miss March gathers them up and takes them to her nurse's office.

"Amelia!"

Darby corners me the moment I step inside. She's a mess, with leaves in her hair and mud up to her elbows.

"Amelia, this *has* to be him, right? What are we going to—"

"We?" I ask. "*We?* There's no *we,* Darby, not after what you did."

"What I did?" She blinks. "What are you talking about?"

I shake my head, tired of the games she and Mia are playing with my brain. I'm tired of trying to be friends with people who just want to use me for their personal joke.

Pushing past her, I shove open my own door and resist the urge to throw myself onto the bed. I'm covered in mud head to toe. Even my hair is clotted with dirt.

But as I bend down to peel off my filthy socks, I notice a black card resting on my pillow, along with another dead rose. I pick the note up resignedly. The silver lettering is now all too familiar.

You owe me a spell, Amelia Jones.
This is your final warning.

CHAPTER TWENTY-SIX

All That Jazz

THE ASSEMBLY THAT AFTERNOON is solemn, with the whole student body gathered in the Shell along with the staff, teachers, and Maestros, from the cafeteria workers to Coach Phil. Nobody was spared from the earworms' spell.

Except, of course, for me. But no one knows that except Jai.

Everyone's quiet and still, eyes haunted. There's a heaviness in the air, as if we're sitting at a funeral.

The ice spell was viewed as an accident at best, a bad prank at worst, the same as the hallucination spell a month earlier. Or maybe those events were just accepted as the sort of inexplicable things that happen at a school for Musicraft.

But the earworm incident is on a whole other level. The Maestros are at a loss to explain it . . . and only Jai and I know the truth—and probably Darby and Mia, if they've put two and two together.

That truth turns in me like a snake, till I feel sick with it.

"We will be placing stricter curfews on campus until this matter is fully resolved," Mrs. Le Roux says from the stage. "The Echo Wood is off-limits, and no one is allowed outside after dark. Dinner will be served earlier, so you can all be in your rooms by the time the sun sets."

"Welcome to Mystwick Prison," whispers Jamal in the row behind me.

"Think it's ghosts again?" asks Amari.

I feel sudden pressure on the back of my head, as if several dozen pairs of eyes are boring into my skull. If ghosts *were* involved, they'd know exactly who to blame. Shrinking lower in my seat, I chew on the cuff of my sleeve and watch the headmaestro.

"We *will* get to the bottom of this," she says. "A full investigation is underway, and every one of you will be questioned in the days to come. Until we know the full story, nobody is above suspicion. Not students, not staff, not Maestros. Even *I* will undergo scrutiny."

Surely she can hear my heart pounding, even from across the concert hall. Surely everyone must see the cold sweat on my face. All I want to do is crawl under the seats and hide.

But as the assembly is dismissed and everyone files out, no one gives me a second look.

Still, I remain glued to my chair. The rest of the Aeros in

my row scowl as they have to climb around me. It's like I've turned to stone from all the guilt built up inside me. I'm too heavy to move.

"Amelia?"

Darby stops in the aisle next to my seat, but I don't look up at her.

"Amelia, what's going on? You've been avoiding me."

Mia appears right on cue. "Darby, let's go play a cleansing duet. I feel like I *still* have dirt under my nails, and the water pressure here just doesn't cut it."

Darby looks torn, and she starts to speak to me again.

"Just go, Darby," I whisper. I can't bear to talk to her right now. Even if she has some explanation for betraying me to Mia, I don't want to hear it.

It still hurts too much.

She stares at me for a few heartbeats, then shrugs. "Fine. Whatever."

They go together, and I'm left alone in the great auditorium. Letting my head fall back, I stare up at the starry music notes on the ceiling. Deep inside, I feel the pulse of the angry, dangerous spell. I can't remember the last time it was really quiet. It's been so constant that I've almost gotten used to it. It reminds me of the old tree behind my house that grew around the ax my grandfather sank into it long before I was born. The blade is permanently buried in its trunk, as much a part of it as its own branches, so only the tip of the handle is still sticking out.

Will this music become a permanent part of me?

For once, I hear Miss Motte's quiet footsteps before she can sneak up on me. She sits in the chair across the aisle. Saying nothing, she just waits, wrapped in a vibrantly patterned caftan, her gray dreadlocks in a twisty bun studded with music-note pins.

After a long, silent minute, I lower my head.

"I guess it's time for our lesson," I say softly.

"It is indeed that time, Amelia."

Does she know? Can she read the guilt written all over my face? She must. She's acting like she's waiting for a confession.

"Okay." I stand up, but she raises a hand to stop me.

"Why don't we do our lesson here today?"

"Oh. Sure."

She goes onto the stage and sits at the grand piano. Her fingers do a quick dance over the keys, warming up. "I was thinking maybe we'll try something new today. A little bit of cooperative Composition, for fun, to shake off some of this gloom. What do you say?" She plays an inviting measure, then lifts an eyebrow. "Join me for a little jazz improvisation?"

I pull myself out of the seat and slog onto the stage, where I take out my flute. "I don't know how."

"Sure you do. You're a Composer, aren't you? This isn't any different from the way you'd normally Compose, except we work together. Play off each other. You see, jazz is about listening and feeling together. Jazz is about *trust*."

Trust.

If she knew how many secrets I was keeping, she wouldn't trust me to even *hold* a flute, much less Compose with her.

She plays a bit more of the tune, leaving it unfinished—so that, I suppose, I can pick up the spell.

But I don't.

I just stand there with my flute assembled and stare at the floor.

"Amelia?" She turns on the bench, tilting her head.

Music storms inside me. I press my eyes shut against it.

"I can't do it," I say. "I can't Compose anymore. I—I think I'm broken."

Tears run from my eyes.

Miss Motte pulls her hands from the keys. "Amelia, what's going on?"

"I thought I could pretend I was fine and everything would go back to normal, but it hasn't, and it won't. It just gets worse and worse, like I can't do anything *but* break things."

"My dear—"

"There *is* music inside me, Miss Motte!" Something deep in my chest cracks open, and the words tumble out. "You were right. But it's not good music. It's bad. It's dark and angry and . . . it scares me. And I can't Compose anymore, because *that* music is all I hear, all the time, but especially when I'm angry. That's when it gets loudest."

I must sound like a babbling fool. I wait for her to say as much.

But she just waits in silence, her eyes full of empathy, and that only makes me feel worse. Why can't she see how messed-up I am?

"This is about your daddy," she says. "You're still angry at him."

I inhale sharply, about to deny it, to tell her it's none of her business like I did before.

But I can't. I just can't keep pretending.

"That's just it, though," I say. "I'm not just angry at *him*. Don't you see? *I'm* the reason my mom died. He blamed me, it's *my* fault. I told you and Mr. Pinwhistle that I'm not broken, but I am—*I am*. My dad saw that, and that's why he left me. Because of what I did. Don't you get it? It's *me* I'm angry at!"

My voice echoes through the concert hall. "Getting into Mystwick wasn't just about being like my mom. It was about proving I'm not the messed-up loser kid my dad left behind. That I was—*am*—worth staying for. But look what's happening! Everyone's in danger because of me. He was right. I break things, and I hurt people. He was better off without me, just like Mystwick would be."

"Oh, Amelia." She rises, walks straight to me, and wraps her arms around me in the biggest hug I've had since I left Gran to climb aboard the Mystwick zeppelin months ago. She holds me tight until I can't stand it anymore—I let go and cry. All the worry and fear and anger that's been storming inside of me pours out through my eyes. I must go on for ten minutes like that, and all through it, Miss Motte just holds me close.

"I'm tired of keeping secrets," I say at last, my voice muffled by her shoulder.

She pulls back, holding me at arm's length. Her eyes shine with tears too.

"That is the thing about secrets," she says. "They tend to get heavier the longer you carry them."

Stepping back, I wrap my arms around myself, my gaze lowering. "I didn't mean for things to turn out like this. I really thought I could do it on my own. And then everything started going wrong." Now that I've started confessing, it's like I'm powerless to stop. You'd think she'd played a truth spell over me. "I didn't Compose the fire dragon spell. At least, not exactly. I played the notes, but they weren't really mine."

She nods, as if she's suspected as much. "It just wasn't your style, was it?"

Why does everyone keep saying that? It's like they all know my style better than I do. I didn't even know I *had* a style.

"Let me guess," she says. "You used an enchanted feather? A spiderweb? A butterfly's wing?"

My head droops. "Dandelion puff."

"Ah, yes, a classic. All those little filaments—perfect for trapping delicate memories." She sighs. "Memory stealing is, alas, not uncommon among Composers. It's the pressure, you see, of constantly producing new spells. That's what happens when you let others control your voice. They demand more and more until you're drained dry, and then, in desperation, you turn to less than honest methods."

I look at her curiously. "Have *you* ever . . ."

"No, though I have had my chances. You're hardly the first to use one—unfortunately, it happens more than most Composers care to admit—but still, it was wrong. It was worse than musical plagiarism. It was *emotional* plagiarism. But I won't lecture you about it more because I can see your conscience has done quite enough of that for you."

I hang my head, my face hot with shame. "I'm so sorry. Are you going to tell the headmaestro? Will we be disqualified from the Trials?"

"Well, now. Let's not get hasty. I think my sister's a mite occupied with today's events. Which . . . you don't know anything about, do you?"

My heart freezes.

If I tell her about the earworms, the Necromuse, the Midnight Orchestra . . .

The truth balances on the tip of my tongue—the whole messy story.

"Amelia?" She looks at me intently. "Is there something you need to tell me?"

I'll tell everyone, Mia had said. *Mystwick will be disqualified . . . and it will be all your fault.*

More guilt to add to the mountain I already carry.

I imagine everyone at school hating me for ruining their chance in the Trials.

And the Maestros, who have already given me every chance in the world, who believed in me when most people would have given up . . . I can envision their disappointment. Their disgust. Their realization that I was a mistake.

Just the way my dad did.

I look out across the auditorium, where the doors have been left open. There are still holes all over the grounds beyond, piles of dirt beside them. The handle of the pitchfork I wrestled away from Jai is sticking out of the lake.

I can't do this on my own. I can't stop the Necromuse from reaching his hand into Mystwick and doing whatever he wants. Maybe everyone *will* hate me. Maybe I'll even get expelled.

But I can't risk more people getting hurt.

"Yes," I whisper. "I do have something to tell you."

Pacing up and down the stage, twisting my flute in my hands, I spill everything.

And I do mean everything.

I tell her about the portals, the Midnight Orchestra, Mr. Stewart. I tell her about the memory seed and how I almost left it in the desert, but at the last second changed my mind. I tell her how I used it to Compose the fire dragon spell and about the memory I saw when I did. I even tell her about Jai and Darby getting swallowed by the second portal with me, and about Mr. Midnight turning out to be the Necromuse. By the time I get to the part where he told me to Compose a resurrection spell, that there would be consequences if I didn't, Miss Motte is looking a little seasick.

But she doesn't say anything. Not a word. Not even a sound, until I've reached the part about the earworms and the note from the Necromuse on my pillow.

After a long, heavy silence in which Miss Motte doesn't seem to breathe, she finally shifts her weight and looks at me straight on.

"All right, Amelia. All right. Let's just step back and take a deep breath." She presses a hand to her lips, then to her chest, her face scrunching as she thinks.

I wait, blinking, for her to tell me it will be okay, that she can fix everything. But she just stares hard at the top of the piano, as if she's arranging a mental jigsaw puzzle.

"I'll admit," she says at last, "that I, uh, I was not quite prepared for the full extent of your . . . escapades."

"You mean you believe me?"

"Of course I believe you. Why wouldn't I believe you?"

Well, for starters, maybe because for all their talk of wanting to hear the truth, half the time adults won't even believe you when you *do* tell it. But Miss Motte doesn't ask questions, doesn't even ask for proof. She trusts that everything I told her is the truth, just like that.

It's like a weight I didn't know I was carrying lifts off my shoulders.

"As for the rest of it . . ." She shakes her head. "I suppose I can understand why you didn't tell me or any other adult sooner, or trust us to keep you safe. After all, there was another adult who was supposed to keep you safe a long time ago, and he didn't do that, did he?" She thumbs her lip absently, as if talking more to herself. "Maybe we're the ones who need to prove to you we're *worth* trusting."

Here she goes again, turning everything inside out. Here I am explaining to her all the ways I've messed up and how many secrets I've kept—and she thinks *she's* the one who has to prove something to me?

"So what do we do now?" I ask.

"I'm afraid this is bigger than I am, Amelia. Perhaps bigger than anyone here at Mystwick. But first things first. We need to talk to my sister."

CHAPTER TWENTY-SEVEN

Call Da Capos

MRS. LE ROUX'S OFFICE has its own fireplace, where flames crackle softly. The headmaestro leans on the corner of her desk, fingers steepled. Wynk the musicat sits on the floor beside her, staring through narrow eyes at the two suited agents who walk through the door, one as slim as a flute, the other as round as a tuba.

The first has a stern expression, with her dark hair in a tight bun and her black suit pristinely ironed. The second has a ketchup stain on his collar and a bald spot.

They exchange nods with Mrs. Le Roux and Miss Motte, then turn to me, Jai, and Darby, who stand in a row, eyes wide. Jai's absentmindedly sucking on his thumb again. I cough, and he yanks it out.

"You just *had* to tell the adults," Jai whispers.

I shrug helplessly.

"I'm Agent Rebecca Alvarez," says the lead agent in a crisp

tone. Turning back to the headmaestro, she flashes a badge with a bronze music note pinned to it. "Maestric Bureau of Investigations. Mrs. Le Roux, I presume?"

The headmaestro shakes her hand. "Thank you for coming so quickly."

I'm still having a hard time believing that Mrs. Le Roux called in the Maestric Bureau of Investigations. The actual *MBI.* If I could melt into a puddle and soak into the carpet, I would. I'd almost rather face the Necromuse again than these guys. I've seen enough TV to know the kind of people they track down. I'm not sure there *is* a higher authority than the MBI.

It dawns on me in a whole new way just how much trouble I'm in.

Agent Alvarez looks around the office. "So, which one of you is Amelia Jones?"

I lift a hand, swallowing.

"What, this tiny thing?" says the other agent, raising his bushy eyebrows. "Lotta ruckus for someone so short. I'm Agent Nedim Rahim. Yes, I know, it rhymes. Yes, my parents did do it on purpose. You can call me Agent Ned. Lollipops?"

He produces three yellow lollipops, which we take uncertainly. Jai opens his right away, while Darby pockets hers and I stand there holding mine.

Taking out a fourth, Agent Ned pops it into his mouth and winks.

Agent Alvarez gives him a sidelong look. "Let's get straight to business, shall we?"

"Amelia, tell them everything you told me," Mrs. Le Roux instructs.

"No detail is too small," adds Agent Alvarez. "I want to know the when, where, why, how, and who."

"What about the *what?*" Jai asks. "Isn't that the most important one?"

Agent Ned laughs.

His partner cuts him a sharp look. "Yes, that too."

So, for the third time today, I go through the entire story again. Jai and Darby add a few details. Agent Alvarez asks about a hundred questions, most of which we can't answer, like what color socks was Mr. Stewart wearing, and what was the position of the moon in the sky, and how many guests were there, and precisely what flavor were the madeleines the Necromuse offered me. Every time I shrug, she pinches her lips together and makes an angry mark in her notebook. I feel like I'm failing some kind of test. Beside me, I can feel Darby getting madder and madder.

"We weren't there to play detective," Darby snaps, resulting in a tense glaring contest between her and the agent.

Remarkably, it doesn't end in either of them spontaneously combusting.

Agent Ned beams at us. "Now, now—I'm sure you're all doing your best!"

"Are all these details necessary?" asks Miss Motte.

"Everything helps. We've been tracking this so-called Necromuse for years," says Agent Alvarez. "He's considered very dangerous, very slippery. No one knows his real name, and he uses at least a dozen aliases. Deals in illegal spells and items, blackmail, forgery, theft. You name it, he's committed it."

"What she means is, every detail *does* count, on account of us having, um, not many details to go on," adds Agent Ned. "Always a step ahead of us, this rascal."

"But not for much longer," says Agent Alvarez, viciously underlining something in her notebook. "Though I've never known him to target *children* in his extortion schemes before."

"Amelia has . . . unique talents," says Mrs. Le Roux.

"Yes," says Agent Alvarez, eyeing me. "The little girl with a knack for black spells."

I widen my eyes. "You know about me?"

"We keep a file on all musicians known to have meddled with such magic."

I sway on my feet, as if I might pass out. The MBI has a file on *me?*

"First offense, you're a minor, you've nothing to worry

about," says Agent Ned kindly. "But clearly this Necromuse has taken an interest in you, little lady. You did the right thing, telling your teachers."

I nod, looking down again. I'm starting to wonder if maybe I should have kept my mouth shut. Judging by Jai's and Darby's looks when they were hauled into the headmaestro's office, they certainly think so. I dragged them into this mess without warning, which means no doubt that their parents will find out, and who knows what kind of trouble that'll put them in.

"You really have no idea who this man is?" asks Mrs. Le Roux.

Agent Alvarez squirms a bit. "Well . . . we've known for some time that he is Barred, but we've already cross-referenced every person in the MBI's registry, with no luck. He must have somehow erased all records we or any other agency had on him. And we know that this orchestra of his has been around for decades."

"And you've never managed to catch him in all that time?" Jai whistles. "He's good."

Agent Ned nods, looking tired, while Agent Alvarez looks at Jai like she's thinking of arresting *him*.

"Anyway," she says, "it seems our guy is intent on getting a spell out of Miss Jones here. I say we use that to our advantage."

Miss Motte's eyes narrow. "What do you mean?"

"We'll set a security detail around Miss Jones until he makes his move. Then we'll make *our* move and finally put this guy away for good."

"A trap," says Mrs. Le Roux with a disapproving quirk of her lips. "With Amelia as bait."

Bait!

I don't like the sound of that. Not one little bit.

"We will be ready to spring into action before he lays a finger on the girl," Agent Alvarez assures us. "With Miss Jones's help, we can bring this criminal to justice at last."

"And I can *finally* take my vacation to Patagonia," adds Agent Ned wistfully.

Nobody asks me what *I* think, which, given how big a part of this plan involves me, I find a little rude. But that's how it goes with adults. Tell them the problem and they'll take all the power to fix it out of your hands. I remind myself that that's what I *wanted.*

"We're attempting to contact her legal guardian," says Agent Alvarez.

"Gran is on a cruise," I say. "She sent me a postcard from Malta saying she dropped her phone overboard."

"I'll speak for Amelia until her grandmother can be reached," adds Mrs. Le Roux. "We'll do whatever we have to, to keep Amelia safe."

"Of course, of course." But Agent Alvarez doesn't look

very interested in my safety. She looks like a hungry lioness contemplating an antelope.

"What about the Trials?" I ask. "And . . . my fire dragon spell?"

Mrs. Le Roux's nostrils flare slightly. "Though it pains me to think of Mystwick performing anything less than ethical, we will proceed, and you will play your fire dragon spell in the Composium."

Agent Alvarez nods. "Yes. You'll do everything as you normally would, so the target doesn't get suspicious. We will accompany you, of course, to the Trials."

Right. Because they *want* him to come after me. Because I'm bait.

"Sounds exciting!" says Agent Ned, rubbing his big hands together. "Love a little interscholastic competition, I do. We'll cheer for you from the stands! But—you know. Silently. On account of us being undercover and on duty and all that."

"What about us?" asks Jai, waving his lollipop. "Darby and I went to see the orchestra too. Do we get a security detail?"

"Sure, bud!" says Agent Ned, giving Jai a fist bump.

"Cool! Can I get sunglasses like yours?"

"Sure, I don't see why—"

"Nobody gets sunglasses!" Agent Alvarez interrupts, exasperated. "Agent Rahim, may I remind you we are not here to make friends? We'll keep an eye on each of you kids, but the bureau can only spare the two of us for this job. Stick together as much as you can, no sneaking off. And of course, keep this between the three of you, hmm? We don't want to tip the target's hand. No one—and I mean *no one*—outside this room should know about any of this."

Darby looks at me, and I look away, still unable to speak to her. How are we supposed to "stick together" without Mia going ballistic?

"If that will be all, agents," says Mrs. Le Roux, "we leave for the Trials in the morning, so we have packing to do."

Agents Alvarez and Ned nod and shake her hand before leaving.

"We will be nearby," Agent Alvarez adds as she goes out the door. "If you kids see anything—and I do mean *anything*—out of the ordinary, find us. He could send you a letter, emails. He could have someone working on the inside, for all we know. Anything out of the ordinary, *we want to know about it,* understood?"

"Does she *know* this is Mystwick?" Jai murmurs to me out of the corner of his mouth. "We'll be tugging their sleeves every five minutes."

Mrs. Le Roux dismisses us at last, and we leave with sighs of relief. I check the clock as we go out; we've been up here for hours.

"Wait a moment, Amelia!" Miss Motte calls out.

I wave to Jai and stop on the landing outside the headmaestro's office. Darby looks up at me, her brow furrowed, as if she's about to ask a question. Or maybe to explain why she told Mia everything. We still haven't spoken to each other since the ice spell froze the school.

But Miss Motte arrives then, and Darby lowers her head and goes without a word.

"Now that that's all settled," says Miss Motte, "why don't you and I have a chat."

We walk down the stairs, which are open to the great front windows of Harmony Hall. There's not much of a view today; the mountains are hidden behind a thick wall of gray clouds. Sparse snow flurries drift softly through the air.

"Before all this Necromuse business," Miss Motte says, "we were discussing something else."

"We were?"

She puts a hand on my arm. "Your dad, Amelia."

"Oh. Yeah, I guess. We don't really need to talk about that anymore."

"Is that so?"

"I was just upset about the earworms and the Midnight Orchestra and all that." I brush my hair behind my ears. "But I'm fine. Really."

"Are you?" She stops me, a hand on my shoulder. "Amelia, it's not your fault that your father left you."

My stomach clenches, and I start descending the stairs faster, one step ahead of her. "I know. Of course."

"Amelia—"

"I need to go pack for the Trials. Leaving in the morning, you know."

"Amelia."

I stop at the bottom of the steps and look up at her. She leans on the balustrade, her eyes probing.

"He's gone, Miss Motte," I say. "And I never have to deal with him again. So why waste any more words, any more thoughts, on him? He's ancient history. I'm *fine*."

I rush out the front doors before she can say another word.

CHAPTER TWENTY-EIGHT

Break Allegro

The Orphean Trials are held at a ski resort not far from Mystwick, in a pretty, snow-laden vale between three high mountain peaks. After a short trip in the school zeppelin, the *Purple Bumblebee,* we disembark into a chaotic frenzy of instruments, magic, and puffy ski jackets.

For a moment, we stand blinking in the sunlight, as all around us, the students of the other Musicraft schools run and throw snowballs.

There are Maestros milling around, chatting, and lots of parents too. Several kids from our group spot theirs and run to greet them, including Darby, whose mom waits in a red coat, her black hair the exact same shade as Darby's. She tows Mia along with her, and her mom grabs them both in a big hug.

"Right, then! Inside with the rest of you!" orders Mr. Pinwhistle. He, Miss Motte, and Mrs. Le Roux are our three chaperones. Looking around, I try to spot the MBI agents, but they must be well hidden—or disguised. I haven't seen them since this morning, when they teleported ahead of us in a dark black car to "scout ahead." What I think they really meant was "lay the trap."

Jittery, I look around, wondering if the Necromuse is lurking somewhere nearby, just waiting to jump out.

"Relax," Jai tells me. "It's not like we're on our own out here—not after you *told all the grownups*."

Yeah, Jai still hasn't totally forgiven me for that.

"Do you have any idea what their plan is?" he whispers.

I shrug. "Proceed as normal is all they'd tell me."

"Right, proceed to be *bait*."

I grimace, nodding.

Leave it to the adults, Amelia, is how Mrs. Le Roux had put it. We know best. Just do your homework and practice your flute and everything will be fine.

Well, I guess we'll find out soon if they're right.

We deposit our bags in a large dorm room lined with bunk beds; all the Mystwick girls are sharing the space. Soon after, the room clears out as almost everyone heads for the ski-rental shop. We have vouchers from the school, good for one day of skiing, but *fun* is the last thing on my mind—and besides, I've never skied in my life and I don't intend to start this competition with a broken arm.

Instead, in a state of total paranoia, I find a cozy spot in the grand lobby and study my library book of defensive spells. There's not much in it that would really be useful, since I think it was compiled several decades ago, when people were more worried about fending off polio or packs of wolves. But I study the melodies anyway, figuring too much preparation never hurt anyone.

The lobby is quiet except for groups of students who wander in to ogle the Crystal Lyre. It's set in a glass display case in the center of the room, gleaming under carefully positioned spotlights. I'm tucked in next to a big fireplace overlooking the south ski slope, where Mia and Darby are racing each other down the slalom course.

"All study and no play makes for dull competition, you know," says a voice.

I yelp, startled out of my skin as an older boy flops down beside me.

"Luca D'Alessio?" I recognize the Souza Composer from the videos Mr. Pinwhistle made us study.

The boy gives a flourishing wave of his hand. "And you are Amelia Jones."

"You know about me?"

"How could I not? The first Composer from Mystwick in a generation. My primary competition. The little girl who summoned an army of the dead all with a flick of her flute."

"It wasn't an army," I mutter. That description sounded *way* too close to what the Necromuse does.

Shaking the thought away, I glance down at Luca's clothes, which are silk and velvet, like some kind of old-fashioned opera star, yet at the same time, ridiculously modern and cool.

"I've seen your Compositions," I say. "I don't think you have much to worry about."

He gives me a calculating look, then shrugs. "Pity. I'd hoped for some real competition finally. But I think you're right. You are just a little girl in *way* over her head."

With that, he pops up and swans breezily away.

My eyes narrow, a rush of indignation warming my skin. Just a little girl, huh? In way over my head? What a self-obsessed jerk.

And yet . . . he's probably right.

I've been so focused on watching for the Necromuse's next attack that I've barely thought about the competition. My head's not in the game, as my old basketball coach would say before he benched me for the thousandth time. To be fair, I'm a tragedy at any sport.

Noticing that everyone's starting to move to the other end of the room, I sit up and look to see what's going on. Kids are buzzing around a cluster of Maestros and medics in white uniforms by the front doors.

My heart climbs into my throat.

Is this it? Is this the Necromuse's move? Did he hurt one

of my friends? I don't see Agent Ned or Agent Alvarez anywhere.

Panicking, I push closer and find Jai coming in fresh off the slopes, his hair dusty with snow.

"It's Chad," he says breathlessly. "He fell down. As in, off the ski lift and onto his leg. It's broken."

"The guitarist from Rebel Clef?" I feel a rush of relief, followed by a touch of guilt. I feel bad for Chad, but at least it wasn't the Necromuse.

"Jai Kapoor!" yells a voice.

Rosa Guerrera appears, her eyes blazing. She grabs hold of Jai and stoops down to look him in the eyes.

"I'm only going to ask you this once in your pathetic lifetime, Kapoor," Rosa says. "So don't screw it up." She draws a deep breath, looking pained, then says, "Do you wanna rock out with us?"

"Er . . ." Jai looks like he's been hit with a ski.

"Scratch that. Rephrase," says Rosa, gripping him even tighter. "You're *gonna* rock out with us. I remember how you disrespected my guitar back when the school froze over. You'll have to do."

"You really thought I was that good?"

"Whoa, fact-check: the sound you made was *tragic,* and I wished I could die so I wouldn't have to hear it ever again. But at least you know which end of the guitar is up, which is more than can be said for most of these other nerds. So you're filling in for Chad. Battle of the Bands is tomorrow afternoon, and you're already signed up."

"I—I can't do that!" Jai protests.

"Why not?" I ask. "Jai, this is like your wildest dream come true!"

"Because." He runs a hand over his face, then peeks at me between his fingers. "My dad's here."

"What!"

His voice goes shrill. "I didn't think he'd come. He was supposed to have a thing with the Philharmonic of someplace or other, but I guess it got canceled. I saw him arrive an hour ago, and I've been avoiding him ever since."

"You're gonna have to tell him the truth, sooner or later."

"Later, then. Later sounds great."

Rosa groans. "Forget it. We'll just get someone else to play. It's not like we have a shortage of talented musicians around here. I'll get Gregory."

"Gregory," he echoes flatly. "The same Gregory who puts mayonnaise on his ice cream and can't even say the word *toilet* out loud without turning red?"

"Yep. That Gregory." Rosa points across the lobby, where the tenth-grader in question is crying because he apparently just sipped hot cocoa that was too hot.

"Gregory doesn't have the soul of a rocker!" Jai protests. "Gregory will ruin everything!"

"Rosa's right," I say. "This is for the best. Gregory should do it. I mean, face it, Jai. You're a classical violinist, and that's probably all you'll ever be."

"Amelia . . . Why do I get the feeling you're trying to manipulate me? *You,* who doesn't have a devious bone in your body?" He frowns deeper. "Worse, why do I feel like it's *working?*"

Shouldering my flute case, I begin walking away. "See you around, Jai. I'm going to go shower while the bathroom's empty."

"I'm not touching that guitar."

"Okay. Fine. Whatever." I keep walking.

"Yeah, whatever! Who cares?"

I wave my hand but don't turn around. "Not me!"

"Well, me either! So there!"

As I head up the stairs to our dorm, I smile, knowing my work is done.

"We're screwed," whispers Victoria, her fingernails anxiously drumming the armrest of her wheelchair. "No guitarist, no band. No band, no battle. Are we really going to forfeit?"

The arena where the Battle of the Bands is held is an impressive sight. Bleachers circle a wide, round stage where four bands are set up at each cardinal point. We're sitting in the northern quadrant, above Rebel Clef. Our school band is ready to go: mikes checked, amps on, drumsticks poised . . . but Chad's lonely guitar rests in its stand, front and center. Rosa Guerrera looks ready to chew nails.

The other bands—the Souza Academy Sonogoats, the San Diego Conservatory Warblers, and the Miami School Muses—are all accounted for and getting restless. The rest of their school teams sit behind them, along with any parents or other supporters, holding banners and signs with slogans like ROCK 'EM DEAD! and NO DRUMS, NO GLORY! Luca D'Alessio catches my gaze and gives me a mocking, pouty look. I stick out my tongue at him. Trash talk zings around the arena like spitballs—mostly directed at us in the Mystwick section.

"We wanna battle, not a surrender!"

"Yo! Too scared to face the music, Mystwick?"

"Hey, Musicows!" yells a Souza kid. "Or is it Musi*chickens*? Cuz your guitarist *chickened* out!"

He starts clucking, and it quickly spreads until the entire arena is giving us their best chicken impressions.

"This is humiliating," groans Jamal.

Mr. Pinwhistle is growling under his breath. Miss Motte smiles blithely in her seat. I scan the crowd restlessly, chewing my pinkie nail. The Necromuse could show up any minute. Heck, he could already be here, blending into the crowd, and I'd never know it until it was too late. Where *are* the MBI agents?

Below us, in the first five rows, are all the parents and families of the Mystwick students. Jamal and Amari's family alone takes up an entire row, and the twins moan and slump in their seats every time one of their aunts or grandparents turn to beam at them. There's nobody there for me, or for Mia. I wonder where her dad is, and if she's thinking about her mom, still missing somewhere out in the sea. Darby sits with her mom, and Jai's dad is in the third row from the front, scowling. I recognize him from my Mystwick auditions, where I'd seen him lecture Jai.

"Jai will show," I say.

"How d'you know?" asks Victoria.

I know because the seat next to me, which was reserved for him, is empty.

I know because he didn't say a word all through breakfast, even though they were serving his favorite—waffles and bacon. He just stared at his plate with his eyebrows all scrunched up.

I know because Jai is my best friend, and I have complete confidence in his ability to make bad decisions. At least, *bad* by most standards. After all, openly defying your strict dad in front of hundreds of spectators isn't exactly smart. But what kind of friend would I be if I discouraged him from chasing his dreams, even when it means doing something colossally stupid?

Still, after ten minutes pass, my nerves start to wobble. What if Jai psyched himself out of showing up? What if his dad found out what he meant to do and locked him up or something?

What if the *Necromuse* . . .

"He's not coming," sings Mia quietly.

I bite my lip as one of the judges walks grimly onto the stage. I can only hope Rosa doesn't tackle the guy; she's staring at him like she's a tiger and he just stepped on her tail.

"Unfortunately," says the judge, "the rules state that each band must consist of —"

"Wait!" shouts a voice.

I grin as Jai comes running down the aisle.

CHAPTER TWENTY-NINE

The Trill of the Fight

EVERYONE TURNS AND WATCHES as my best friend hauls butt, panting by the time he reaches the stage. I glance at his dad to find Mr. Kapoor's eyes nearly popping out of his head.

"I'm here, I'm here!" Jai gasps. He wraps a hand around the neck of Chad's guitar.

"Ahem," says Mr. Pinwhistle, rising to his feet. "I believe the Mystwick band is all accounted for."

The judge sighs and returns to his seat. Rosa gives a triumphant strum of her bass string.

Down in front, Mr. Kapoor stands up, his hands in fists at his sides. But Jai, fiddling with his guitar, seems to be avoiding looking at the audience. Which is good—because if anybody looked at *me* the way Mr. Kapoor is looking at his son, I'd poop my pants.

"Listen up, nerds!" Rosa yells while Jai loops the guitar over his shoulder. "We're Rebel Clef, and we are gonna *ROCK. YOUR. NIGHTMARES!*"

All of us in the Mystwick section jump to our feet and cheer, as above our heads, an announcer calls out in a booming voice, "Families and guests, contestants and Maestros, welcome to the forty-fifth annual Orphean Trials Battle of the Bands!"

Now the whole arena is cheering, jumping, and whooping. Onstage, the four bands glare at one another and crouch over their instruments as if they're about to draw swords.

The lights go out, plunging us into darkness. The cheers fade into silence. For a minute, nothing happens, and I wonder if this is part of the staging or if the power's been cut. Whispers fill the arena, and I just hope Mr. Kapoor doesn't run onstage to drag Jai off.

As the silence and darkness drag on, my worries shift in another direction.

What if the Necromuse—

Then, all at once, the stage explodes with sound.

All four bands begin playing their spells at once. Since the speakers are directed toward their respective sections, we can mostly just hear Rebel Clef's music, the others just garbled noise in the background. Screaming guitars, thrumming drums, and wailing keyboards erupt with music and magic.

I've never seen a Battle of the Bands in person. It's not much different from Sparring, just bigger, louder, and way more chaotic.

Rockets of yellow light shoot from the band sets and explode over our heads in dazzling fireworks. The accompanying smell of hot asphalt follows in a nauseating wave that nevertheless has people roaring. The raining sparks fall, glittering, to the center of the arena, where they expand into different shapes.

The San Diego Warblers conjure the glowing outline of a massive, hairy tarantula. Its pincers slash at the air and its eight eyes burn with golden fire.

In front of the Miami Muses, a great white shark leaps and snaps its enormous teeth.

The Souza section lets out a roar when their band delivers a snarling saber-toothed tiger, all claws and fangs.

Last to appear is the Rebel Clef's fighter. Sparks of light zigzag through the air like over-caffeinated fireflies, tracing the outline of something *huge*. I hold my breath, fists raised in anticipation.

Finally, in a burst of magic, a twenty-foot-tall T. rex comes to life on the stage, propped up by streamers of light flowing from the members of Rebel Clef, Jai included. We let out a floor-rattling cheer as the dino opens his giant mouth and lets out a savage roar.

"LET THE BATTLE BEGIN!" shouts the announcer.

Like puppets on strings of fire, the four huge creatures lurch across the arena. The four bands play furiously behind them, their music directing their fighters' movements. Soon, all four are charging full speed at one another.

The clash is *blinding*.

I raise a hand to block the flash of light. A collective "*Whoa!*" rises from the audience.

The T. rex snaps at the tarantula, while the shark leaps up from the floor, only to have its tail chomped by the sabertooth tiger. The creatures let out realistic roars and shrieks, their glowing outlines flickering where they're wounded. The faster sabertooth and tarantula scurry and slash, avoiding the stronger jaws of the T. rex and shark.

When the shark bites off one of the tarantula's legs, it releases an earsplitting scream. Hands slap over ears in every section of the audience. The tarantula isn't defeated, but it limps around, the San Diego band looking panicked as they try to keep their fighter in the match.

"This makes absolutely no zoological sense!" yells Victoria, though I can barely hear her over the noise.

I glance away from the spectacle at Mr. Kapoor, hoping to see that he's coming around to how cool this is, but he sits like a stone, staring at the back of the seat in front of him.

Uneasily, I watch Jai instead. His hair sticks to his face with sweat, his school cardigan is unbuttoned and hangs loosely off one shoulder, and he's never looked so in his element.

Something warm pounds deep in my chest, pride for my friend and admiration at this talent he's been hiding for so long. He pours *everything* into that guitar until there's smoke practically curling from the strings.

With another scream, the tarantula ends up caught between the T. rex and the sabertooth; together, they rip the hairy spider in half, and it dies in a shower of sparks. The strings of magic that had been controlling it backfire on the San Diego band, scattering their instruments and knocking the drummer off the stage altogether. A roar of triumph sounds from the other three sections as the San Diego Warblers throw up their hands in surrender.

The remaining three fighters circle one another warily, looking for angles of attack. The sabertooth is limping now too, and the shark is missing a fin. The T. rex roars, then charges at the shark, only to swerve at the last minute to chomp the sabertooth's tail. I bet no real-life T. rex *ever* moved so quickly, but under the expert control of Rosa and her band, it practically pirouettes.

But the Souza band was ready, and with a crashing drum solo, they send the sabertooth streaking through the air to clamp its jaws on the T. rex's throat.

Oh, no . . .

The T. rex stumbles, its entire body flickering, on the verge of going out. Seeing their chance, the Miami Muses clamp their shark's teeth on the dino's tail. The T. rex lets out a choked cry of pain.

Chaos in the Rebel Clef band.

The drummer breaks tempo, sweat making the drumsticks slip in his hands. Rosa shouts something, then points at Jai.

I press my hands to my mouth as Jai jumps forward and rips into a blistering guitar solo. His sweater hangs from his elbows like a cape, and when he shakes his head, sweat flings from his hair. His fingers move in a blur, coaxing a flurry of notes from the strings. He drops to his knees, bent over the guitar.

The whole audience is completely silent, eyes fixed on the seventh-grader playing like he's performing frantic CPR on his own instrument.

And slowly, the magic flowing from Jai to the T. rex grows brighter and brighter, until all at once, with a furious snarl, the dino erupts with light that sends the sabertooth and the shark reeling backwards.

Every Mystwick spectator howls in triumph—except, of course, Mr. Kapoor.

But his radiating disapproval can't touch Jai now.

Jai's a king holding court, his music infusing every inch of the T. rex. As the rest of the band resumes playing, the dino seizes the shark in its jaws and reduces it to sparks and smoke, knocking the Miami Muses out of the battle.

All that's left is Souza's saber cat, circling and snarling, trying to draw the T. rex closer to the Souza band, where their magic is stronger. But instead, Rebel Clef sends another wave of magic rolling to the T. rex—and from its back sprout two massive leathery wings. With a mighty flap, the dino lifts into the air.

"Okay," says Victoria, rolling her eyes, "this just got *mega* ridiculous."

But the crowd *eats. it. up.*

Even the Miami and San Diego crowds are cheering now, as the flying T. rex dive-bombs the sabertooth and crushes him beneath its huge clawed feet.

The sabertooth struggles, the Souza band red-faced and panting as they try to maintain their spell, but it's not enough.

The T. rex bends its neck down and bites off the sabertooth's head in one clean snap, and just like that, the tiger disintegrates into fading sparks—and Mystwick wins.

As they bring their rock spell to a triumphant close, we all scream and hug and pump fists. The T. rex lets out one last roar, then dissolves into shooting streamers of light that burst in a dazzling array of fireworks.

Jai, sweaty and glowing with victory, lifts his guitar over his head. Rosa pounds him on the back, and the keyboardist runs over to plant a kiss on Jai's head.

I've never seen him so gloriously happy.

But then, like a cloud moving across the sun, his smile droops. He lowers the guitar, and his entire body sags. I follow his line of sight to the audience, where Mr. Kapoor stands up and stiffly marches out of the arena.

CHAPTER THIRTY

The Flat Hits the Fire

THE RANKINGS ARE LISTED in the grand lobby of the hotel.

Souza is in first place, having won the Gauntlet and Sparring events. Nobody who wants to keep their head attached to their spine will dare speak to Kjersten. She came in a close second after a record-setting two-hour Spar against Souza's best cellist. Jamal and Amari did their best in the obstacle course but placed third after Jamal twisted his ankle. Musical Arts also got us a third place, when Phoebe's earnest efforts to sculpt a majestic ice stallion ended up more . . . well, a melted frog. Souza came in second, and San Diego first, with a brilliant sculpture of a mariachi band, complete with frosty mustaches and fringed ponchos.

Mystwick is in second place overall, with our win in the Battle of the Bands boosting us from third.

Which leaves one event remaining: the Composium.

Which will decide *everything.*

Based on the current scores, Souza, San Diego, and

Mystwick all stand a chance to take the win. Miami will still perform, hoping for a second-place finish.

Tension is high at dinner.

The cafeteria is divided into four factions, and this time, there's no trash talk flying around. Instead, the teams huddle to strategize, with their Composers the center of attention. Luca D'Alessio holds court, perched atop a table, where he laughs and flings his hands around as if this were all a big joke.

I may have only just met him, but I really can't stand that kid.

The Mystwick group, dressed in our black performance outfits, is jittery with excitement. Rumor has it that Luca's spell isn't as amazing as his previous ones, which means we might actually have a shot at taking Souza down with my fire dragon spell.

"We can *do* this," whispers a member of the ice sculpting team. "We might actually pull this off! I heard the San Diego kids talking. They're betting on *us* to win it all."

"Don't get cocky," warns Trevor, but he's grinning along with the rest of them.

I sit at the far end of the table, poking at my ham and mashed potatoes. I can't seem to muster up the same excitement. Instead, my stomach feels squirmy with nerves.

"Hey, Trevor?" I call.

"Hmm?" He looks over at me, lifting his eyebrows. "What's up?"

"Have you seen Jai? Was he in the guy's dorm?"

"Kapoor?" He shrugs. "Haven't seen him."

Weird.

After the Battle of the Bands this morning I tried to reach the stage to talk to him, but by the time I fought my way through the crowd, he was gone. That was hours ago, and I haven't seen a sign of him since.

I have a sinking feeling where he might be.

"I'm going to check on him," I say, picking up my untouched food.

"You've got ten minutes," says Trevor. "Then we're heading over to the concert hall for the Composium. Don't be late, Jones."

I have to pass the rest of the team to leave, and they give me high fives and fist bumps as I walk by. They're acting like we've already won the Lyre.

"We're gonna *crush* Souza!" Kjersten gives me a fierce smile. "And it's all because of you, Jones!"

"Uh . . . thanks."

I rush out of the cafeteria, my heart thumping.

First I go to the front desk of the hotel and wave down the receptionist. "Excuse me. Mr. Kapoor told me to ask you to send more towels up to his room."

"You got it, sweetie." She checks her computer, then picks up a phone. "Housekeeping? Set of towels to Room 203, please."

Before she's even hung up, I'm gone, the number memorized.

I find Room 203 and hesitate in front of the door. Everything in me wants to turn around and run. Mr. Kapoor scares me almost as much as the Necromuse. But if Jai's in there getting the lecture of his life, I owe it to him to be at his side. After all, I'm the one who practically pushed him onto that stage. He'd stand by me no matter what; I have to do the same for him.

Before I can lose my nerve, I knock sharply on the door.

It opens at once, so quickly I jump.

"Yes?" It's Mr. Kapoor, and he looks a whole thunderstorm of mad. His eyes are wild, his eyebrows clenched together.

"Um, sorry. I—I was just looking for Jai?"

"Who are you?" he demands, opening the door wider.

"I'm Amelia Jones. Jai's best friend."

"Amelia Jones," he says in a flat tone. His eyes narrow. "So. In addition to defying me and fooling with crude, vile magic, he's also been running around with some *girl,* getting up to who knows what!"

"Huh?" I shriek. "No! Oh, gosh, Mr. Kapoor—it's nothing like that! We're just friends. Honest."

Oh, by Bach's curly wig. You could fry an egg on my face, and that's a fact.

"I only came by to tell you it's my fault that Jai helped the band out today, and also that he's really good at it, and even if you hate him for it, I think he's brave for—"

"Fresh towels?" chirps a cheerful voice.

I turn to see a short housekeeper holding a stack of towels and smiling from ear to ear.

"What?" booms Mr. Kapoor. "Get out of here!"

The housekeeper's smile vanishes. She blinks once, then hurries away, looking over her shoulder.

Drawing a breath, I turn back to Mr. Kapoor. "Look, sir, what I'm trying to say is, I think you should go easy on Jai, or at least be mad at me and not him."

"Enough!" Mr. Kapoor pinches the bridge of his nose. "So was it also you, then, who helped him escape?"

I blink. "Huh? I did what now?"

He gives me a disdainful look. "Ten minutes ago Jai went to take a shower, here in our room. But I got suspicious when the water never started running, and I went in. Jai was gone."

"Out the window?" I guess, since that's kind of a habit of Jai's.

He shakes his head. "You know full well there's no window

in the bathroom. He had no instrument, either, so the only way he could have escaped his punishment was by magic. It must have been *you* who helped him!"

"Jai's gone?" Sticky, terrible dread fills my throat. "And there's no way he could have got out on his own? Are you sure?"

"Do I look like I am *joking?*" he thunders.

I shake my head wordlessly. Honestly, he looks like he's never told a joke in his entire life.

Enormous, swelling terror rises like a monster behind me. Its shadow darkens the hallway and stretches as far as I can see.

I gasp. "I have to go."

"Oh no you don't!" says Mr. Kapoor. "I want an explanation! I want to know where my son is!"

You and me both, mister.

Only unlike Mr. Kapoor, I have an idea where Jai might be—or who might have taken him.

My flute case thumping against my leg, I sprint through the hotel, pushing through the cluster of Mystwick kids emerging from the cafeteria.

"Hey, Jones!" shouts Rosa. "The Composium's in five minutes and you're going the wrong way!"

Ignoring her, I charge into the dorm we've been sharing and fall on my knees by my bunk. I search the pillow, then under it, then all through the sheets, ripping them off the bed. When I find nothing, I look around the bunk, in my suitcase, and everywhere I can think of—but there's nothing.

No dead rose.

No black note card.

I sink to the floor, my legs sprawled wide, and grip my hair with both hands. I don't know whether to be relieved or even more worried.

Did Jai escape his dad on his own, and if so, where is he and why didn't he come find me?

Unless he's waiting at the Composium, where he knows I should be.

I race through the hotel and outside, headed for the glassy concert hall at the heart of the resort. The place is dead quiet, with everyone gathered inside for the grand finale. Velvety white snow flows down the mountainside and around the hall. I'm steps away from the door when it flies open and Trevor steps out, his face white and his eyes panicked.

"Amelia!" he shouts. "*There* you are! We're on next!"

"Sorry." I step past him into the red-carpeted lobby. Glimmering crystal chandeliers hang overhead, casting pebbled light over the walls. "Is Jai here, by any chance?"

"His dad pulled him from the performance, didn't you hear? Lucky he wasn't essential or—"

"I know that, but is he *here?* In the audience or backstage maybe?"

Trevor shrugs. "How should I know? I've been losing my brain just trying to track *you* down. C'mon! We're missing Souza's performance!"

He drags me down a curving hallway that leads backstage. We slip through a door into the darkened wings, where the rest of the Mystwick orchestra is waiting. They all sigh in collective relief at the sight of me, and Rosa grabs my wrist like she's going to keep me from disappearing again.

"Where have you *been?*" she hisses.

We're standing just offstage, behind the three rows of tall velvet curtains. In the glow of the footlights, the Souza Musicraft Academy orchestra is in the midst of a grand symphony, with Luca D'Alessio up front, his eyes shut as he plays a white grand piano. Honestly, he's overselling it, as if he's on the verge of tears listening to his own music.

But his spell!

Okay, even I can't deny he's an incredible Composer. The music is rolling and triumphant, sending out white waves of magic that sweep through the audience like snowy winds. People start standing up in their seats, pointing and gasping all around them. Rumor had it Luca's spell wasn't as good as his past ones, but it doesn't sound like that to me.

I blink a few times as a stray wisp of white magic coils around me, and my mind goes foggy . . .

Then a pair of hands claps over my ears, blocking the music, and the fog dissipates.

"Didn't you hear the announcement?" asks Trevor, bending over me, his hands still clamped over my ears so I have to read his lips to understand him. "Earplugs!"

Oh, right. He didn't want us going into *our* spell with Luca's white magic still fogging our brains, so he gave us all earplugs this morning. I fish mine from my pocket and pop them in.

Satisfied, Trevor steps back. "Get ready," he mouths, tapping his wrist as if indicating the time. "And relax. Jai's probably in the audience."

Immune to the magic now, I take the chance to scan the audience for any sign of my best friend, but the glare of the stage lights hides everyone out there.

"Amelia!" Miss Motte swans my way, draped in a fuzzy shawl that makes her look like an elegant moth. "There you are! Isn't the energy here *inspiring?* So many nerves! So much excitement!" She inhales deeply. "Mmm, the air is *humming,* wouldn't you say?"

I stifle a groan.

"I'd wish you luck, but you don't need it. You have all the power you need. Don't forget that." She flicks something my way, and I catch it automatically.

It's one of the mood beads from my necklace. She must have saved it after I scattered them everywhere. It rests like a dull pearl on my palm until I drop it in my pocket.

"Thanks, Miss Motte, but have you seen—ugh, never mind, then."

She's already fluttering away as if I weren't even speaking—patting cheeks, thumping shoulders, reminding the other students to *embrace the silence between heartbeats* and *breathe deeply the marrow of the moment.* My teammates stare after her in bewilderment.

Sighing, I go backstage and sit cross-legged beside a pile of amps and cords. The others are all getting their instruments out, silently preparing for our turn with all the weird little rituals musicians do before a big performance. Everyone has their own thing they think will give them good luck. Kjersten meditates, her viola perfectly balanced on her knees. Victoria clutches her guitar and prays, her lips moving soundlessly. Amari and Jamal do a cat's cradle with their lucky string, loosening up their fingers. If Jai were here, he'd be carefully resining his bow with exactly forty-two strokes.

My lucky thing, I guess, is looking at my mom's picture, still taped to the inside of my flute case. I open it up to see, but . . . there's something else there now, covering it up.

A familiar black note card.

Sucking in a breath, I peel it carefully away from the picture and turn it over, my stomach sinking. Nestled in the velvet beside the flute is the single dead rose.

Dear Miss Jones,

This is between you and me — so let's keep it that way.
I want the spell for the boy.
This is your last chance.
Tell anyone, especially those bumbling agents, and your friend pays the price.

CHAPTER THIRTY-ONE

Say It Isn't Solo

THE NECROMUSE HAS MY best friend.

He has *Jai.*

I stand in the dark folds of the stage curtain, numb from head to toe. Around me, the Mystwick students make way for the exiting Souza kids, who are clearing their instruments from the stage. But I'm rooted to the spot, unable to move even when a boy yells at me for blocking him and his tuba.

"Good luck, little girl," Luca D'Alessio says in my ear.

I look at him, barely hearing his words

"Whoa." He steps back. "You look *terrified.* Don't puke while you're out there."

Laughing, he throws an arm around one of his classmates and they leave out the side door. A cold gust of wind blows in when it slams shut, making my teeth chatter.

"Five minutes, Musicats!" Trevor calls out. "Set up, then tune up!"

"Let's do this!" says Kjersten. "This is it, team! This is where we win it all!" She drops her voice to a whisper. "I saw the judges' faces when Souza finished. They did *not* look impressed. His spell was weak, and they know it."

"If we just do this the way we practiced," Trevor adds, "that Crystal Lyre is *ours*. Mystwick will be the champions again!"

My teammates buzz with excitement as they set up for our performance.

But to me, their voices are like the distant drone from a TV. Don't they understand how terribly unimportant all this is now? That the Composium is the last thing they should be worrying about?

The Necromuse *took Jai.*

Phoebe pats my shoulder and says something. Then Kjersten tugs my sleeve, leading me onto the stage. I'm immediately blinded by a spotlight.

The Mystwick orchestra is set up, ready to perform. Pages rustle, instruments shine, people in the audience cough. None of it feels real.

And then, somehow, I find myself standing at the front of the stage, flute in hand, with hundreds of faces staring up at me. At the piano, Mia waits with a bored expression. Darby is poised with her baton, ready to Conduct. Everyone's there—Trevor, Phoebe, Rosa, Kjersten, Victoria, the twins.

Mrs. Le Roux, Mr. Pinwhistle, and Miss Motte look on from the wings. They're all waiting for me to start the spell. It's the Composer's job to announce the piece to the audience, then play the opening measures.

"Amelia!" Trevor hisses from the Percussos' section.

There's an empty chair in the violins, where Jai should be sitting.

Someone in the front row of the audience starts laughing.

"C'mon!" shouts a voice in the back. "Play!"

I can't breathe. The heat from the stage lights seems to burn my eyes.

"I—I can't," I gasp out. "I'm sorry."

With that, I turn and run, my flute in my hand.

A dozen Mystwick students jump up, calling to me, but I rush past them all, knocking over a music stand with a clang.

Before anyone can stop me, I shove open the back door and stumble into the backstage hallway.

Why hasn't the Necromuse sent a portal for me? Is he waiting somewhere nearby? Did I miss some sign? What if I have to wait until the next full moon? *Where* are those MBI agents, and why did they let him take Jai? They were supposed to protect all of us!

"Amelia!"

Miss Motte runs after me like a fluttering bird, her

assortment of scarves flowing behind her. Panting, she waves me down. "Cheese on a cracker, girl, let me catch my breath a minute. Tell me what's wrong."

"I—I can't."

"Can't what, dear?"

"Amelia!"

I whirl to see Agent Alvarez approaching, dressed in a housekeeping uniform.

"Is everything all right?" she asks. She pulls a small pan flute from her pocket, clearly ready for trouble.

Tell anyone, especially those bumbling agents, and your friend pays the price, the Necromuse wrote. He knows about the agents. Their trap is so much smoke in the wind. That he could grab Jai and leave a note *in my flute case* is proof of that. If I tell the adults . . . Jai could get hurt.

"I can't go up there," I say. "It's stage fright, that's all. I'm sorry, I just need be alone."

"Amelia!" Agent Alvarez raises a hand. "Wait!"

I run farther down the hallway, cutting left into the first open door I see—the green room where the Mystwick students left all their backpacks and instrument cases. I lock the door before anyone can come in, just so I can have a few minutes to think.

"Amelia!" Agent Alvarez pounds on the door.

"I'm fine!" I shout. "Just give me a few minutes, *please!*"

I hear Miss Motte whispering, and then the sound of their

footsteps as they leave. Finally. I sink down, my face in my hands.

He took Jai.

Fury rises in me. The Necromuse has been playing me for weeks with his notes and his portals and his "deals." He's messed with Mystwick, with my classmates and friends.

My angry spell spins in my mind till I'm dizzy with it. Miss Motte called it my *power,* but I don't know what to *do* with it. Jai's beyond my reach. I'm helpless.

With a growl, I kick the wall, rattling the pictures hanging there. Rows and rows of previous Trials winners smile down at me, lifting the Crystal Lyre.

My heart stops.

I press my fingertips to one of the pictures, which has a small plaque under it reading CHAMPIONS: THE MYSTWICK SCHOOL OF MUSICRAFT.

It was taken the year before Mystwick lost to Souza's tampering. And their Composer that year?

My mom.

She grins in the photo, surrounded by a crowd of students in Mystwick blazers, the Lyre in her hand. They're celebrating their victory, their shoulders sprinkled with confetti, balloons all around.

Among them is my dad, standing off to one side, a small smile on his face.

My finger trails down the photo to his hand, which clutches a violin, and then stops.

I never knew my dad played violin.

Something uneasy turns in my stomach, a strange feeling . . . Shaking my head, I push it away and turn around. My fingers grip my hair as I try to keep from spinning into senseless panic. What do I do to save Jai? What *can* I do?

I *hate* feeling powerless.

Power.

That's what I need—the power to make everything right. The power to save Jai.

And I know where I can get that power.

Amelia, it seems you've found a mighty source of fuel, Miss Motte had told me.

For weeks—no, *years*—I've avoided the anger I feel toward my dad. I pushed it down, pretended it wasn't there. But now I need to *feed* that anger. I need to stoke it into a raging inferno until I have enough power to rip Jai out of the Necromuse's hands if I have to. If that's what it takes . . . I'd do anything to save Jai. *Anything.*

I look back at my dad in the picture. Then my eyes slide to everyone's bags on the floor. I toss through them until I find Miss Motte's tie-dye tote bag. My heart fluttering, I take a peek inside.

The yellow folder is there, just as I'd suspected.

I don't want to open it. I don't want to remember. I definitely don't want to learn new things about him.

But Jai needs me, and there is nothing else I can do to help him.

Taking the folder out with shaking fingers, I open it and begin leafing through the pages. My abdomen clenches with distaste, but I press on, seeing my dad's name over and over. There are class schedules, report cards—with mostly failing grades—disciplinary sheets. He skipped class a *lot,* and curfew just as much. On one page I find a handwritten note from some bygone Maestro.

ERIC IS A GENIUS; UNFORTUNATELY, HE KNOWS IT.

I swallow hard and keep leafing through. One of the disciplinary sheets catches my eye. He got three months of detention for playing an ice spell *into* the pipes running beneath Mystwick, causing the magic to spread across the whole campus—and completely covering the school in ice.

My body goes cold.

The squirmy feeling returns, just like when I saw him holding the violin in the photo above.

My heart beginning to race, my hands clammy, I keep searching, faster now, through more disciplinary reports, detention logs, test scores. I tear pages out and let them fall to the floor. In the back of the folder I find a sheet that simply reads DISMISSED DUE TO ABSENCE. THE STUDENT'S ECHO TREE HAS BEEN UPROOTED ACCORDING TO PROTOCOL. That must have been when he dropped out. I remember Mrs. Le Roux once telling me that if a student is expelled, their tree is forcibly removed from the Echo Wood, to ensure that they can never return to the campus.

There's one more sheet in the folder, some kind of legal document. I frown, not sure what it is.

Then I see it.

My hand shakes so badly I drop the page. I back away from the folder, the pages scattered across the floor. Looking again at the picture on the wall, I stare at his face, the violin in his hands.

My heart feels like it's being squeezed.

No, no no no no no . . .

I think back over the last few weeks, every clue, every little hint I completely missed. But the pieces fall together so quickly and easily that I wonder how I ever missed it. How I was so *stupid.*

The document on the floor flutters in the draft blowing through a floor vent. The words on it seem so mundane, a mess of jargon and big legal words. But hidden in them, like a thorn in the leaves, is a single sentence:

Eric Neal is hereby Barred from Musicraft in all its forms in perpetuity.

Barred.

My dad was *Barred.*

The date of the document is one year after my mom died. Sick to my stomach, I read it again, to be sure it's real.

You will Compose for me a spell to raise the dead, the Necromuse's voice echoes in my memory. *This magic must come from you. It was always you.*

Now I know why he targeted me, how he knew where to find me, why he was so interested in the ghost-summoning spell I Composed. I even know why he really wants a resurrection spell—and why he thinks *I* have to be the one to play it.

Because the Necromuse . . . is my dad.

CHAPTER THIRTY-TWO

Do Re Mia

SHARP KNOCKING RATTLES ME from my daze.

I look at the door, numb to the bone, with no idea how long I've been sitting here staring into space. The world is unreal and distant while I seem to be floating a hundred miles up in the air. My breathing is stalled; my heart has forgotten how to beat.

The Necromuse is my dad.

My dad is the Necromuse.

The person at the door knocks again.

Shuddering, I bolt into action, gathering up the incriminating papers and shoving them into a trash can. I don't know if Miss Motte read them all, but if not, I don't want her to. I don't want anyone to know what I know. The last thing I need is everyone looking at me and seeing the Necromuse's daughter.

So what's the plan, Amelia?

What do I do now?

How do I save Jai? How do I make everything right?

I have this anger inside of me, this power Miss Motte says I have to control, but I don't yet know what to do with it. Maybe if I knew where Jai was, I could Compose something to free him. But I have no idea where that might be, or even where to start.

The knocking gets louder, as if the person on the other side of the door is panicking.

"I just need a minute!" I call out.

"Amelia, it's me! Please let me in!"

Darby?

I go to the door, cracking it open.

"What's going on?" she whispers, her dark eyes wide with concern. "And don't tell me it's just stage fright. Something's seriously wrong, isn't it?"

My anger at her for telling Mia my secrets has evaporated over the last few minutes. I can't afford more enemies right now; what I really need is a friend. I don't know if I *should* trust Darby, but at that moment I choose to anyway.

"I need help," I whisper. "I don't know what to do."

"What happened?"

Tearing up, I open the door fully to let her in, then shut it behind her. "The Necromuse took Jai. He left this."

I show her the note.

She looks at it for a long moment, her hand over her lips. "Do the Maestros know?"

"No, and they can't know. You saw what he wrote."

She nods. "Where do we start?"

"We?"

"We're going to get him back, Amelia. Don't you doubt that."

Tears well in my eyes. "You'll help me?"

"Of course I will. Look, I don't know why you've been angry with me these past few days, but I'm still your friend, and Jai's too. We'll save him together."

I throw my arms around her, not caring that she can feel how badly I'm shaking. I almost tell her the rest of the truth—that the Necromuse is my dad—but I bite my tongue at the last minute and instead whisper, "Thank you."

She pats my shoulder. Darby's not a hugger. "What's your plan?"

"I don't know." Sniffing, I pull back. "The Necromuse must be waiting for me somewhere, but I've only ever reached him through a portal *he* sent for me. I don't get how he took Jai at all, with the agents and Maestros on high alert. He managed to slip that note into my flute case—which has been with me the entire time. How did he get close enough to . . ."

Something tickles in the back of my mind, and I tilt my head, focusing on it.

"What?" Darby says, seeing my expression change. "What is it?"

"Agent Alvarez said something about the Necromuse maybe having someone on the inside. Meaning someone at Mystwick could have been helping him all along . . ."

My voice slows as a terrible idea dawns.

Darby and I match gazes.

"His specialty is bringing people back from the dead and making them work for him," I whisper. "Do we know someone like that? Someone who was gone, then *wasn't?* Someone who shouldn't have turned up . . . but did?"

Her eyelashes flutter as she shakes her head. "No, Amelia. *No.*"

"Darby. Do you know why I was mad at you all week?"

She keeps shaking her head, her eyes starting to water.

"I was mad because I thought you told Mia everything about the Midnight Orchestra and the Necromuse. Only . . . you *didn't* tell her, did you?"

The blood drains from her face. And I know I'm right.

"Because Mia knows. She knows *everything.*" My voice shaking, I say what has to be said. "Darby, what if Mia—"

"What if Mia *what?*" asks a voice.

Darby and I jump as the door opens again and Mia slips inside. Her hair is tied up with a black ribbon, and her black performance dress is threaded with tiny crystals, so she sparkles when she moves.

"I'm not *dead,* if that's what you think," Mia says. "And I'm definitely not a zombie."

She leans on the door, her arms folded, as Darby and I back away. My heart beats faster, and I look around the room. There are no other doors.

Darby draws a deep breath. "Mia, what's going on?"

"Why couldn't you just *stay away* from her?" sighs Mia. "I told you again and again—that girl is trouble."

"Amelia's my friend," Darby breathes. "What are *you?*"

"I'm who I've always been," Mia says. "I swear it."

"*You* opened the portals to the Midnight Orchestra," I say. "It was you all along."

The glass piano in the woods, the keys swirling around the portal . . . I should have guessed that *she* was behind the magic.

Mia glances at me, then back at Darby. "All I ever wanted, Darbs, was to keep you safe. You have to believe me. You were never supposed to get involved."

"Involved in *what?*" Darby asks. "Is Amelia right? Are you somehow connected to the Necromuse?"

Mia swallows, and for the first time since I met her, she looks unsure of what to say.

"I know you're hiding something from me," Darby says. "I knew it the day you appeared at Mystwick, acting like everything was normal. I knew it when you refused to tell me how you ended up shipwrecked. You're keeping secrets, and I guess that's not strange for you, but this time it feels different. You've changed, Mia. You're paranoid and . . . *mean,* like you never were before. And I don't know why. I want to help you, but you won't be honest with me!"

Mia looks ready to explode. I cringe, bracing for the eruption . . . but it doesn't come.

Instead, Mia *wilts.*

Her face crumples. Her shoulders slump. And I see the last thing I ever expected to see—Mia Jones *crying.*

Are the tears real or another manipulation? I have no idea. But Darby softens, putting a hand on Mia's arm.

"Sh-she doesn't deserve your help," sniffles Mia, shooting me a hateful look through her tears. "I know things you don't. I know things about *her.*"

I go stiff, eyes wide.

She couldn't possibly know . . .

My secret, my new secret that's so huge and terrible and ugly, pounds in my head till my vision blurs.

Does Mia know who my dad really is?

"Tell me, Mia," Darby says softly. "What is going on?"

I shut my eyes, bracing for the worst.

But instead of blurting out my terrible secret, Mia says, "You're right, Darbs. I didn't tell you the whole story about my shipwreck. Or why I'm really at Mystwick, or why all of it is *her* fault."

Mia's eyes glitter with angry tears as she continues. "If you understood, you wouldn't judge me. But you don't know what it's like to grow up with parents who only see you as a cash cow. You don't know what it's like to have your mom inject your aching wrists with steroids so you can put on another performance. You don't know what it's like to never be allowed to *rest,* to just be yourself, to take a break from performing and practicing and photo ops. That's why we went on that yachting trip. I needed an escape, a few weeks to just *exist* without constantly being put on display."

"What *happened?*" Darby presses.

"We were on the yacht, just sailing along, when this storm comes out of nowhere." She pauses, her face crumpling as she relives the memory. "It was bad. Really bad. I jumped on the piano and tried to play a weather-calming spell, but it's like someone was actively fighting me, making the storm stronger. I could hear, over the thunder and the waves, the sound of an *orchestra.*"

"The Midnight Orchestra?"

Mia nods. "Then *he* appeared, the Necromuse, playing his

awful violin. He split my piano in two, and it was over. Our yacht sank.

"We all survived, of course. I don't know whether he meant for that to happen or not, but my parents and I woke up the next day on the island. We spent the next three months stuck there. And then, out of the blue, the Necromuse shows up again and tells me he has a job for me."

"What job?" whispers Darby.

Mia points at me. "Her. I was ordered to go to Mystwick and open a portal to send this other Amelia Jones to the Midnight Orchestra. So I did that, but it didn't end there. He kept giving me new orders, and I've had no choice but to carry them out."

"The ice spell," Darby murmurs. "It was *you* who froze Mystwick."

"And you planted the earworms," I say, realization dawning.

I think back to that day, remembering Mia covered in dirt. But I *don't* remember actually seeing her digging a grave. She could have been hiding the whole time.

"And the cards on my pillow," I whisper. "You put them there. And you played the hallucination spell so the Maestros wouldn't believe me about the orchestra."

Suddenly I understand everything.

All this time, Mia was trying to keep Darby safe. She knew

the Necromuse had set his sights on me, and she didn't want her best friend caught in the cross fire—the way Jai was. All the mean remarks she made to me, the angry looks, the bullying . . . was because he had turned *her* life upside down to get to *me.*

Still, one thing doesn't make sense.

"Why did the Necromuse maroon you in the first place," I ask, "then abandon you for three months? He couldn't have known I was a Composer then. *I* didn't even know. So it couldn't have been because he wanted to use you to trap me."

"I don't know. That's the part I can't figure out."

"Why are you helping him?" asks Darby.

"I had no choice! He has my mom." Mia shivers. "That's what the Midnight Orchestra really is—people he's taken as hostages to make people like us do his dirty work. That's why they look like zombies, playing so perfectly. They're being controlled by earworms. It's like they're in a deep trance, *always,* until their loved one on the outside does whatever job the Necromuse has asked of them. But some of them have been in the orchestra so long, they're presumed dead to the outside world."

"That explains the whole *army of the dead* thing," I whisper. "The rumors about the Necromuse are true, in a way. And now he has Jai too."

"If I finish the job he gave me," Mia says, "he'll release my mom and I'll never have to deal with him again."

"What does he want from you next?" I ask, sickened with dread and guilt.

"He wants me to send *you* back to him. Only I can't do that now, can I? Because someone, like an *idiot,* told the Maestros everything." She fixes me with a glare that could melt icebergs. "And now those MBI agents have locked down every piano in this place because they suspect someone is using them to help the Necromuse. If you'd kept your mouth shut, you'd already be with the orchestra, and this would all be over!"

She doesn't know.

I feel at least a touch of relief that Mia is apparently still unaware that the Necromuse is my *dad.*

"What will happen to Jai if I don't reach him in time?" I ask.

She shrugs. "Maybe we'll never find out. Jai and my mom are long gone."

"No. No no no—you *will* send me to the Necromuse, and you'll do it now! I can't leave Jai all alone!"

Darby lays her hand on my arm. "Maybe we should tell the Maestros. He could be bluffing."

"No. I can't put Jai in more danger."

"The Maestros won't find the orchestra anyway," scoffs Mia. "Neither will the MBI agents. Are you kidding? He's been doing this for *years* and nobody's caught him. He'll only be found when he wants to be."

"*You* know the spell to find him," I point out. "You could tell it to Agent Alvarez and Agent Ned."

She folds her arms. "And risk him hurting my mom for double-crossing him? Yeah? Not gonna happen. We play by his rules, or we don't play at all."

It really does have to be me.

If I'm going to save Jai, I have to do the thing I've been avoiding for years—I have to face my dad.

"She's right," I say. "If I don't show up, he could go into hiding, and we might never get Jai back, or Mia's mom. It has to be me. Mia, how can we open that portal?"

She looks stunned, as if she'd expected me to run or put up a fight—not *help* her finish her dirty work. But there's no time to be angry at her for the part she played. It's not like I can blame her anyway. We've wasted enough precious minutes as it is. I need to get to Jai *now.*

I grab her shoulders. "*Mia!* Think!"

Startled, she shrugs. "I need a piano, and they're all—"

"You're supposed to be a prodigy, right? Can't you think outside the box?"

Mia looks around the room, but it's pitifully bare. There's a table and chairs, the photos on the wall, the Mystwick team's backpacks and empty instrument cases, and a bunch of glasses, pitchers of water, and fruit trays to keep everyone fed.

"You'll really give the Necromuse the spell he wants?" Darby asks me.

I shake my head. "Not if there's another way. Not if I can . . . figure something out."

"Like what?"

Like use the only advantage I have left—the fact that I know who the Necromuse really is.

Not that I'm going to tell *her* that.

"I'll work that out once we get there. Mia. Any ideas?"

Her eyes fix on something across the room, and a slow, sly smile spreads across her face. "Hey, Darby? Remember the fireworks spell we played at my parent's fifteenth wedding anniversary? Or rather, do you remember *how* we played it?"

Darby's eyes widen. "You don't mean . . . Mia, that's impossible!"

"Didn't you hear?" Mia cracks her knuckles. "I'm a *prodigy*."

CHAPTER THIRTY-THREE

A Spell as Smooth as Glissando

BEWILDERED ABOUT WHATEVER PLAN they cooked up via their best-friend telepathy hotline, I stand and watch as Darby and Mia arrange dozens of glasses on the conference table.

"Uh . . . how is playing tea party going to help?"

Mia picks up one of the pitchers and starts pouring water, paying close attention to the amount in each cup.

"It's a glass harp," says Darby. "Since we don't have access to a piano, this will have to do. It's a weird instrument, but it's also one of the strongest ever created. Something to do with the way the water affects the sound—it amplifies the magic. Making it perfect for portal spells."

Still confused, I bite my tongue and watch them finish filling the glasses. When they're done, they step back and exchange grins.

"Just like we did at my parents' party," says Mia. "If I play the spell, can you bring the harmony?"

Darby nods, looking nervous. "But Mia—"

"No time," Mia says. "We have to make this work before the Maestros figure out what we're doing. Ready, Wondergirl?"

I look up. "For what?"

"Even if this works, the portal will probably be small and weak. We'll have to jump through it before it collapses."

"We?"

"I'm coming with you. I have to make sure he frees my mom."

I nod, my heart jumping like a grasshopper in a frying pan, and sling my flute case over my shoulder.

"Here we go!" says Mia as she begins dragging her finger around the rim of a glass. A high, sweet note sounds out. She runs through a few measures, teasing out the melody. "Got it?"

"Yep." Darby begins playing too, adding harmonies. The girls' hands carefully move between glasses, the notes coming faster and faster. The sound is crystalline and sweet, high treble notes that begin to produce faint purple lights.

"Is this safe?" I ask.

"Well, the guy who invented the glass harp *did* die in a fire when his spell went sideways," says Mia, grinning nastily.

"We have no choice," says Darby, concentrating hard. "It's the only way to reach Jai."

The music is eerie and almost *too* sweet, the glass harp's tone as delicate as a spider's web. I wonder how such fragile sound can possibly open a doorway through space-time.

Purple magic rises like steam from the glasses. It spreads foggily through the room and gathers on the other side of the table.

"We need more magic," says Mia through gritted teeth.

"Amelia!" Darby says. "Give us more harmony!"

"I don't know how—"

"Do it, or the spell's as good as dead!"

The fourth rule of Musicraft. *The more who join into the spell, the greater will its power swell.*

Swallowing hard, I put my hands down and tentatively drag my fingers over the rim of the nearest glass. A discordant note sounds out, and Mia growls. But I try the next one and hear it harmonize with the melody she's playing.

Harmony adds strength to a spell without changing its actual purpose. So I find my way through the music, adding tones here and there to support the melody, and as I figure out which glasses play what notes, my confidence grows. Soon, all three of us are playing, fingertips and palms moving over the glasses as delicately as if they were made of . . . well, glass.

Purple lights spin around us, brightening as the magic of the spell strengthens. Magic dust sparkles on the rims and spills over onto the table. The air is fuzzy with the stuff.

Then, on the other side of the table, a sliver of white light shines in the air—a tear in the fabric of space.

"Yes!" Mia cries. "More, give me more! We're nearly to the end!"

I've never worked so hard to be so delicate. One clumsy move and I could dash away half the glasses, shattering them and spilling the water inside. If that happened, the portal might fail and Jai would be lost forever.

Sweat beads my face and stings my eyes, but I can't afford to wipe it away. I can only play on, drawing music from this strange instrument while sandwiched between Darby and Mia. They look as strained as I feel, Darby pale and sweating, Mia's teeth clenched and her eyes blazing.

"That's it, that's it," Mia says. "C'mon, last measures . . ."

As we near the end of the spell, the magic around us grows more and more unstable. A glass tips over and shatters. The tear opens wider, and wind rushes into it as it pulls the air from the room.

"Almost there!" shouts Mia. "Whatever you do, don't stop playing!"

The portals widens, opening reluctantly, as purple lightning crackles around it.

At that moment, someone starts pounding on the green room door.

"Amelia?" calls Mrs. Le Roux. "What's going on in there?"

"Hold . . . *on* . . ." Mia shouts. *"Just a bit more . . ."*

All at once, the portal snaps into a perfect circle, the sides stabilizing.

"Amelia Jones!" the headmaestro shouts.

"GO!" Mia roars.

I dive across the table, scattering glasses, and throw myself into the portal. Tumbling head over heels, I drop through a tunnel of swirling colors.

CHAPTER THIRTY-FOUR

Going for Baroque

THIS ISN'T LIKE THE other times I went through the portal, which were a matter of stepping from one place into another with little more than a slight chill.

This time, the magic is chaotic and unstable. I'm buffeted around as I fall. My heart lifts into my throat, and my organs jumble around as if they're being stirred into soup. If I'm screaming, I can't hear it over the rushing wind around me. All I can think is that if Mia screwed up the spell, I'll be forever falling through space-time, like a mouse trapped in the walls between rooms, never to land.

Then, suddenly, I collide with something solid, the wind punched from my lungs. My vision goes starry.

I hear thumps on either side of me. Darby and Mia must have made the jump too.

The blurry colors around us condense into solid shapes—walls, windows, doors, furniture. I blink away the lights in my vision and make out the other girls lying on the floor, groaning. I'm slumped against a wall, my hair a frizzy mess and my clothes rumpled, but a quick check reveals that all my body parts have come with me. Thank Bach. The portal is gone, collapsed almost as quickly as it opened.

Darby pushes her hair back and stares wide-eyed at the ground, like she can't believe we made it.

Mia grins smugly. "Piece of cake," she says. "Now, just need to figure out . . ."

". . . where we are," I finish.

We're in a huge lobby of some kind, with windows boarded over and large double doors barred from the inside. Stained, moldy carpet covers the floor, and faded, peeling wallpaper hangs in tattered sheets, revealing glimpses of chipped brick walls. Old velvet chairs are scattered around, tipped over, most of them broken, and the Turkish rug under our feet is almost gray with age.

I stand up, brushing dust from my black pants.

"It's a box office," murmurs Darby, pointing to a booth with glass windows, the panes either shattered or glazed with a thick layer of dust and grime. On either side of it are two arched doorways covered in moth-eaten red curtains.

"This place was pretty glamorous once," says Mia. She lifts the corner of a poster that's peeling off the wall. It's hard to read the faded ink, but it appears to be an advertisement for an opera called *Orpheus and Eurydice.* I remember studying it in our opera section of Musicraft history. It's the story of the god of music, Orpheus, whose beloved Eurydice is killed, so he journeys to the underworld to try to bring her back to life.

Spoiler alert: it doesn't end happily.

I shiver.

Darby gives a low whistle. "It's dated 1941. This place has been closed for a long time."

A thump sounds from the other side of the room, and all three of us shriek.

Clutching Darby's arm, I stare as one of the thick curtains rustles aside to reveal Mr. Stewart, dressed in his tux jacket and kilt. He thumps his cane again.

"Come," he rasps. "He is waiting."

As we walk across the ruined lobby toward Mr. Stewart, Darby whispers, "You know we're walking into a trap, right?"

"Yep," I reply.

"And you know there's really no reason the Necromuse couldn't just take us *all* prisoner?"

"Yep."

"*And* you know that nobody knows where we are or how to find us?"

"You're starting to sound like Jai," I point out, feeling a pang.

"Have you figured out a plan yet, Wondergirl?" Mia asks.

My voice shoots up an octave. "Nope!"

Mr. Stewart holds aside the curtain, allowing us to step into an enormous concert hall. The place is in worse shape than the lobby. Dust covers the thousands of velvet seats arcing around a grand stage. The peeling walls and the upper balcony look ready to cave in, and large swaths of fraying blue silk that had been pinned to the ceiling now hang in tatters. On the stage, ragged curtains frame a painted backdrop depicting an ancient Grecian city, the colors faded to pastels. Wooden beams hang down like sagging tree branches, and on the floor, old bricks, cloth, and broken furniture are piled beneath layers of dust.

But the Midnight Orchestra, arranged neatly on the stage, is spotless.

"Jai!" I shout, catching sight of my friend. He sits in the violin section, his instrument propped on his knee. He's wearing the same creepy doll mask as the other musicians—or *hostages,* rather—but I don't need to see his face in order to recognize those ears. He's clearly in a trance, no doubt thanks to an earworm. Every one of the hostages sits as still as a statue, almost lifeless.

"Wait, is that your mom?" Darby whispers to Mia, pointing at the masked pianist.

Mia nods, her eyes hard. "She always wanted to be a

concert pianist, but she didn't have the talent," she says bitterly. "I guess she got her wish, in a way."

Once I've seen that Jai is present and breathing, I can focus on the figure standing in front of the orchestra. My eyes slide to him, full of dread.

Mr. Midnight.

The Necromuse.

Dad.

He's dressed in a black suit, his mask white porcelain from his nose to his forehead. Before, his masks had covered his whole face, but this time I can see the scruffy beard on his jaw and the grim line of his mouth. His dark hair is combed to mostly cover his ears, hiding the Bars I now know are there. In his hands he holds his violin and bow, the latter lightly, rhythmically tapping his leg.

Our footsteps echo in the tattered concert hall as we walk down the aisle. We're grouped close together, with Darby in the middle. I don't even remember grabbing her hand. I squeeze her fingers so hard her bones practically crunch.

I have so many questions.

How long has he been the Necromuse? Does anyone else know his real name? How many people has he kidnapped over the years?

Has he ever thought of me?

Has he ever regretted leaving?

We stop in front of the stage, staring up at that blank white mask. Dad sure doesn't *look* regretful. He looks as emotionless as a gargoyle.

My heart drums in my chest. My flute, still tucked inside my coat, feels as heavy as lead.

"Miss Jones, you've come to bring me my spell."

I nod once, my mouth too dry to speak.

Darby gives me a sideways look, eyebrows raised. I return a small, tight smile, hoping she can see I'm not serious. I'm just buying time. Every minute is precious, another chance to spark an epiphany of what, exactly, I *am* going to do. Because I honestly have no plan, no idea, no clue how to get Jai and the three of us safely away from here—and still do something to help Mia's mom and the other hostages. Every one of those people is someone's father or mother or son or daughter, a person probably dearly missed. Mia told me that some of them have even been presumed dead, they've been missing for so long.

Revulsion surges in me, hot and spiked. That man may be my father, but he's also a monster who has hurt a lot of people.

It won't be enough to simply escape.

He has to be stopped.

Dad gestures toward a curving stair on the side of the stage. I take a deep breath, nod to Darby and Mia, then walk up alone, nervously running my fingers over the keys of my flute. The wooden stairs creak under my shoes.

On the stage, I pause, staring at Dad across the expanse of floorboards between us. He waits motionlessly.

My hands are sweating. I wipe them on my pants, but the flute is still slippery in my grasp. Swallowing hard, I take a few steps closer, as cautious as if I were crossing a thin layer of ice over a deep river. Every footfall sends creaks and pops echoing through the old floorboards.

Finally I stop a few feet away and stare at his shiny black shoes.

"Give me my spell, Miss Jones, and we can part ways with no more trouble. You can see that your friend is unharmed. But to ensure his continued safety, you must pay off your debt to me."

For the first time I can remember, I look at my father. *Really* look at him, face-to-face—or *mask,* I suppose—as I've always been too afraid to do in the past, even when he was just a memory. Now here he is, real and in person, the shadow that's lurked behind me sprung fully to life. Out in the light at last.

I look at him, and I realize . . . I understand him.

Once I look past the mask, the drama of the ruined concert hall, and the orchestra of mind-controlled people, behind the grandeur and mystery he's built around himself, the names—Mr. Midnight, the Necromuse, whatever else he's been—and I just look at *him* . . .

I see a broken, desperate man.

I've glimpsed him before, under the northern lights, when he leaned close and told me he wanted me to raise the dead for him. But I hadn't fully understood what he was saying, or what—or rather, *who*—he really wanted.

He wants Mom.

That has to be why he's doing all this: the hostages, the shady deals, the whole Midnight Orchestra thing . . . it's all part of his quest to find a spell that will raise my mom from the dead.

For the first time, I really, truly understand.

It wasn't my fault.

He didn't leave because of anything I did, or because mom died saving me, or because I was broken or not worth staying for.

His leaving had nothing to do with me at all.

He left because *he* was broken, because *he* felt guilty, because *he* was scared and desperate and heartbroken.

My dad left, and it's *not my fault.*

Deep inside me, something heavy crumbles.

More than anger, more than sadness, it was *guilt* weighing me down. I really have been blaming myself for my dad leaving, thinking something must have been wrong with me. Thinking I didn't *deserve* to feel angry at him.

Now it's like wings are sprouting from my back, and suddenly I can fly.

This is why I've been unable to face my anger, to feel it, to let it out the way Miss Motte wanted me to. This is why I couldn't Compose. This is why I was afraid for so long.

The guilt was in the way. But the guilt was a lie.

And now the lie is gone.

Heat against my leg draws my attention, and I peek into my pocket. The mood bead Miss Motte gave me backstage is blazing red—just like the beads that day in her cottage. The day the memory-recall spell took me back to my childhood with my dad.

And now that bead burns brighter and hotter than ever.

With strength like that, Miss Motte told me, *you might Compose a spell to stop time itself.*

Suddenly I know exactly what to do.

I have all the power I need.

"All right," I whisper, raising my flute and looking my father in the eyes. "Here's your spell."

CHAPTER THIRTY-FIVE

A Riff in Time

THERE'S MUSIC INSIDE YOU, *Amelia Jones, that's aching to be let out.*

As usual, Miss Motte was right.

I know what notes to play; I know because they've been singing in my soul for weeks, maybe even years, like the *drip drip drip* of a leaky pipe. Over time, their power has grown like a rising flood.

There's plenty of anger in me, and I pour it into my flute.

Before, when I'd felt this much fury, I pushed it away. Feeling it meant feeling the guilt I was too scared to face. So I'd stuffed it in a box and clamped a lid over it, hoping to find another way . . . but everything I tried only made things worse.

Now here I am, with nothing *but* my anger, ugly and hot and true, and this time I can't be afraid of it. It's power I've kept trapped inside for years, music I've never had the courage to play. But now there's no guilt to hold me back from it.

My spell is so big and hungry, it demands more. The magic begins pulling at *me,* trying to drain my strength away, so I reach deeper, searching, prying up sadness and pain that has been buried for years, flinging it into the spell's ravenous mouth. Things I'd pretended didn't hurt. Moments I'd almost forgotten now come tumbling out of the shadows.

Every Father's Day, when Gran tried to distract me by taking me out for ice cream. Career day at school when everyone else's dad showed up to talk about their jobs. The father-daughter dance in fifth grade, when I had to awkwardly waltz with the principal, Mr. Hodgekiss. All my birthdays, awards ceremonies, swim meets and basketball games and art shows, the concerts and recitals.

I know my dad by the holes he left in my life.

I know him by the empty chairs where he should have been sitting.

I know him by what he's not.

That's what I pour into my spell.

My chest aches from feeling so much at once. All the words I've kept bottled up become notes in my flute. The music is everything I am: tight and angry and sad and uneven. It's not a particularly pretty piece, and my playing isn't going to win any competitions, but I've already learned that it's more important to be genuine than to be perfect.

As if he can read the words behind the music, my father takes a small step backwards, his lips parting below the edge of his mask.

Or maybe he's just reacting to the magic that tumbles from my flute.

It comes all at once—no gradual glow or trickle of sparks. Instead, a cascade of light erupts from my instrument and spreads through the air, misty fog the color of violets, smelling of burning plastic.

Time magic.

"What—" He lifts a hand, glittering purple light pooling on his palm and draining through his fingers. "What is this?"

He wants Mom? I'll give him Mom.

Just not the way he expects.

Take us to her, I tell the music. *Show him what he lost. Show him who she was.*

My magic is like a combination of the time-window spell I played in the Composing classroom and the memory-recall spell Luca D'Alessio created. At least that's how I want it to play out. As usual, I push my magic in the direction I want it to go, but there's always a point where it takes on a life of its own.

As my melody deepens, the lights pouring from my flute begin swirling between me and my dad, a tight, glowing sphere that spins dizzyingly fast.

"Enough!" orders my dad. "What are you doing? You'll give me what I asked for, Miss Jones, or your friend will remain in my orchestra for—"

He shouts as the ball of light suddenly expands outward, enveloping us both in its hazy glow. My eyes grow wide, and after one final, piercing note, I lower the flute, panting.

The two of us stand inside a bubble of filmy lavender light, the walls of the sphere translucent and sparkling like a net of stars. Outside the spell, Darby and Mia stand at the stage's edge, Darby reaching up toward me. But something's not right.

It's like they're both *frozen.*

Mr. Stewart isn't moving either, nor any of the orchestra members.

Outside the bubble, I realize, time has stopped completely. Or rather, *we've* slipped outside of time.

"What is this?" whispers my dad. He pushes a hand to the wall of the bubble, but though it stretches a bit under his palm, it doesn't break. A network of lights spread outward from his touch, like glowing veins.

"I don't know," I answer truthfully.

It looks a little like the time window—the color and burning plastic smell of the magic is the same. But this is no window. It's more like a snow globe, with my dad and me trapped inside.

"Hey!" someone shouts.

My dad and I both whirl around to see a boy sitting cross-legged on the stage behind us, just inside the bubble's edge.

Dressed in a black hoodie and jeans, he's got a violin propped on his lap, and he shakes back his shaggy dark hair to peer at something offstage.

Oooookay.

That kid was definitely not there a minute ago.

And even weirder—he's *see-through.*

Not like, invisible. Just kinda hazy, like he's a hologram or . . . a ghost. And what's more, he doesn't seem to see us at all. His eyes pass right through me without a hint of surprise or awareness.

My dad's reaction is stronger. He gives a little strained gasp. I can see his teeth clench under the edge of his mask.

The boy stands up, pointing his bow like a sword. "Come out where I can see you!" he orders. His voice sounds wavy, like it's echoing underwater. "I know someone's sneaking around back there."

I glance at the tattered curtains, which begin to ripple, and then out from behind them steps a girl dressed in overalls and a bright pink headband.

At first glance, it's like looking in a mirror. But this girl's hair is darker, and she's shorter than I am. And there's a very familiar flute case slung over her shoulder.

Mom!

Which means . . .

The boy is my dad, Eric.

"Who are you?" the boy demands, lowering his bow but looking at my mom suspiciously. They're both no older than I am, maybe even a little younger.

"I'm Susie," says the girl. Like the boy, she's slightly see-through. "I heard you playing. You're pretty good. What's your name?"

"You're not supposed to be in here."

"Neither are you."

This isn't just any old day. This is the day they *met!* Right here in this moldy old concert hall. And here I stand, watching my parents meet for the first time, as clear as if I were there.

My dad didn't choose this place randomly. It has meaning for him.

I look at my dad. He's staring at the pair of kids like they're, well, ghosts. Which they aren't, of course. They're as real as we are, seen through time the way I'd seen my dad in the Composing classroom. Only instead of viewing them through a window, we're *in* their time, or at least halfway there. The two kids can't see us or hear us. It's kind of like a scene from *A Christmas Carol,* with me, I guess, as the Ghost of My Parents' Past.

"You shouldn't be in here," young Eric says to young Susie.

She shrugs, plopping herself down on the edge of the stage and swinging her legs. Her toes nearly clip Darby in the nose; my friend is still frozen outside the time bubble's walls. "I was looking for someplace to practice before my audition

later. Saw this place, figured it'd be empty. Then I heard your spell."

"Well, it's *my* place. I got here first, so you can shove off."

"Don't you want to know what I'm auditioning for?"

"No."

She leans toward him, eyes sparkling. "It's called the Mystwick School of Musicraft. It's the most wonderful school in the—"

"I've heard of it. Snooty school for snooty kids."

Susie raises an eyebrow in an expression so much my mom's that it hurts. "Then *you* should have no problem getting in." Seeing his scowl, she laughs and pats the stage beside her. "Come play a duet with me."

"Huh? Why?"

"It'll be fun!"

"Are you always this annoying?"

"Are you always this much of a scaredy-butt?" Susie takes out the flute—the same flute I'm holding now—and slides the joints together.

"I'm not a—how *dare* you—"

She begins playing, but the sound is muted and warped; I can't even tell what spell it is. I think the time spell that brought us here must be breaking down, getting weaker. Their bodies are starting to be more see-through, their edges blurring away.

Eric—the younger one—must recognize the music,

because he relents, raises his violin, and begins playing with her. Within seconds, they're both smiling, as their spell takes effect and blue magic begins swirling around them.

The walls of the time bubble start shimmering, further proof that the spell is weakening. Outside its bounds, Darby and Mia start moving in really, *really* slow motion, as if time is just starting to flow again. Darby's fingers push through the air, and Mia's eyes grow wider and wider.

We don't have long before the spell breaks completely.

My dad doesn't seem to notice the weakening magic around us. Instead, he stares at the two kids on the edge of the stage as they play their duet, their spell conjuring a small ship of glowing magic that sails in circles around them.

Slowly, he reaches up and removes his mask.

I suck in a breath, a splinter running through me as I see his face for the first time in eight years.

He's got a long nose, sharp cheekbones, dark eyes chiseled deep, and thick black eyebrows that scrunch together. His scruffy beard is short and speckled with gray, and a deep worry line carves down the center of his forehead.

How can he look so familiar and so strange at the same time?

"How long have you known who I am?" he asks.

I swallow hard. "Not long."

We look at each other for a minute. And despite everything he's done, and how much anger I have for him, in that moment, all I want in the world is for him to . . .

Impossible, silly pictures fill my head—of all of this going away and him telling me he's sorry, that he actually loved me all this time, that everything will be different now and he's going to stay and we'll make things be okay, and we'll be a family again.

Silly, stupid Amelia. Obviously that won't happen. Obviously he's more broken and messed up than I can imagine, and anyway, it's not like he's just been off on some road trip for the last eight years.

He's the *Necromuse.*

That's not something you just walk away from with an apology and a trip to the ice-cream shop.

Dad looks back at the kids, his eyebrows pulling even tighter together. If he *is* sorry, even the tiniest bit, there's no sign of it on his face. "Then you must know why I need that spell."

"I know why you want it," I whisper.

His jaw is tight, and a vein in his temple visibly tics. "She was the best thing—the *only* good thing—I ever had."

I look at my mom's past self, making silly faces over her flute while she plays.

"Me too," I say. "But I won't bring her back for you."

His hand clenches into a fist as he picks out the word. "*Won't.*"

The time spell is getting weaker by the minute. The kids on the stage are almost completely see-through.

"She made me promise not to."

"You saw her, didn't you, when you Composed that ghost-summoning spell?"

I nod. "She doesn't want to be brought back. Even if I *could*—and I'm not sure I could—would she come? Are you even the same person she would remember?"

He gives me a startled look but quickly hides it with a scowl. "You forget, I'm not asking. You'll give me what I want, one way or another. I see now that it *has* to be you. That's why the others failed me. You're the one who's meant to bring her back. You're connected to her the way no one else can be." He takes a step toward me; I step back. "You owe me this, daughter."

"No I don't," I say, blinking back tears. "I don't owe you anything: not my magic, not my guilt, not my forgiveness. No. *You're* the one who owes *me!*"

My shout echoes off the thinning walls of the time spell, bouncing back to me all wobbly and warped.

My dad stares at me.

"Today is the day you start paying *me* back," I say, breathless. "You'll start by letting me leave with Jai and everyone else in your horrible orchestra. And you'll leave me alone after that. Never look for me, or talk to me, or even *think* about me. You should be pretty good at that by now. You hate me, after all."

He opens his mouth, but no words come out. Finally, his stony expression begins to crack, and I see . . . *something* beneath. Regret? Shame?

Or is he just mad that I won't give him what he wants?

"It was more complicated than that," he mutters. "I don't hate you. That's not why I . . . You were better off with your grandmother. I'm not a good man. I come from a bad place, bad people. You won't understand. I was better, with Susie. Don't you see why I need her? Why the world needs her? She made everything better for everyone. *She's* the parent you deserve, not me."

"But she's gone," I say. "And you were all I had. Then you left."

"Yes," he replies softly.

"If you wanted me to help you bring her back, why didn't you just *ask* me? Why all this?" I gesture at the orchestra. "Why the lies, the deals, the consequences?"

"So you'd never have to know who I was," he murmurs. "*What* I was. At least not until your mother was back. It was meant to keep you at arm's length, same as all the other guests of the Midnight Orchestra. Safe."

"Safe!" I give a bitter laugh. If there's one thing I haven't felt these past weeks, it's *safe*.

"I would never harm you, A-Amelia."

He stumbles over my name, as if it hurts him to say it. I'm as much a stranger to him, I realize, as he is to me.

"Too late for that," I reply quietly. "Maybe if you'd let her go, you could have seen *me*."

He puts his mask back on, his lips parting to speak, but before he can, the walls of the time bubble come crashing down. It's kind of like the way Mia's teleportation bubble burst when we landed in the concert hall—an explosion of magic rippling outward. My mom's and dad's childhood figures vanish, washed away in that glittering tide. Then the magic fizzles out, sounding like dying fireworks, all sizzles and pops and smoke.

Within moments, the last of my time spell fades into the air, leaving only the faintest scent of burned plastic.

"Amelia!" Darby gasps, suddenly bursting into motion again, along with Mia. Time in the real world resumes, only a split second passing. "What—what just happened?"

My dad and I watch each other warily.

"What happened," I say slowly, "is that we have an understanding, right? Me and my friends are leaving. In fact, *everyone* is leaving—the whole orchestra. Or"—I lean toward my dad and whisper so Darby can't hear—"I'll tell everyone your real name. I bet they find you pretty quickly then."

The corner of his mouth quirks, as if my threat has only amused him.

"Actually, Miss Jones," he says, "*we* are leaving. You and I."

With that, he grabs hold of my arm, pulling me close. Darby yells, trying to climb onto the stage, but Mr. Stewart jumps forward and takes hold of her and Mia. The girls struggle, but it's like being undead has given the old man super strength. He barely flinches when Mia slaps his arm.

"I'm not giving you what you want!" I yell.

"On the contrary," my dad replies, "you already have."

CHAPTER THIRTY-SIX

Fever Pitch

STILL HOLDING ME TIGHT, Dad opens his coat and takes a little box from its inner pocket. When he pops it open, I try to peer inside, but he angles it out of my view. But there's no mistaking what it *is,* not when he twists a little knob on the side and it starts to play a tinny melody.

"A music box?" I ask, confused. Music boxes are mechanical; they can't produce magic.

He shuts the box and replaces it in his pocket, then flings an arm toward the Midnight Orchestra players—who sit up straighter, apparently alert now. Whatever he did with that music box, it's somehow linked to the hostages.

"The spell you just heard," he tells them, "play it."

I gape as the enchanted musicians begin playing *my* spell, the one I just Composed minutes ago, transforming it into a full symphony. How are they even doing that? It's like *they're* a giant music box, playing on command.

"A spell to take one back in time," my dad murmurs. "I should have thought of that ages ago. It's *perfect*."

"What are you doing?" I gasp.

"Not me, Amelia. *We*. We are going back to save her."

"But—"

"April ninth," he says as he drags me closer to the orchestra. Purple magic is beginning to sparkle on their instruments. "Eight years ago. If we time it right, we can reach her just after she resurrects you, and we can pull her into the present with us before the spell can backfire on her. You'll both survive that night."

"I'm pretty sure every movie about changing the past ends really badly!"

"Ah, that's the beauty of it! We *aren't* changing the past, we're just pulling her *out* of it. Instead of her dying that night, she'll only disappear. But everything else will be the same. It's simple, and it's brilliant, and it's all thanks to you!"

I'm starting to really panic now. Darby and Mia can't help; they're still struggling with Mr. Steward, oblivious to the conversation between my dad and me. And as the Midnight Orchestra's magic grows, swirling clouds of purple dust encircling us, I know it's only a matter of minutes before we're zapped away into the past.

"But you just saw my spell play out! We weren't really *in* the past, just looking at it!"

"Yes, yes, but that was magic conjured by one girl with a flute. An entire orchestra as powerful as mine? They just might take us *all* the way back."

He's got a crazed look in his eye.

"We'll be a family again, Amelia," he says softly. "The three of us, as we were meant to be together. Don't you want that?"

My arm goes limp in his grasp as I consider it. *Could* this crazy plan work? Could we really save Mom before she's killed?

He seems to take my response as agreement, because he lets go of me and picks up his violin, putting it to his chin. "I knew you'd understand. You're more like me than you know, daughter."

I suck in a breath, my blood running cold. "No, I'm not."

But his idea, the *possibility* of it, makes me breathless with longing.

"They can provide the magic," he says, tilting his head toward the orchestra. "But you and I need to guide them to the right moment in time. Play with us, Amelia. Concentrate on that tonight. Concentrate on *her*. We can see this through, together."

He adds the soulful tones of his violin to the symphony, and soon the shining instrument glitters with magic. His graceful fingers dance over the strings, pulling from it all the vibrato and tone it will give. I stand by him, frozen in place, my mind racing.

I glance at Jai, just steps away from me now, his face completely hidden behind his doll mask, his bow scraping away at his own violin as he dutifully obeys the Necromuse's order. I can see the faintest glow in his ear, where the worm controlling his mind is hidden.

The earworms.

What did Jai tell me about how they work?

Somewhere nearby, there must be a queen worm, the one transmitting the mind-control spell to the rest of the colony. When everyone at Mystwick had been enchanted, Jai told me to look for the queen. *Find her, and you can break the whole spell.*

And I have a pretty good idea where she is.

But what if Dad's right?

What if this plan could work?

"Wait a minute . . ." I say. "What about the law of equal . . . something something?"

"Law of Equal Consequence," he says. "Yes, yes, I'm aware." He stops playing just long enough to point his bow. "You! The pianist!"

Mia's mom raises her head, staring blankly at my dad.

"Come here," he orders.

She rises and walks toward him, her eyes completely vacant.

"Mama!" Outside the haze of magic now surrounding us, Mia struggles harder against Mr. Stewart. "What are you doing with her, you creep? I did everything you wanted! Let her go! *Mama!*"

Ignoring Mia's screams, my dad looks Mrs. Jones over. "Same height, same build, even the same last name. Can't get more equal than that."

"You're going to swap her for Mom?" I ask, horrified.

"For us," he says. "For our family, Amelia. Don't forget that. Now pick up your flute and help us."

Mrs. Jones stands by passively, not even looking at her daughter, who's still calling to her.

The magic grows thicker with every measure the orchestra plays. My dad's obviously fighting against the power of the bars in his earlobes; a drop of blood trickles from his ear canal. But he plays on, bow arcing gracefully over the strings of his violin, his eyes closing as he concentrates.

I look from him to Darby and Mia. To Mrs. Jones.

Back at my dad.

He's really going to dump Mia's mom into the past as if she's nobody at all, forever separating her from her family. Breaking his word to Mia. Proving he really isn't a good man. That no matter what, he'll always be the Necromuse—using people like game pieces to get what *he* wants.

But . . . what if he and I want the same thing?

What if we could bring Mom back with us and be together again? If anyone could make him better, she could, right? And it's not like he'd be *hurting* anyone, just . . . moving them around in time.

"Amelia," he says, his chin still pressed to his violin. "Isn't this what you want?"

Would my happiness be worth such a price?

It's not a question I even need to ask. I already know the answer.

So, as hard as it is, I force myself to step closer to my dad and put my arms around him. He breaks off playing, startled.

"There's nothing I want more in the world," I whisper truthfully.

He smiles and starts to put his arm around me in a hug—a real hug, a *dad* hug, something I've dreamed about in my sleep but never dared imagine awake.

I really could have everything I want, if only I were willing to become like him.

But I'm not.

My hand slips into his coat's inner pocket, pulling out the music box I'd seen him fiddle with earlier. Whipping it out, I turn and fling it through the air.

"Darby!" I yell.

She looks up just in time, catching the box with her free hand.

"No!" roars my dad. He pushes me aside and lunges toward Darby, but he's too slow.

Darby pops opens the music box and pulls out the wriggling white worm inside, casting it to the ground and crushing it under her shoe.

Just like that, chaos erupts in the concert hall.

The members of the Midnight Orchestra begin howling and clutching their ears. Instruments drop to the ground, clanging and splintering. Mrs. Jones yelps and clutches her head, dropping clumsily to her knees.

"No, no, no! *Susie!"* Dad resumes playing his violin, desperately trying to control the magic still burning all around us. But it's too much for one musician to handle.

"Get down!" I yell, dropping to the floor.

Because . . . boy, do I know what happens when you let a time spell go sideways.

Magic shoots through the concert hall like fireworks.

Wherever it hits, it explodes, sending bricks and mortar raining down from the walls. A jet of power blasts through the piano, splitting it in half with a loud *twang.* Twisting to look at Darby and Mia, I see the girls using Mr. Stewart like a shield. He stands immobile, as if completely oblivious to the explosions of magic going off all around him.

My hair crackles with static electricity as I crawl over the stage's splintery floorboards. Jai is fighting to remove the mask over his face, and I yank him down beside me and pull it off for him.

His eyes blink at me, bewildered. "Wha—what's happening? Where am I?"

"Long story. Duck!"

I smash his head into the floor just as a ball of magic blasts over us. It blows apart the chair he'd been sitting in, sending splinters of wood flying.

"Sorry," I whisper.

He groans, pressing a hand to his bruised forehead.

The other hostages, having managed to remove their masks, look just as confused as Jai. But at least they have the wits to notice the uncontrolled magic sizzling through the air. People dive under chairs and curl up on the floor, screaming.

"Watch out!" shouts Darby as a massive blast shoots toward the ceiling and explodes through the roof, ripping open a massive hole. Beams of wood and ceramic tiles pour down with a loud crash, crushing a whole section of old seats in the theater.

Sunlight lances through the hole as we all cough and choke on the dust raised from the destruction. One last pulsing blast of magic is still zinging back and forth in the air, as if searching for the perfect target. It's bigger than all the rest, burning like a purple fireball.

Mrs. Jones rises to her feet, coughing hard, just as the ball of magic shoots her way.

"MAMA!" screams Mia. She finally breaks free from Mr. Stewart and throws herself onstage, tackling her mom to the ground.

The magic speeds over their heads—aimed directly at my dad. He is still playing his violin, his faced creased with desperate concentration, determined to somehow pull my mom back into his world.

The blast hits him full in the chest.

A bright burst of purple lightning dashes the bow out of his hand and envelops him head to toe, and for a single moment he's completely suspended in its purple glow, holding only the violin. His eyes grow wide and lock onto mine.

And then, in a puff of magic, he vanishes.

CHAPTER THIRTY-SEVEN

Two Truths and a Lyre

THERE'S NO TIME TO digest what I just saw.

Dozens of frightened people are still shouting in confusion. I stumble to them and start helping them up, doll face masks and instruments crunching underfoot. I sit one old woman down; she's shivering and looking around in a daze.

"It was earworms, wasn't it?" asks Jai. "The Necromuse got me?"

"Yeah, and about that . . . they're still sort of . . . *in there.*" I try to smile, but it comes out a grimace. "Darby squished Her RoyalWorminess and broke the spell for you."

He sighs. "Well, good thing I've had practice at this."

Turning around so I don't have to watch him pull the worm out of his own ear, I check the old woman over for injuries and ask for her name, but it's like she can't even hear me. Wincing, I extract the earworm from her and crush it under my shoe, even though it's useless now without its queen to control it.

Darby tries to explain everything to the other freed hostages, but it's not going well. A large man with sweaty armpits is demanding to speak to an adult in charge.

"YOU!" he roars, pointing at me. "I want to speak to your superior, or else—"

At that moment, the hole in the roof darkens with shadow. Everyone looks up, where the sky fills with a wonderfully familiar, deeply purple sight.

"The *Bumblebee*!" I shout.

The Mystwick zeppelin hovers over the roof, propellers churning, and a moment later, a rope ladder unfurls.

Agent Alvarez and Agent Ned come zinging down like superspies, dressed head to toe in black combat gear and carrying shiny black instruments—hers a bassoon, his a violin.

"Secure the area!" Agent Alvarez snaps, and Agent Ned salutes and lumbers away, his violin looking tiny in his large hand. "You, girl!" she says to me. "Is he here?"

I shrug helplessly. She growls and darts off, searching the crowd for a man I already know she won't find.

Next, Mr. Pinwhistle comes clambering down awkwardly, followed by Miss Motte, Mrs. Le Roux, and the captain, Jenkins, with his parrot Captain flitting around his head.

"Amelia Jones," grunts Mr. Pinwhistle when he lands on the ground. "You are determined to see me in an early grave, aren't you?"

Miss Motte descends more gracefully, her shawls aflutter. "Still doubt me, Mr. Pinwhistle? I told you my locator spell was foolproof."

He reddens. "You teleported us to *Greenland* first!"

"And wasn't the view lovely? All those polar bears." Miss Motte gives the air a little sniff. "Hmm. I smell *time magic*." She looks directly at me and raises her eyebrows.

"Are you all right, students?" Mrs. Le Roux asks, looking over Jai, Darby, Mia, and me.

"Yes, um . . ." I look around helplessly. "It's a bit of a long story."

"Well, we've been sounding alarms across the countryside and teleporting from one end of the globe to the other looking for you small walking nightmares," grumbles Mr. Pinwhistle. "So *start talking*."

While Jenkins helps calm the hostages and Mia sticks close to her mom, I sit on the edge of the stage with Darby and Jai and tell the Maestros our story.

Well, most of it.

I *kinda* leave out the part where the Necromuse turned out to be, you know, *my dad*. Not even Darby or Jai know that part, since my whole conversation with him happened inside the time bubble.

Mrs. Le Roux frowns. "And you say this man just vanished?"

"Into thin air." I make my fingers explode outward. "The time magic hit him and . . ."

He was just *gone.*

Again.

And not a single part of me believes he's dead. I have no idea what happened to him, exactly, but I can't shake the feeling that he's still out there somewhere.

Or some *when.*

"Why was he playing a time spell?" asks Miss Motte, looking at me curiously. "What does he want?"

I look down at my hands. I've told Miss Motte things I've never told anyone else, secrets and feelings I've carried for years.

But I just can't tell her this one.

"I don't know," I mumble.

Mr. Stewart had disappeared not long after my dad. Darby saw him slip out the back while everyone else was looking at the zeppelin. If the Necromuse had any other undead followers in the building, they must have scattered too.

"He's given us the slip again," says Agent Alvarez, walking over, her bassoon clenched in one hand like a club. She looks ready to spit nails at being foiled once more by the infamous Necromuse. "Nobody leaves this place till I've questioned everyone, got it? I've called for backup, and they'll be here within the hour."

I don't think interrogations will do her much good. I've already learned from Jai that not a single member of the Midnight Orchestra has any memory from the time they were first kidnapped until now. In fact, most of them don't remember being grabbed in the first place.

I swallow, knowing the agents will want to question *me* again. The last thing I need is the MBI digging around, asking questions, like maybe whether anyone in this room might be *related* to the guy who kidnapped and blackmailed dozens of people and also, oh, *illegally raised the dead.* It wouldn't happen to be the girl who already has a reputation for Composing black spells, would it?

"Make it quick, agents," says Mrs. Le Roux. "We're getting these students out of here and somewhere safe as soon as we can. If you have further questions, you can ask them back at Mystwick, under proper supervision."

Agent Alvarez looks ready to argue, but Agent Ned puts a hand on her arm and nods. She finally relents.

"Back to Mystwick, then, and a hefty round of detention, I should expect," adds Mr. Pinwhistle.

"Detention!" Miss Motte clicks her tongue. "Fred, don't you think they've been through enough? After all, they *were* only trying to help poor Jai. I think they acted admirably."

"Admirably!" he splutters. "They deliberately disobeyed direct instructions from—"

"Oh, you old hypocrite!" Miss Motte waves him off. "I could tell a tale or two about Mr. Pinwhistle's youthful exploits, believe me. What about that time you and I snuck off campus to—"

"Miss *Motte!*" Mr. P. is as red as a turnip.

"Or that time we broke curfew and met up in Harmony Hall to—"

"Mathilde! Stop!"

"All I'm saying is, you were no model student, were you?"

"Every one of those occasions was *your* idea, might I remind you! That's Matti Motte for you, they warned me. Stay away from her, Fred. She's always breaking things. Rules, curfew, instruments . . . She's got a butterfly heart, that one."

Wait a minute . . . Butterfly heart? I've heard that phrase before.

I straighten, my eyes popping open wide.

"It was *you!*" I shout, pointing at Mr. Pinwhistle. "You're the one she left at the altar! You two were supposed to get married!"

"Wait, *what?*" cries Jai, delighted.

If Mr. Pinwhistle was red before, now he flushes a dangerous shade of purple. "Now, missy, I don't know who told you—"

"Yes, of course Amelia's right," says Miss Motte. "I broke your heart, Fred."

"We are *not* discussing this!" he growls. "And that's final!"

Without another word, he storms off toward the former Midnight Orchestra members and sets about trying to organize them. The three of us take the chance to jump down from the stage and evade further interrogation. I'm still reeling at the thought of Miss Motte and Mr. Pinwhistle being *in love* once upon a time. It's like imagining a parrot falling for a porcupine. They couldn't possibly be more different.

"I think I'll take a piece back as a souvenir," Jai says, plucking a chunk of brick off the ground. "How about this one? To always remind me I got kidnapped by the actual Necromuse and totally got away with barely a pinkie flex."

"Well, duh, because *I* was the one doing all the work!" I point out.

He laughs, and then the smile drops from his face. "I guess I gotta go back and face my dad again. I'd rather take on the Necromuse and his whole zombie army."

I *almost* tell him right then and there. It's on the tip of my tongue.

He's my dad. The Necromuse is my dad and I think he might still be out there. I think he won't ever stop looking for me.

But I don't say it.

There are some things just too terrible to share, even with your best friend. Especially when that secret involves your own dad *kidnapping* that best friend.

"You're turning all red," Jai says, squinting at me. "What's wrong?"

"Nothing. I—I was just thinking of how I sort of ran out on the entire Mystwick orchestra back at the Trials, to save *you*."

"Wait." He raises his hand. "You didn't compete in the Composium?"

I shake my head.

Jai groans and slaps his forehead. "Oh, Amelia, c'mon! You could've let me be kidnapped for *ten more minutes* if it meant bringing home that trophy!"

"You're welcome!" I roll my eyes. "I hope you won't mind being friends with Mystwick's biggest social outcast."

"Ah, well. At least I got to totally rock out. Did you see me rock out?"

I grin. "It was epic."

"The *epicest!* And . . . I would never have gone up there if it weren't for you." He gives me a sidelong look. "You know, you're pretty scary when you use your powers for evil."

"E-evil?" I stammer.

"Hello? Convincing me to completely blow off every rule my dad ever gave me, all in one afternoon? While he's sitting *right there?*" He laughs as he wanders off to pick through more rubble for the perfect memento. "You're truly wicked, Amelia Jones."

I smile weakly, even as my heart still pounds on my ribs. Of course he's joking. Of course he doesn't mean I'm actually evil. Which would be ridiculous, anyway.

You're more like me than you know, daughter.

No, no, no. He's out of my head now. I'm just being paranoid.

My friends are safe. The hostages are safe.

My dad is gone, along with his creepy followers.

And the angry music in my heart has finally gone quiet.

CHAPTER THIRTY-EIGHT

Coda of Silence

IT'S GOOD TO BE back at Mystwick.

Even if I am standing over the sink in the cafeteria bathroom, miserably scrubbing pea soup out of my cardigan.

Kjersten swore it was "totally an accident" when she dumped her bowl of soup on me in the dinner line, but her eyes told a very different story. Not that I was surprised. Don't even ask how many mean notes I found in my desk, calling me everything from a chicken to a traitor. And we only got home from the Trials this morning.

Yeah, I guess you could say I'm not exactly *popular.*

I try to remind myself that if everyone knew the real reason I ran away from the Composium, they'd be acting very differently right now. But they don't know, and they can't.

The Maestric Bureau of Investigations made sure of that.

Before Agent Alvarez would let any of us leave the ruined concert hall, we all had to sign papers saying we wouldn't talk about what happened there, about the Midnight Orchestra, *any* of it. I was ready to sign anything, whatever it took to stop her from asking *more* questions. She seemed to believe me when I said I didn't recognize the Necromuse, that he'd never taken off his mask.

Now the only people I can actually talk to about it all are Darby and Jai, and then only in whispers.

The soup's not coming out of the sweater.

Sighing, I ball it up and stuff it in my backpack, then slip out the back door of the cafeteria into the chilly night. I'd rather spend the rest of the dinner hour outside, where at least nobody can "accidentally" snip off my ponytail or fill my flute with ketchup.

It's going to be a *long* week before winter break starts.

I sit on the dock on Orpheus Lake, my legs swinging over the frozen water. The sky is as clear as crystal, with all its cold winter stars. The moon, half full, shines down on the ice, turning it into a softly gleaming mirror. Lamps glow on each of the dock's posts, making it feel like an illuminated raft floating in the dark.

Hearing footsteps crunch on the snow, I turn around.

Darby walks down the dock toward me, her oboe slung over the shoulder of her gray peacoat. She's got a tartan scarf wrapped around her neck and a matching beret neatly placed on her dark hair.

"I saw what happened in the cafeteria," she says. "You okay?"

"Yeah. It's no big deal."

She nods, looking distracted.

"Are *you* okay?" I ask.

"Yeah. I just . . . I thought you might want this." She takes her hand out of her pocket, holding the music box I stole from my dad.

I swallow. I'd totally forgotten about it. How in the world did she smuggle it past Agent Alvarez? "Oh. No, I don't think I—"

"Trust me, you want it."

"O . . . kay? Why?"

"You'll see."

Reluctantly taking it from her, I run my hands over the lid. It's made of dark, almost black wood, polished to a shine, with the initials ENS on the top. Weird. Eric Neal . . . secret last name I don't know about? Or maybe it's someone else's initials, and he stole the box from them. Given what I know about him, either seems just as likely.

The box is short but as wide as my hand. All it takes is a press, and the lid opens. It starts to play its eerie little tune, and there doesn't seem to be a way to turn it off. Then I notice a little drawer on the bottom. Sliding it open, I find a bunch of carefully folded papers.

Darby sits beside me and says nothing. Glancing at her, I get the sense that she's already seen whatever is hidden in these pages.

My fingers shake a little as I unfold them in the dim light of the lamps.

The first thing I find are my mom's old Compositions, the ones I saw my dad steal from her notebook. I wonder if he was hoping one of them might be the resurrection spell she played to save my life, but if so, he was out of luck. There are spells for straightening hair, making the bed, conjuring a breeze . . . but nothing nearly as big and dangerous as resurrection.

I press them to my chest a moment, then set them aside to see what else he stored in there. What I find makes my heart drop into my shoes.

Newspaper clippings.

About *me*.

They're all stories and pictures from my hometown newspaper, about my recitals at my old school, the story about how I was invited to play with the high school band, a snippet titled LOCAL GIRL ACCEPTED TO PRESTIGIOUS MUSICRAFT ACADEMY. There's even a page of Mr. Pinwhistle's handwriting—DISASTROUS PERFORMANCE, IMMEDIATE REJECTION, MUSTACHE EVERYWHERE. Wincing, I realize that they're the notes he must have taken during my terrible audition for Mystwick.

But not all the stories my dad collected were about my

music. There are also excerpts about my swim meets, my Girl Scout troop, and that one disastrous season I played basketball. And there are pictures I've never seen, of me and my mom and my dad, obviously from *before*. I was just a baby in most of them, as bald as an egg and smiling from ear to ear, in Mom's lap, on my dad's shoulders, wearing a bunny costume, sitting inside a carved-out pumpkin . . .

He's been following my whole life, carrying these things in his pocket all these years.

And now Darby knows who he really is.

I replace the papers in the box and shut the lid; the music finally goes silent. It takes me a minute to find my voice. "I, uh, guess I should thank you for not telling anyone."

She glances at the music box, then back at me. "I suppose you heard by now that Mia's not coming back this school year. Her parents are going to keep her home for a while."

"I heard."

"Which means . . . your old bed's open again. You know, if you want it."

My eyebrows knit together as I rub the edge of the music box. "You sure? I mean . . . you know my secret now. Who I really am."

"Who you really are?" Darby's head lifts, her eyes widening. "Amelia . . ."

I let out a long breath. "I know what everyone else would say if they knew. How they'd look at me."

You're more like me than you know, daughter.

Darby stares at me for a long moment. "Do you think you'll look for him? There are spells . . ."

"No," I say quickly. "I'm done with him. Wherever he is, and preferably that's far, far away from me, he can stay there."

She chews her lip, as if wrestling with what to say next. "You know, those papers in there. Those aren't the kinds of the things you keep when you want to forget someone. I'm not saying your dad is a good guy, but . . . I think he still cares about you. In a weird, messed-up way."

"You're wrong."

She points at me, a challenge in her eyes. "Mia's acceptance letter."

"What?"

"Mia's acceptance letter. How did you get it?"

"There . . . was a mix-up."

She shakes her head. "That's not an explanation, not if she didn't actually die. But you know what *is?* Your dad found out you failed your audition, so he marooned Mia on that island in order to steal her letter, send it to you, and get you into Myst-wick anyway."

My stomach twists.

It does make sense. It explains the letter perfectly. He *did* have Mr. Pinwhistle's notes, the ones that made it clear I'd never get into Mystwick on my own. And it explains why he attacked Mia's yacht long before he knew I could Compose.

But I don't want to believe it. I don't want to know that any part of my dad still loves me, especially enough that he'd ruin someone else's life to give me what I want.

Has my dad been behind the scenes my entire life, helping me from afar when I didn't ask for it, moving pieces around me like I was part of some game? Somehow the idea is more chilling than the thought that he truly abandoned me without a second look.

"You know, there *is* something that doesn't add up," I say. "Jai told me that rumors about the Midnight Orchestra go back fifty years. According to George, the stories about the Necromuse go back even further. So what I don't get is . . . how could my dad have been running around with his orchestra long before he was even born?"

"Sounds to me like you *aren't* done with him."

"No, I am. I really am. It's just . . . Forget it. I don't want to know the answers. He may be my father, but he'll never be my dad."

She nods, staring across the lake for a long moment.

"This was all about your mom, wasn't it?" Darby says. "Your dad wanted to bring her back."

She really can't let this go. Sighing, I push the toe of my shoe into the ice beneath the dock, making cracks spread across it. "Yeah, till I gave him the idea to grab her out of the past with a time spell."

She nods. "So when he grabbed Mia's mom . . ."

"The Law of Equal Consequence."

"Yep." Darby fiddles with the handle of her oboe case. "You could have let him do it, too. But you didn't. You saved Mia's mom instead."

I wonder if I should tell her how hard that decision was. That a strong part of me really wanted to let him go through with it.

"Amelia, you're not like him. You're a good person." She puts her hand on my arm and squeezes. "If anything, it should be *you* who doesn't want to room with *me,* after the way I let Mia treat you."

"Darby! No! I'm not mad at you."

"And I'm not scared of you, no matter who your dad is."

I look down at my hands. "If everyone finds out . . ."

"They won't. Not from me, anyway. I promise."

We look at each other for a long moment; then I smile. "Thanks, *Darbs*."

"Don't ever call me Darbs. I've always hated that stup name." She sighs a little, then adds, "It's weird how I co never tell Mia that, but I can tell you."

"Tell her what?" Jai asks.

We look up as he comes bounding across the dock to drop beside me, out of breath. He sets his violin case next to him. "What's this? Lake party, and you didn't invite me?"

"More like pity party," I say. "Everyone at school *hates* me."

He shrugs. "They'll get over it. Eventually. Maybe. Okay, probably not."

Wrinkling my nose, I lean slightly away from him. "What's that smell?"

"Huh? Oh." He gives a sheepish grin, then sticks up his thumbs, which reek like they've been drenched in . . .

"Hot sauce," he confirms. "To keep me from, uh . . ." He wiggles one thumb over his lips. "You know, when I'm asleep."

"Oh . . . right." I wince. "Sorry about that. Again."

"At least I've stopped craving milk all the time." He shudders. "What *are* you doing out here, you strange girls? Plotting your next disaster, Amelia? What's it to be next time? Aliens? Talking kangaroos? A trip to the North Pole to save Christmas?"

"Nope! No more disasters for me. No more adventures. No more weirdness. From here on, I am totally, one hundred cent *normal*. As boring as lettuce in salad."

You are a lot of things, Amelia Jones, but *normal* isn't one m." With a chuckle, Jai lies back and locks his hands head, grinning at me. "I think that's pretty great."

"Yeah," Darby adds. "Who wants to be normal when you can be *magic?*"

She takes out her oboe and begins to play a spell, sweet and slow. Blue magic flows from her instrument and curls through the air like frosty filigree.

Grinning, Jai takes out his violin, and at his urging, I put together my flute.

We join Darby's spell, our music weaving together and threading through the air. Glittering blue light twists and spirals over the frozen lake. The lights play over the ice, shimmering reflections spreading in all directions. Where the magic is thickest, snow flurries appear one by one, then in swirling gusts.

Our magic presses and molds the snow, sculpting it with hands of blue magic until three snowmen are standing before us on the ice. Darby's is expertly shaped, not a snowflake out of place. Jai's has a crooked, goofy smile and crossed eyes. Mine is a bit crooked, and a bit lumpy, and nearly falls over, but at the last minute Darby adds a flourishing harmony and her snowman tips just enough to prop mine up.

They're perfect.

TRAVEL TO ANOTHER WORLD WITH THESE MUST-READ FANTASY BOOKS

FIND YOUR STORY